D0819083

HERE I AM

ROCHELLE
ALERS

HERE I AM

ARABESQUE®

Recycling programs
for this product may
not exist in your area.

HERE I AM

ISBN-13: 978-0-373-53441-8

www.kimanipress.com

Printed in U.S.A.

To my editor, Evette Porter—
thanks for the encouragement, chats and the laughs
as we continue this incredible journey together.

Dear Reader,

In *Here I Am*, we revisit the Wainwrights and meet another hunky scion, who is heir to the family's New York City real-estate empire. This time it's Brandt Wainwright—an NFL quarterback and Super Bowl MVP—who has chosen professional sports over the family real-estate business.

Always in tip-top shape, Brandt faces his greatest challenge when he is forced to endure months of physical rehabilitation after a horrific automobile accident. Unable to take care of his most basic needs, he is forced to rely on the assistance of no-nonsense nurse Ciara Dennison.

Unimpressed by his celebrity-athlete status, Ciara tries to repress her feelings toward Brandt—both as a patient *and* as a man. Despite the spotlight and tabloid rumors, Brandt must convince Ciara that true love is worth fighting for and that there is a happily-ever-after.

Of course, there are more Wainwrights whose stories are yet to be told. In the meantime, look for my Hideaway summer wedding trilogy in 2012, and get reacquainted with the Cole family.

Read, love and live romance,

Rochelle Alers

WAINWRIGHT LEGACY

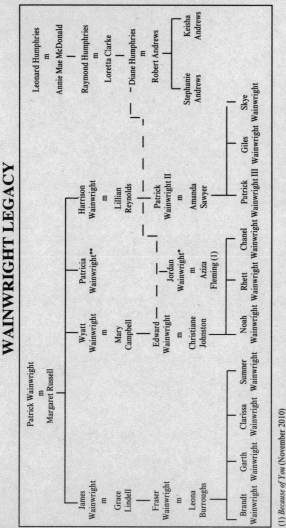

(1) *Because of You* (November 2010)

* Jordan Wainwright, the eldest of Edward Wainwright's children, is the result of an extramarital affair between Edward and Diane Humphries

** Deceased

When I say, my bed shall comfort me;
my couch shall ease my complaint.
—*Job* 7:13

Chapter 1

Brandt Wainwright gritted his teeth. It was as if he had ten thumbs instead of two. He had tried three times before, but he was unable to secure the striped, silk tie into a Windsor knot.

He'd given up wearing ties, or as he called them, corporate nooses, the day after he was drafted by the NFL. That was more than ten years ago. Now, as his cousin's best man in a wedding that was certain to make the Vows section of the Sunday *New York Times,* he'd agreed to wear a tuxedo.

He wasn't completely surprised when his cousin had asked him to be his best man, but what had shocked him was Jordan Wainwright's announcement that he'd planned to marry Aziza Fleming. Brandt had introduced the two of them at the New Year's Eve party he'd hosted earlier that year. Seven months later, and in less than half an hour, they would become husband and wife.

Brandt ran a hand over the back of his neck. He felt practically naked having cut his hair, which usually covered the nape of his neck. He hadn't wanted to, since like many athletes he was superstitious about things like that. But then again, he had to when Jordan asked him to get a haircut like the other groomsmen in the wedding—his brothers, Noah and Rhett, and Jordan's law partner, Kyle Chatham.

If it had been anyone else, Brandt would've told them exactly where they could go and what they could do in the most colorful language imaginable. He was used to that kind of language in the locker room, on the gridiron and on occasion at family gatherings, much to the chagrin of his straitlaced mother. Brandt usually didn't make New Year's resolutions, but this year he'd made a promise to himself to watch his language.

Two quick taps on the door caught his attention. Turning, Brandt smiled as Jordan Wainwright leaned against the doorframe in one of the guest suites in the landmark Fifth Avenue mansion. After a raucous Vegas-style bachelor party at Brandt's penthouse, the groomsmen managed to clean up well enough to attend the rehearsal and the dinner that followed in the magnificent four-story greystone mansion where Jordan had grown up with his brothers and sister. Instead of returning to his place, Brandt had spent the night in one of the guest suites to ensure he would make it to the wedding on time.

Brandt's pearly white teeth were a stark contrast to his deeply tanned face. He smiled at Jordan, who wore a pair of dress trousers, black patent leather oxfords, a white tuxedo shirt and a platinum-hued silk tie. Jordan's looks were dark and dramatic. His raven hair, hazel eyes and olive complexion made him stand out among the Wainwrights, who were mostly blond and fair-skinned.

"I came to see if you needed help with your tie."

Brandt frowned. "You've got jokes?" The question was laced with sarcasm. "You should've had a beach wedding so we wouldn't have to wear tuxedos, ties *or* shoes."

"You can have a destination wedding once you decide to stop chasing skirts," Jordan replied, with a smile.

Brandt's frown deepened. "For your information, I only chase skirts during the off-season. Did you come to check on my Windsor knot–tying skills, or are you getting cold feet?"

Jordan folded his arms over his chest and shook his head. "Not even close. My mother would have a minor breakdown if I didn't go through with this wedding. Initially, she wanted to invite three to four hundred people from my side of the family, but Aziza was adamant. She told her no more than one hundred fifty. After all, it is her wedding."

"Which mother?" Brandt asked. The question was out before he had chance to think about it. "I'm sorry about that."

Jordan waved a hand. "Don't apologize, Brandt."

It wasn't until he'd announced his engagement to Aziza that Jordan decided to put the skeletons from his past to rest. It had taken thirty-three years for him to finally meet his birth mother.

Jordan walked into the bedroom and sat on the tufted bench at the foot of the bed.

"Christiane is leading the way, and Diane is hot on her heels," Jordan admitted.

A decades-old feud ended when Jordan brokered a real-estate deal in which the Wainwright Developers Group and RLH Realty had formed a fragile partnership, resulting in the companies agreeing to jointly own and manage four properties in Harlem. Once the deal was finalized, Wyatt Wainwright, the family patriarch, had summoned anyone with a drop of Wainwright blood to attend a family gathering. It was to stunned silence that Wyatt disclosed the circumstances surrounding his eldest grandson's birth. It had been Diane Humphries-Andrews and not Christiane Johnston-Wainwright who was Jordan's birth mother.

Brandt sat next to his cousin, stretching out long legs and crossing them at the ankle, while staring at the tips of his shoes. "I know it's not easy for you to talk about it, but how does it feel to have two mothers?"

Jordan sandwiched his hands between his knees. "I really don't give it much thought." He gave Brandt a sidelong glance. "Ironically, I feel closer to my half sisters than I do to my biological mother. I don't hold it against Diane that she gave me up at birth, because she had unwittingly been sleeping with a man who was engaged to another woman. What I'm still dealing with is my grandfather Wyatt's *and* Diane's fathers' underhanded wheeling and dealing. When I discovered what they'd engineered, I couldn't help but think about what would've happened if my father had ended his engagement to Christiane and married Diane."

Brandt managed a wry smile. "You'd still be a Wainwright. And what made the lie so easy to pull off is that you look like Wyatt—even down to the black hair."

Jordan smiled. "Maybe, as long as I don't start acting like him."

"Are you that certain you're not like him?"

Jordan's deep-set eyes stared at his cousin. Brandt Wainwright was the NFL's golden boy. In the sports world he was known as "The Viking," with his rakish good looks and long, blond hair. A hefty two hundred fifty-five pounds were evenly distributed over Brandt's muscular six-foot-five frame. Although Jordan was just a few days older than Brandt, there were times when he'd felt a few years older. Jordan attributed the difference in maturity to the fact that Brandt had chosen to become a professional football player, while he had decided to become a lawyer.

"What's that supposed to mean?" Jordan asked.

Brandt smiled. "Don't get your nose out of joint, cuz. After all, I don't want you to get a headache—especially on your wedding night."

"When did you become a comedian?"

The uncomfortable silence seemed to grow with each passing second. Rarely did the two cousins argue or disagree about anything. Jordan had been an only child for ten years before his brother Noah was born, so in the meantime Brandt had been Jordan's unofficial brother.

Brandt had lost count of the number of times he'd stayed over at Jordan's family's mansion across from Central Park. Back then, he'd been too young to understand why his aunt and uncle had slept in separate bedrooms before the birth of Noah Wainwright, who was ten years Jordan's junior. But what no one had known at the time was that Christiane was not Jordan's biological mother. And it had taken Edward Wainwright's wife almost a decade to forgive her husband for his indiscretion.

"Jordan, I'm not trying to be funny," Brandt said. "I know it can't be easy for you to see family members who were once at each others' throats come here today. And I saw you go through hell when you had to decide whether to invite Diane and your half sisters to your wedding. All I can say is better you than me."

Jordan nodded.

"I know you blame your grandfathers for being puppet masters who manipulated the lives of their children, but you have to put that behind you," Brandt continued. "Especially today when you're beginning a new life with the woman you love."

The room grew quiet again.

"You asked me whether you should invite Diane Andrews to your wedding and I said yes," Brandt continued. "Every family has its secrets and the Wainwrights and Humphrieses are no exception."

Jordan put his arm across Brandt's shoulder. "You missed your calling, cuz. You should've become a lawyer rather than let a bunch of three-hundred-fifty-pound linemen beat the crap out of you every Sunday."

Brandt chuckled. "I may play football, but I do know how to read and write."

"What do you plan to do when you stop playing ball?" Jordan asked.

Brandt shrugged his broad shoulders. "I don't know.

I suppose I'll have to cross that bridge when I come to it."

"Noah said there's a position for you at Wainwright Developers whenever you're ready to hang up your jersey."

"I'll think about it."

Jordan patted his cousin's back. "Don't think too long, cuz." He didn't want to remind Brandt that there was always the possibility that his career could end with him being carried out on a stretcher.

"I won't," Brandt said after a reflective pause. "I plan to play for another two years and then I'm out." Aziza, Jordan's soon-to-be wife, had renegotiated his contract for three years instead of five. He wanted to retire at thirty-five while he was still at the top of his game. He'd entrusted his legal affairs to Aziza Fleming after he'd asked his teammate Alex whether his sister would be willing to negotiate his contract extension. Aziza proved her worth when she'd stood firm on what she'd wanted for her client, and in the end he'd been rewarded by becoming the highest-paid quarterback in the league.

Jordan exhaled audibly and stood up. "I guess I'd better finish getting dressed."

"Are you nervous?" he asked.

"Is the Pope Catholic?" Jordan replied.

"Damn," Brandt drawled. "You've always been cool and calm, never let anyone see you sweat. What's up with you?"

A wry smile spread across Jordan's face. "When I woke up this morning, I finally realized the enormity of what it means to become a married man. It's no longer about what I want or need, but also what Zee wants and needs. We've talked about starting a family, and it scares the hell out of me when I try to imagine being a father. Will I be too hard on my kids, or too easy? And what if I have girls? Do I chase away every boy who looks sideways at them?"

"You have a long time before you have to worry about your daughter going out with a boy," Brandt said.

Jordan nodded.

"I don't know about your father, but every time my dad saw me with a new date he'd say, 'think of her as your sister.' Do you how that can mess with your head? Once, I did go out with a girl who reminded me of my sister, and even though I'd wanted to sleep with her it never happened."

Jordan chuckled. "That's what you get for dating blondes. They're all going to remind you of your sister."

A sheepish expression spread across the quarterback's face when he smiled. "Some really weren't natural blondes."

"That's why I prefer brunettes," said Jordan. "I've never been surprised once we decide to take our relationship to the next level."

"I'll keep that in mind the next time I get involved with a woman." Brandt waved his hand dismissively. "Thanks for coming to check on me, but I think I'm good here. As soon as I'm dressed, I'll come down to see you."

Jordan checked his watch. "I'll see you downstairs in twenty minutes."

Brandt nodded.

Aziza Fleming had hired wedding planner Tessa

Whitfield-Sanborn of Signature Bridals and Event Planners to plan the ceremony, which was being held in the Wainwright mansion, as well as the cocktail reception in the small ballroom and dinner and dancing in the larger ballroom. Although the well-known wedding planner was on maternity leave, she'd agreed to oversee Jordan and Aziza's wedding since Jordan's law partner had been her husband's law school mentor.

Brandt reached for the gold monogrammed cufflinks, a gift from Jordan to his groomsmen, and fastened them to the French cuffs of his shirt. Then he reached for his tuxedo jacket and slipped each arm into the sleeves. He stopped to contemplate his cousin's wedding, unable to understand why once their children reached a certain age, their mothers suddenly became obsessed with marrying them off. Brandt had to assume it had something to do with wanting grandchildren.

Lately he'd had to suffer through his father's lengthy discourses about taking responsibility for his actions. What he hadn't wanted to mention to his father was that since he'd become sexually active, he'd never slept with a woman without using protection. If he wasn't ready for marriage, then he was even less prepared for fatherhood.

The clock on the mantelpiece chimed on the quarter hour. Everyone in the wedding party had been instructed to meet in the antechamber on the second floor overlooking the entrance hall at five forty-five. Leaving the suite, Brandt walked the length of the hallway to a rear staircase. The groomsmen were huddled together, waiting for their boutonnieres, which were fashioned from miniature white roses and lilac. The sound of feminine laughter floated from a nearby room.

There had been two rehearsals—the first time for the wedding party to familiarize themselves with the logistics, and the second time to confirm that everyone knew what they were to do. Brandt and Jordan were to enter the foyer through a hallway leading from the west wing of the mansion. The groomsmen and bridesmaids were to descend the curved staircase and walk along the white carpet to a floral-covered canopy where the bride and groom would exchange their vows.

The wedding planner touched the earpiece in her left ear. Although she was a new mother, Tessa had decided to personally coordinate the Fleming-Wainwright nuptials. Her wedding planning business had grown so much that she'd had to hire two assistants. Both young women were bright and had quickly learned the business. But Tessa continued to closely monitor important clients, especially those who were part of her elite social circle.

She raised her hand to get Jordan's attention. "Jordan, it's time for you and Brandt to head out."

The bridesmaids filed out of the room and into the hallway wearing flowing silk chiffon strapless bias-cut gowns in varying shades of blue, ranging from cobalt to robin's egg to periwinkle to sapphire. Each woman wore a large cushion-cut sapphire-and-diamond pendant that had been her gift from the bride. As a gesture designed to bring the Humphrieses and the Wainwrights together, Aziza had asked Jordan's two half sisters—Stephanie and Keisha Andrews—to be her bridesmaids. Jordan's sixteen-year-old sister, Chanel Wainwright, resplendent in sapphire blue, was maid of honor.

Brandt leaned closer to whisper to Chanel. "Remember you're right behind the flower girl and ring bearer." The ring bearer was one of Aziza's nephews, and one of the younger Wainwright cousins was the flower girl. "Are you going to be all right, Chanel?"

Her blue-green eyes shimmering excitement and her face flush with color, Chanel nodded as she shifted her bouquet of violets, irises and white roses to her left hand. "I hope I don't faint."

Brandt smiled at the slender young woman who seemingly had grown up overnight. He'd always remembered her as a tall, skinny girl with a waist-length ponytail. She was now quite the young woman, her round face framed by a short mass of curls, which were adorned with baby's breath and tiny white roses.

"Stop being a drama princess, Chanel."

"What if I make a mistake, Brandt?"

"You're not—"

Whatever he was going to say was preempted when Tessa signaled for him to follow Jordan. Leaning over, he pressed a kiss to his cousin's hair. He squeezed the tiny hand resting on the sleeve of his jacket, then turned on his heel, and with long strides he walked into the entrance hall to stand next to Jordan.

A minute later Rhett and Noah, followed by the rest of the wedding party, descended the curved staircase as the string quartet began playing "One Hand, One Heart" from *West Side Story*.

Chapter 2

As the music began to play, Brandt experienced a strange, unsettling feeling. He'd attended plenty of weddings involving family members, friends and teammates. But this was the first time he'd been part of the wedding party. As he stood next to Jordan, the love between bride and groom seemed so palpable, Brandt felt as if he was the one exchanging vows with his future bride. It was the first time he'd ever thought that.

When Aziza's father escorted her down the rose-petal-strewn carpet, Jordan released an audible sigh upon seeing his bride for the first time. Because it was her second marriage, Aziza had insisted that everything be low-key. But there was nothing simple about the bride, with her flawless brown skin and the body and face of a runway model, as she walked down the aisle effortlessly exuding grace and elegance. She wore a platinum-colored, strapless mermaid gown with silk tulle that wrapped around the skirt and a waist-length veil. Her thick, dark hair was brushed off her face and pinned into a chignon with jeweled hairpins.

Brandt smiled when his gaze went to the magnificent pear-shaped blue-and-white diamond earrings and the matching pendant, nestled between Aziza's breasts. He'd accompanied Jordan to a jeweler where they'd spent a couple of hours going over designs for his bride's wedding jewelry, and then another hour examining a collection of loose stones. When they left Brandt was more than familiar with intricacies of diamonds' cut, color, clarity, carat weight and certification.

He turned his attention back to the proceedings, and he smiled when Jordan cradled Aziza's face between his hands and pressed his mouth to hers, sealing their vows. They were no longer bride and groom, but husband and wife.

"Ladies, gentlemen, friends and family, I'm honored to present Mr. and Mrs. Jordan Wyatt Wainwright," announced the black-robed judge in a voice that carried easily in the expansive space.

Thunderous applause quickly followed as Christiane Wainwright dabbed at the corners of her eyes with a linen handkerchief. Her blue-gray gown complemented her summer tan and ash-blond hair that was pinned up in an elaborate twist at the nape of her long, slender neck. Leaning to her right, she hugged Diane Humphries-Andrews, the two women sharing a bond as adoptive and birth mother.

Diane, only two years younger than Christiane, was stunning in a royal blue sheath dress that showed off her still-slim figure to its best advantage. Her hair was cut into a becoming style reminiscent of First Lady Michelle Obama. Her features were delicate, but it was her large light brown eyes framed by a face the color of golden-brown autumn leaves that garnered the most attention.

How very civilized, Brandt thought. If it had been left up to his great uncle Wyatt, he doubted whether the two women would've ever met. He felt the utmost respect for Jordan and Aziza in bringing the two families together.

The wedding party proceeded out of the expansive foyer to the elevator that would take them to the solarium, where they would spend the next hour posing for photographs. Meanwhile, the guests were escorted into the ballroom where cocktails and hors d'oeuvres awaited them before they were seated for a seven-course dinner. The menu included filet mignon, Alaskan salmon, lobster tails, stone rock crab and carving stations with roast turkey, prime rib and trays of foie gras and caviar.

Brandt escorted his mother to an area of the ballroom that had been set up like a large parlor with sofas, settees, floral arrangements, candles and enormous floor pillows and ottomans scattered around the marble floor. He led his mother to a settee, and sat down next to her. He watched Leona Burroughs-Wainwright's impassive expression. His mother didn't smile during dinner, when the many toasts were made, or when wedding cake was cut and passed around to the guests.

"What's bothering you, Mom?"

Leona forced a smile. "What makes you think something is bothering me?"

His eyebrows lifted a fraction. "First of all you're

answering a question with a question, and secondly you look as if you've just lost Smooches."

"Bite your tongue, Brandt Wainwright. My baby may have a few years on her, but the vet said there's still a lot of life in her."

Brandt rolled his eyes. Smooches was overweight, visually impaired and eighteen years old. Seemingly the only thing the toy poodle lived for was low-fat treats. "If it's not Smooches, then why the long face?"

Leona patted her coiffed silver hair. "I would have liked it if you were the one getting married tonight instead of Jordan."

He shot his mother an incredulous stare. "Don't tell me you have your nose out of joint because Christiane married off one of her children before you did?"

"Jordan and Aziza know Clarissa's wedding is scheduled for the fall, so why couldn't they have waited until next year? It's not as if Aziza is pregnant."

"Whether Zee is pregnant or not has nothing to do with you," Brandt chastised in a soft tone. "They didn't need to check with you to get the go-ahead."

Leona pouted, a gesture that never failed to get her whatever she wanted. "How do you expect me to compete with this…this extravaganza? When I contacted Signature Bridals more than a year ago I was told they have a two-year waiting list. Jordan gets engaged in February and yet he manages to get them to plan his wedding."

"That's because Jordan and Zee know Tessa Sanborn personally."

Leona turned to her eldest son. "You're just like your father. You have an answer for everything."

"The difference is you don't like my answers," Brandt countered. Leaning to his right, he kissed his mother's cheek. "Clarissa will have a beautiful wedding. You've waited a long time to marry off your daughter, so come November it will be your turn to be the mother-of-the-bride. And what a magnificent mother-of-the-bride you'll be."

Leona's expression brightened. "Do you really think so?"

Brandt smiled. "I know so."

He couldn't understand how a woman who'd managed to marry one of New York's most eligible bachelors and had given him four children whom he adored continued to compete with her in-laws for status. Most of the Wainwright men had married women who'd gone to finishing school, had coming-out parties, were in the Social Register and had attended elite colleges. Leona had been the exception, and most times she'd tried too hard to become a high-society grande dame. What she hadn't realized was that Fraser Wainwright had chosen to marry her because she was different. She wasn't affected or a snob. During their thirty-five-year marriage, however, Leona had changed—becoming a social climber in the hopes that her mother-in-law would accept her. Unfortunately, it hadn't happened. And in Leona's mind, the only thing she had done right was to give her mother-in-law, Francine Wainwright, grandchildren.

Leona, whose natural beauty hadn't faded despite having recently celebrated her fifty-fifth birthday, flashed a dimpled smile. The fuchsia-colored silk suit complemented her smooth, peaches-and-cream complexion. "Brandt, you're going to make a wonderful husband for some very lucky woman."

"I'm going to have to find that very lucky woman first before I can even consider getting married."

Leona sobered. "Are you against marriage?"

His mother's question had caught him off guard. He'd never been one to advertise his relationships, but it had been a long time since he'd brought a woman home to meet his family. It was just that he wasn't ready to settle down.

"No." The single word answer hung in the air. "Why would you ask me that?"

"It's just that it's been a very long time since you've introduced us to one of your girlfriends. By the way, I ran into Courtney Knight last week and of course she asked about you."

Brandt averted his gaze. He'd been engaged to Courtney for less than two months when he'd discovered that she was sleeping with one of his college buddies. In response, Brandt had issued an ultimatum: either she break off the engagement or he would disclose why he wasn't going to marry her.

"That's nice," he drawled sarcastically.

"There you are, Brandt. I thought you'd left."

He turned to find his sister standing a few feet away. Rising to his feet, he smiled at her. "What's up, Clarissa?"

The enormous diamond on Clarissa Wainwright's finger sparkled like a headlamp. She was a tall, blue-eyed blonde with striking features. But every time Brandt saw her, she appeared thinner than she'd been before. Tiny blue veins were visible under her eyes, which were framed by long, dark lashes.

Slipping her hand into her brother's, Clarissa gave him a tender smile. "Do you plan to host any parties at your place before the end of the year?"

"I don't know. Why?" Aside from the New Year's Eve bash at his penthouse, get-togethers were usually spontaneous. In the off-season, he would sometimes invite his teammates and their wives or girlfriends to his place for a casual dinner party.

"My friend Tonya wants you to introduce her to Alexander Fleming."

"Clarissa!" Leona gasped.

The younger woman waved a hand. "Please, Mother. Let me handle this."

"There's nothing to handle," Brandt retorted. "You know I'm not into matchmaking."

Clarissa rested her hands at her narrow hips. "But you introduced Aziza to Jordan."

"I'm not going to discuss their relationship with you." He'd asked his attorney to talk to his cousin because he'd believed Jordan would be able to help Aziza with a sexual harassment suit she sought to bring against her former employer. Brandt hadn't known their involvement had segued from business to personal until they'd announced their engagement six weeks after first meeting. He also made it a rule not to introduce any women to teammates, because if the relationship soured he would never hear the end of it.

Leona touched her daughter's shoulder. "Let it go, darling. Let Tonya find her own boyfriend."

"What harm would it do for Brandt to introduce his

friend to my friend? I'm beginning to believe all the hype. It's always Brandt this and Brandt that in this family. If I'd decided to go into professional tennis instead of getting degrees in art history and interior design, then maybe someone would pay attention to me."

Brandt didn't want to believe that his sister was pestering him to introduce her best friend to his best friend. Alexander Fleming was not only his teammate, but he roomed with him during away games. He was also the bride's brother and in the wedding. It had been Alex who'd introduced him to Aziza when he was thinking about getting a new attorney.

Alex Fleming, who despite being a much sought-after bachelor, had always managed to keep a low profile when it came to his relationships. He'd recently split with a woman who he'd been seeing for several years, and had just begun dating again. What Brandt had noticed during the rehearsal and the dinner that followed was that Alex appeared enthralled with Jordan's half sister, although Stephanie Andrews hadn't given him a passing glance.

"Please excuse us," he said to Leona, who sat slack-jawed at her daughter's request. Reaching for his sister's hand, Brandt led her out of the ballroom.

"Where are you taking me?" Clarissa asked, breathing heavily as she tried keeping up with Brandt's long strides. If he didn't slow down, she would certainly turn an ankle in her four-inch stilettos.

"Somewhere where we can't be overheard," he said over his shoulder. Maneuvering around two couples who were standing in the hallway outside the ballroom, they made their way to the suite where he'd spent the night. "Sit down." Clarissa sat in a club chair, crossing one leg over the other. Brandt pulled up a straight-back chair, and reached for Clarissa's hands. They were ice-cold. "What's going with you?"

Clarissa averted her eyes. "What makes you think something is wrong with me?"

"I didn't say wrong. Something has you on edge, and I'm willing to bet it has nothing to do with me refusing to set Alex up with your girlfriend. Every time I see you you're thinner and thinner. How much weight have you lost?"

She lifted her bare shoulders. "I don't know."

"You don't know," he repeated. "Is that a new gown?" Clarissa nodded. "What size is it?"

"I think it's a two."

Brandt tightened his hold on her fingers. "What's next, Clarissa? A double-zero?" He leaned closer. "What does Harper say about you losing weight?"

Clarissa stared into a pair of eyes much like her own. Brandt had always been her favorite brother. Garth and Sumner were always too caught up with what was going on in their lives to pay much attention to her. And in a family where the birth of a boy was celebrated like that of an heir to the throne, she had always tried hard to get attention.

"He says he likes me slim."

"Slim or emaciated? You look anorexic, Clarissa. Are you losing weight because Harper asked you to, or is it your decision?"

Although she was thirty, her body now seemed prepubescent. When she lowered her gaze Brandt knew the reason why his sister looked so frightfully thin. He wondered if their mother had noticed the drastic change in Clarissa's appearance. "Why are you letting someone else control your life?"

"I don't want to marry him."

The admission stunned Brandt. July was almost over, and in another four months Clarissa was expected to exchange vows with the man she'd planned to share her life.

"You don't have to marry him, Rissa."

Clarissa's eyes filled with tears. It had been years since Brandt had called her by her childhood nickname. "But Mother expects us to marry."

"This is not about Mother, and what she wants or expects. This is about you. If you don't want to marry the guy, then you don't have to. Whatever you decide, you can count on me having your back. And I'm certain Sumner and Garth will support you, too."

"I don't want any trouble from Sumner. He and Harper can't stand being in the same room together."

"Don't worry about Sumner," Brandt said, hoping to reassure his sister that their hot-tempered brother wouldn't cause her soon-to-be ex-fiancé physical harm. Of all the Wainwrights, Sumner was the one who wouldn't hesitate to use his fists in a confrontation.

"I'm going to talk to Mother and Daddy first. Then I'm going to give Harper back his ring."

Brandt curbed the urge to smile. He'd never liked Harper Sinclair, because the man reminded him of a snake-oil salesman. He talked too much, grinned too much and spoke to Clarissa as if she were a child instead of his partner.

"I'm leaving for North Carolina tomorrow morning. Call me on my cell and let me know how everything turns out. If Harper decides to give you grief, then he'll wish it was Sumner rather than me jacking him up."

Clarissa laughed and a rush of color flooded her face. "No one believes me when I tell them my brothers are thugs."

"Remember, we're only three generations removed from the Wainwrights who fought their way out of the Lower East Side to become wealthy."

"Please don't remind me of the so-called good old days when Grandfather and his brothers were always one step ahead of the police." Leaning closer, she rested her head on Brandt's broad shoulder. "Don't worry about me, Brandt. Saying I don't want to marry Harper aloud is what I needed to end this sham of an engagement. I know Mother will be disappointed, but this is not about her happiness. It's about mine."

"Good girl."

"Let me get back to Harper before he comes looking for me."

"You're going to be all right?"

"I'm good."

Brandt released his sister's hand, and watched as she walked out of the suite. He knew she was going to be all right. After all, she was a Wainwright.

Chapter 3

Ciara Dennison held a small plate filled with spicy shrimp in one hand as she tried balancing a glass of chilled lemonade in the other, slowly wending her way through the throng that had gathered in the ivy-ringed backyard garden called the Ninth Ward. The restaurant, a brand-new New Orleans–inspired restaurant, had become an East Village favorite for down-home cooking.

It wasn't often that she got a chance to hang out with the people who worked at the hospital where she'd begun her nursing career, but she was glad she'd come to her former supervisor's retirement party. Katie O'Brien had given up supervising young graduate nurses to teach.

The glow from the flickering candles and low-wattage lightbulbs behind old hurricane shutters provided the only illumination inside the restaurant. The backyard garden with its fountains, wrought-iron fleurs-de-lis and shrouded, backlit statue of voodoo high priestess Marie LaVeau made Ciara feel as if she was truly in New Orleans instead of the Lower East Side of Manhattan.

"Aren't you going to try the catfish po' boy?"

Ciara felt her heart stop for a few seconds before it started up again, this time at a runaway pace that made her feel slightly lightheaded. It had been more than two years since she'd come face-to-face with the man with whom she'd thought she would spend the rest of her life.

Turning slowly, she glared at him. "Fancy meeting you here," she said sarcastically. "I never would've thought Dr. Eye Candy would come down from his lofty perch to hang out with—what was your phrase? Lowly nurses."

Ciara had been enthralled by the brilliant doctor ten years her senior. He radiated a charisma that made him appear taller than his slight five-foot-nine frame. Victor wasn't classically handsome, but his custom-made suits and shirts enhanced his attractiveness.

Dr. Victor Seabrook stared at Ciara. Her hair was brushed off her face in a ponytail that hung down her spine. His eyes moved slowly from her perfect face to a body women paid him, as one of the best plastic surgeons in the country, in the high six figures to achieve. The black pencil skirt, white linen man-tailored blouse and black-and-white zebra-print slingback stilettos showed off her tall, slender body to its best advantage.

Initially, he'd found himself drawn to Ciara because she was a chameleon. At work, her loose-fitting scrubs, glasses and hair secured in a matronly bun at the nape of her neck gave her the appearance of a no-nonsense nurse.

But away from the hospital, contact lenses replaced her glasses, her hair came down and form-fitting clothes replaced her baggy nursing attire.

"Why are you here, Victor? I'm certain you weren't invited."

Victor blinked. "I came because I knew you would be here. Please hear me out," he pleaded when Ciara turned away. "I came to say I'm sorry, Ciara."

"Two years, Victor. It has taken two years for you to tell me you're sorry," she said incredulously.

"You left the hospital, moved and you wouldn't take my calls on your cell," he replied.

"Well, you see me now. Apology accepted. We have nothing else to say to each other. Now, if you'll excuse me I have to get back to my date."

Victor's eyebrows and the expression on his face lifted. "You're dating someone?"

She let out an unladylike snort. "Did you actually believe I wouldn't find someone after we broke up?" Ciara leaned closer, her head eclipsing the plastic surgeon's by several inches. "Get away from me before I tell my boyfriend that you're stalking me."

Victor held up both hands. "Okay, Ciara. I get the message—loud and very clear." Turning on his heel, he walked back inside the restaurant. Ciara Dennison had done to him what no other woman would think of doing—walk out on him. It was as if history was repeating itself. Victor's mother had walked out on him and his father, destroying the older man, who turned to drugs and alcohol. His father died of an overdose, and Victor became a ward of the state. Eventually he was adopted by his foster parents.

Ciara waited until her ex disappeared, hoping it would be the last time she ever had to see him. What she'd told Victor was only half-true. Although she'd invited her roommate's brother to attend the party with her, NYPD Sergeant Esteban Martinez was not her boyfriend, but just a very good friend.

Pushing a button, Brandt switched from the radio to the playlist in his iPod. He'd left New York City before dawn in an attempt to avoid the morning rush, but had run out of luck when traffic came to a standstill between Baltimore and Washington, D.C. It had taken more than an hour before traffic began to move again.

When he'd stopped in Norfolk, Virginia, to eat a late breakfast and fill up his Escalade, the skies had opened up, with the rain coming down in torrents, flooding many of the local roads. Brandt had considered whether to spend the night in Norfolk or continue on to North Carolina. The decision was made for him when rays of sunlight broke through watery clouds.

The cell phone rang and he pushed a button on the Bluetooth. "Hello."

"Hi, Brandt."

He smiled. "Hey, Rissa. What's up?"

"I did it. I gave Harper back his ring."

Brandt lowered the volume on the music filling the SUV. "How did he take it?"

"He was upset, but there wasn't much he could do with Sumner glaring at him. I'd told Mother, Daddy and Sumner what I'd planned to do, and Mother really shocked me when she said she was relieved."

"You're shi…you're kidding me," he said, before the profanity slipped out.

"No, I'm not. She admitted she found Harper a little too pushy, but hadn't wanted to interfere."

"It looks as if you underestimated Leona Wainwright."

"I know. We're going out for lunch and I'm going to order a burger with bacon, cheese and grilled onions. And, if I'm not too full I'll down an order of steak fries."

"Careful, little sister, or you'll ruin your girlish figure."

Clarissa's lilting laugh came through the speaker. It had been a long time since Brandt had heard her laugh. "I lost whatever curves I used to have. But that's all going to change. Right now it's all about Clarissa Odette Wainwright."

"That's my girl." The skies darkened again and within seconds rain splattered on the windshield. Brandt adjusted the speed of the windshield wipers.

"I want to apologize," Clarissa said.

"What about?"

"Going off on you yesterday."

"I've forgotten about it, so I want you to do the same."

"Consider it done. I have to go, because you know how ticked Mother gets when she has to wait. Bye, and thanks, Brandt."

"Any time, Rissa. Bye." He ended the call, turned up the volume and settled back to concentrate on the rain-slicked road.

Brandt had begun spending more and more of his

off-season time at his modest two-story, three-bedroom house in western North Carolina. He'd come to value the quiet of his retreat, where he took long walks along foot trails, learned to fly-fish from the locals and caught up on his reading. There were times when he'd believed spending so much time alone was turning his brain to mush. But whenever he returned to the endless noise and hustle and bustle of the city he appreciated the pristine wilderness of the Blue Ridge Mountains even more.

He'd purchased the property as a gift to himself for his twenty-ninth birthday. Over the next two years he'd rarely come down to spend time there during the off-season. Then last year everything changed. Not only had he come south several times during the year, but the visits went far beyond his regular weeklong stays. The first visit—a week after the Super Bowl—he'd found himself stranded when a storm downed power lines and trees, making it dangerous to drive on the rural roads.

Brandt thought himself blessed that he'd been able to survive for a week with his backup generator. The pantry had been stocked with essentials—powdered milk, eggs, canned soup—and the refrigerator and freezer had been stocked with vegetables, fruit, juice, meat and fish. He'd spent the time watching movies and reading. Even after the power was restored and the roads had been cleared, Brandt had come to value his privacy and appreciate his own company.

This time he planned to spend a week at the vacation retreat before returning to New York and preseason play. He'd participated in the team's mini-camp several months ago, solidifying his position as the starting quarterback.

He maneuvered onto a two-lane county road. It was going to take longer to reach his destination, but he was sure not to encounter any traffic delays. The distinctive voice of Michael Bublé's "Home" filled the interior of the SUV. One second Brandt was singing along, and a nanosecond later a large object appeared on the road in front of the Escalade. It was a deer. Brandt swerved to avoid hitting it, turned the steering wheel to the right and hit the brake. The thud of the deer landing on the hood sounded like an explosion as the SUV skidded off the road and came to a stop, colliding with a tree.

Brandt didn't know how long he'd been sitting in the smashed car. He didn't know what hurt more—the throbbing in his head, the burning in his jaw or the crushing pain in his legs.

"This is OnStar. We just received a signal that your air bag has deployed. Can you confirm you've been in an accident?"

Brandt heard the voice, but the pain in his jaw wouldn't permit him to open his mouth except to mumble unintelligibly, "Help me."

"Hold on. We're sending someone to help you."

He couldn't count the number of times he'd been tackled, or felt the impact of the wind being knocked out of him. But that pain did not compare to what he felt in the lower part of his body. Each time he tried to move the pain intensified. Then he gave up altogether. The falling rain sounded a rhythmic beat on the roof of the SUV, and Brandt wondered if he could withstand the pain until help arrived. He drifted in and out of consciousness as the disembodied voice from OnStar continued to talk. The last thing he remembered was the sound of her soothing voice and the wail of sirens before he sank into a comfortable darkness without any pain.

When Brandt awoke in a hospital a day later, he learned that in his effort to avoid hitting the deer, he'd crashed his SUV into a tree and broken both legs in several places.

Brandt lay in a hospital bed in his penthouse suite, his legs in plaster casts. He'd spent nearly two weeks in an Asheville hospital before he was flown back to New York in a private jet. Instead of an outpatient rehabilitation facility, Brandt's personal physician had recommended that he do his rehab therapy at home, since he had all the equipment he needed in his penthouse. The news that he would miss the upcoming football season was enough to send him into an emotional tailspin.

"Get out!" he shouted at the nurse who'd come into his bedroom. "Get the hell out and stay out! By the way, you're fired!"

Leona waved to the startled woman. "It's all right, dear. You can leave." She got out of the chaise longue in the sitting area of the bedroom suite and walked over to the bed. Positioning her hands at her waist, she glared at her son. "That's the second nurse you've fired this week."

Brandt turned away, burying his face in the mound of pillows cradling his head. "Please leave me alone."

"You can't be left alone, Brandt."

He closed his eyes. "Well, I don't want her here."

Leona threw her hands up in exasperation. Her fun-loving son had turned into an ogre. He'd refused to take telephone calls or have visitors, insisting that he didn't want to see or talk to anyone. Leona had spent the past three days sleeping in the guest wing, but knew it was time to go home to take care of her own household.

She reached for the telephone on the bedside table, picked up the receiver and dialed the number to the private-nurse agency. Normally she would've made the call in another room, but Leona was past caring about Brandt's feelings.

"This is Mrs. Leona Wainwright. I need you to send another nurse."

"Mrs. Wainwright, are you aware that we've provided you with two excellent nurses this week? Is there a problem?"

She rolled her eyes at her son. "Yes. The patient is the problem."

"If that's the case, then we'll send someone who is an expert in caring for difficult patients. You're in luck, because she happens to be available. Her name is Ciara Dennison."

"When can I expect her?"

"Let me call her, and I'll call you back."

Leona flashed a Cheshire cat grin. "Thank you."

"I told you I don't want anyone in my home," Brandt snarled between clenched teeth after his mother had put the receiver back in the cradle.

"What you want really doesn't matter, Brandt. You're laid up with two broken legs and you need someone to help you get around, give you your medication and make certain you eat. If you want to lie there feeling sorry for yourself, then I'm going home. After you stew in your own waste for a few hours I'm certain you'll change your mind about letting someone into your home. Make up your mind!"

Her words trailed off when the telephone rang. Leona picked it up on the first ring. She smiled. "Thank you very much."

Propping himself up into a sitting position, Brandt reached around to adjust the pillows supporting his shoulders. "When is she coming?"

"Her name is Ciara Dennison and she'll be here between one and two."

Ciara Dennison had the advantage when she'd accepted the assignment as a private nurse for Brandt Wainwright. She knew who he was, but he knew nothing of her nursing skills or unorthodox bedside manner. The agency occasionally called her to deal with difficult patients, and she'd earned a reputation as a no-nonsense nurse who provided excellent care.

When the news broke that pro quarterback Brandt Wainwright had been involved in a car accident in North Carolina, the presumption on most sports news shows was that he'd been driving under the influence. Once it was confirmed that there were no drugs or alcohol in his system, it quieted the skeptics and the gossip.

Ciara arrived at a luxury high-rise overlooking the East River, paid the fare, got out of the cab and walked toward the entrance of the apartment building. As the doorman opened the door to the lobby, she was met with a blast of cool air.

"I'm Ciara Dennison. Mrs. Wainwright is expecting me."

The tall, slightly built man smiled. "I'll let her know

you're here and escort you to the elevator." He reached for the intercom receiver under the lobby desk and punched in several numbers. "Ms. Dennison is on her way up." Ciara followed the doorman past a bank of elevators to one in an alcove. He inserted a card key in the PH slot. "It will take you directly to the penthouse."

The doors closed before Ciara could thank him. The car rose smoothly and swiftly, making her ears pop from the rapid ascent. The car slowed, and then stopped. The doors opened to a panoramic view of the East River bridges linking Manhattan to other boroughs. A profusion of flowers in vases and urns crowded a round mahogany pedestal table between the entryway and great room. For some reason she expected no less from a multimillionaire celebrity athlete.

She was met by a tall, slender woman with hair several shades lighter than her gray eyes. Leona Wainwright was the epitome of casual chic: white silk blouse, black linen slacks and low-heeled Ferragamo shoes. The requisite diamond studs graced her earlobes and a wedding band adorned the ring finger of her left hand.

Leona's eyebrows lifted when she stared at Ciara Dennison. The woman at the agency had said she was tough as nails, but there was nothing about the nurse in the artist's smock that looked menacing. She was younger than Leona had expected and her flawless, dark brown complexion made her appear even younger. The large, clear brown eyes staring back at her behind a pair of glasses reminded her of a cat's. Her hair was brushed off her face and secured in a tight bun. Nurse Dennison had come highly recommended, and Leona realized she was her last hope.

She extended her hand. "Good afternoon. I'm Leona Wainwright, Brandt's mother."

Setting a duffel bag on the floor, Ciara shook her hand, finding it soft and cool to the touch. "Ciara Dennison. And before you say anything, I'd like to meet with my patient—alone."

Leona knew immediately that Ciara was very different from the other nurses. Both had been so awestruck by their patient's celebrity that they hadn't assumed a take-charge position. "Please come with me."

Ciara followed Leona through the expansive entryway that led into a great room. A curving staircase off to the left led to another level. "Is he on this floor or upstairs?" she asked.

Slowing her pace, Leona glanced over her shoulder. "He is in a bedroom on this floor." She didn't tell the nurse that the second floor was usually off-limits to everyone. The only exception was when her son hosted parties in the rooftop solarium. She turned down a wide hallway and walked into one of three bedroom suites set aside for guests.

"I'll wait out here for you."

Ciara nodded and then walked into the room. Brandt Wainwright lay in a hospital bed positioned near the floor-to-ceiling windows, eyes closed, with a sheet covering his lower body, the rise and fall of his bare chest in an even rhythm revealing the steadiness of his breathing. The bedroom was furnished in a traditional style, in contrast to the post-war architecture of the apartment.

She approached the bed. The rapid pulse of the large vein in his neck indicated that he wasn't sleeping. Her gaze lingered on his face. He hadn't shaved and a full day's growth covered his jaw and chin. Ciara wasn't into sports, but only someone completely cut off from civilization wouldn't recognize the NFL's golden boy.

His hair was a mess, indicating it hadn't been combed or brushed. It was also oily, which confirmed it needed to be shampooed. Reaching out, she placed a hand on his shoulder. His skin was cool to the touch. But before she could withdraw her hand, Ciara found her wrist trapped between Brandt's fingers.

"Do you usually shake someone's hand even before you've been introduced?" she said, meeting his angry gaze. His eyes were a startling shade of sky blue.

"Get out!"

"I'm afraid that's not going to be possible. After all, you are holding on to my wrist."

Brandt released her hand. "I've let you go. Now get out!"

Ciara took a step backward, far enough to evade his long reach and folded her arms under her breasts. "I'm not going anywhere, Mr. Wainwright. In case you haven't been counting, I happen to be your third nurse and that means you've just about struck out."

"Wrong sport," Brandt drawled, flashing a sardonic grin.

She inclined her head. "I stand corrected. Maybe I should've said the clock just ran out, sport! Game over."

He stared at the nurse in the tie-dyed smock that overwhelmed her slender frame. His gaze shifted downward to a pair of leather clogs. At least the dark blue scrubs fit. He wasn't exactly sure of her age, but he guessed she was anywhere between twenty-five and thirty.

Brandt had decided on another approach. He knew growling like a wounded bear wasn't going to intimidate this nurse. "Please don't take it personally, but I don't want or need someone taking care of me." His tone was soft, almost soothing.

Ciara wasn't fooled by his sudden change in tone. "Whenever I take care of a patient I can assure you that it's never personal. You have a choice, Mr. Wainwright. Either you let me take care of you here or you can go to a rehab facility."

He snorted. "That's not going to happen."

Her eyes narrowed behind the lenses of her black plastic frames. "You think not? If I walk out of here and file my report with the agency my recommendation will be that you see a psychotherapist and go to an inpatient rehab facility. I'm also certain you don't want to remain on injured reserve next season. And I'm sure you've been cautioned about blood clots. We'll begin by showering and washing your hair. If you want, I can help you shave or you can continue to look like Grizzly Adams."

Brandt sat up straighter. "Did anyone ever tell you that you have a very unusual bedside manner?"

Ciara's expression did not change although she wanted to laugh. "So you noticed. Do you like it when I talk tough?"

He lifted a broad shoulder. "That's something I have yet to decide. One thing for certain is you did get my attention."

"Now that I have your attention, Mr. Wainwright, what do you plan to do?"

"Do about what, Nurse Dennis?"

"It's Dennison. And there's no need to be so formal."

"How shall I address you, miss?"

"Ciara will do."

"Since we're becoming so familiar with each other, then I insist you call me Brandt."

Ciara felt as if she'd scaled one hurdle. Brandt was talking to her instead of yelling at her. "I think it's best that you shower and wash your hair first."

His hand went to his face, absentmindedly scratching his beard. He'd grown the stubble to conceal the bruises on his face from the impact of the air bag. He wasn't certain whether they'd faded, but not having to shave was one less thing he had to concern himself with. Getting out of bed and into the shower was not only difficult, it had become all but impossible.

Brandt's mood changed like quicksilver. "I can shave myself."

"Good," she countered. "I've been known to have a problem with the blade getting a little too close to the jugular."

"Don't tell me you're auditioning as a stand-up comic."

"Very funny, Brandt," Ciara drawled sarcastically.

"You're the one with the jokes. Let's just call a truce."

"You're in no condition to negotiate. Your mother is paying top dollar for me to be your nurse until you're able to take care of yourself. I'll help you with the day-to-day stuff and follow up with the therapist as you progress. I'm required to write up daily reports and give you pain medication, so it's in your best interest to cooperate."

Chapter 4

Brandt continued scratching his face. There was something about Ciara Dennison he liked. There was fire under the dowdy exterior. When he'd yelled at the other two nurses, they'd scurried away like frightened mice. The last one had turned on her heel so quickly she'd almost lost her footing.

What everyone, including his mother, had failed to understand was the feeling of helplessness. Without having the wheelchair at his disposal, he was unable to get out of bed and make it to the bathroom before embarrassing himself. The ultimate humiliation was having to use a bedpan.

During his two-week stay in the North Carolina hospital, he'd believed he would never leave alive. He'd drifted in and out of consciousness from the sedative, unaware of any visitors. When the head of orthopedics recommended his transfer to the hospital's rehabilitation unit, Brandt knew it was time to leave.

He'd returned to New York City, not to a hospital or rehab facility but to his own home. After his personal physician and a leading specialist reviewed his medical records, they approved his convalescing at home with round-the-clock nursing care and physical therapy three times a week for a period of three to four months.

"Are you going to stay here 24/7?"

Ciara hesitated, debating whether to lie or tell the truth. She decided on the former, because she had to know for certain that Brandt would become a cooperative patient. "No. I'll alternate with another nurse. Twelve hours on, twelve off."

"I don't want another nurse."

Ciara took a step closer to the bed, her expression reflected surprise. "You want me to work a twenty-four-hour shift?"

"Will that pose a problem for you?" Brandt asked.

"Not really. But I hadn't planned to work around the clock."

"Well, tell your man that he's going to find something other than you to occupy him while you're at work."

There was no way Ciara was going to admit to Brandt Wainwright that she didn't have a man, husband or boyfriend. After dating Victor Seabrook for two years, she'd decided to not get involved with another man—at least for some time.

"Let's not get personal," she warned softly. "After I help you get cleaned up, I'll have your mother call the agency to change my hours. Then, I'm going to have to return to my place to pick up enough clothes to last for at least a week," she said, lying smoothly. Her carry-on bag contained enough clothes and toiletries to last several weeks.

Unaware that Ciara had skillfully manipulated him into doing something he hadn't wanted, Brandt said, "I have a cleaning service that comes in several times a week. They do laundry. If you need them to take care of anything for you, then leave your clothes in the laundry room." He reached for the sheet, uncovering his legs. He'd changed from wearing boxer-briefs to boxers in order for them to fit over the casts. "I need you to bring the wheelchair closer to the bed so I can go to the bathroom."

Ciara walked around the bed and pulled the wheelchair closer before applying the brake, while Brandt braced his hands on the mattress and pushed himself into the chair. The muscles in his chest, arms and abs were magnificent. She had to remind herself that her patient was a professional athlete, and being in peak physical condition was a major factor in his earning an astounding amount of money for throwing a ball down a football field. He earned as much for one game as most people earned in ten years. She had little interest in sports, especially in jocks with overblown egos.

"Where's the bathroom?"

Brandt pointed to a door on his right. "It's over there. I don't need you to watch me."

Releasing the brake on the chair, Ciara pushed him toward the en suite bath. "I'm not going to watch you. I just want to make certain you make it inside."

"I've made it okay before you got here, and I'm certain I'll make it after you leave."

"Why don't you try dialing down the tough-guy talk, Brandt. You don't frighten me."

"What does frighten you?"

She pushed the chair into a bathroom that was larger than the kitchen and dining room she shared with her roommate in a two-bedroom renovated apartment in West Harlem. There was a free-standing shower, double sinks, a soaker tub with jets and a dressing area. The doors to an antique cupboard were removed to reveal shelves filled with an ample supply of towels and bathrobes.

Ciara wanted to tell Brandt he didn't frighten her in the least. In fact, she found his outbursts rather amusing. There was no doubt he was an imposing figure on the gridiron, but she wasn't a professional football player, and whether or not she was scared of him was irrelevant.

"I'm not afraid of anyone or anything," she stated confidently.

Brandt smiled for the first time in weeks. "I'm impressed."

Pushing him closer to the commode, Ciara positioned Brandt where he could easily get out of the wheelchair. "Are you certain you'll be all right?"

"Yes. I'll let you know if I require your assistance." His words were dripping with sarcasm.

Ignoring his comments, she turned on her heel and walked out of the bathroom, closing the door behind her. Standing next to the door, she exhaled deeply. Going toe-to-toe with Brandt Wainwright was exhausting—it always was that way with a stubborn patient. Dealing with difficult patients always took a lot out of her.

As a psychiatric nurse she knew exactly what Brandt was going through. As an athlete his physical limitations were even more devastating. And although his inability to walk was only temporary, to Brandt it was torture. For most patients in his situation, the feelings of helplessness were often followed by anger and depression. Ciara had to intervene before he succumbed to his emotions. She was certain he would walk again, even if she doubted whether he would be able to play ball again.

His readiness to play football was something she would leave up to the team doctors. Her responsibility was to help with his recovery so that the physical therapist could get him up and walking again. Brandt opened the bathroom door and wheeled the chair into the bedroom. She lowered the bed, making it easier for him to get back into it.

Ciara noticed beads of perspiration on Brandt's forehead and that he'd gritted his teeth when he fell back to the pile of pillows. "Would you like something to help the pain?" She knew he was hurting.

Brandt tried willing the pain to go away, but it'd persisted. It was as if someone was driving hot spikes into his legs. Once he'd left the hospital, he'd resisted taking painkillers, even though he'd been told there was no honor in suffering in silence.

"Please."

Leona arose from the padded bench outside the bedroom where she'd sat waiting for Ciara Dennison to emerge. She hadn't heard Brandt shouting at Ciara, so she prayed things had gone well between him and his latest nurse.

"How did it go?" she asked as Ciara stepped into the hallway.

"Well, Brandt needs to wash his hair, but that's going to have to wait until later. Right now he needs his pain medication."

A sigh of relief escaped Leona. She'd sat praying Ciara Dennison would succeed where the other nurses had failed. She was also surprised Ciara had asked her for Brandt's medication. Whenever she'd asked her son whether he needed something for pain, he'd refused to take anything.

"It's in the kitchen. I'll get it for you."

Ciara took Brandt's pulse as she waited for his mother to return with the painkillers. It was within normal range.

She'd gotten over one hurdle when she had managed to get him to agree to her being there. But she wasn't ready to declare victory just yet. She didn't like getting into his face, but apparently it had worked—if only temporarily.

Ciara waited until Brandt was asleep before she left the bedroom. "He's asleep," she told Leona who popped up from the bench. "Is there some place we can go and talk?"

"We can talk in the kitchen. I could use a cup of chamomile tea to calm my nerves. Would you like coffee or tea?"

Ciara gave her a sidelong glance. "Tea would be nice, thank you."

"After tea, I'll give you a tour of the penthouse. All of the bedroom suites on the first floor have connecting doors. Brandt installed an elevator between the pantry and the kitchen, so you don't have to climb the stairs. If you take the suite next to his it will give you easy access whenever he needs you."

"Does he sleep through the night?" Ciara asked, following Leona into a spacious kitchen finished in an antique white with a coffered ceiling, paneled-door refrigerator, black granite countertops, an eight-burner commercial range and double ovens. The kitchen opened to a formal dining room with the same coffered ceiling.

"I'm not certain." Leona gestured to a quartet of stools at the cooking island. "Please sit down."

Ciara sat, giving the older woman a questioning look. "Why don't you know?"

A rush of color suffused Leona's face. "Since the accident I've been unable to sleep, so my doctor prescribed a sleeping aid. I always make certain Brandt is settled before I take the pill."

So if he were to fall out of bed or need something, you wouldn't know it until the following morning. Ciara shook her head as if to banish the thought. Throughout her nursing career, she had been taught that it was always and only about the patient.

"Is he eating?" she asked, changing the subject.

Leona filled a kettle with water and placed it on the stovetop range. "His appetite is improving."

"What do you mean improving?" Ciara asked.

"During his hospital stay he'd refused to eat, so they fed him intravenously. Since his return, he has been picking at his food."

"Who cooks for him now?" she asked, continuing her questioning, and watching Leona as she moved comfortably around the kitchen, opening cabinets, drawers and removing china and silver.

"I ordered frozen entrées."

Resting her elbows on the countertop, Ciara cupped her chin in the heel of her hand. She decided to reserve comment on the frozen meals. Her mother, Phyllis Dennison, was a registered dietician and abhorred processed food. If it wasn't made from scratch, then it didn't end up on Phyllis's table.

"The pantry and refrigerator are stocked, so if you want to make something for yourself, then please feel free to do so," Leona continued as she placed a bottle of honey and a sugar bowl on the countertop. "If you prefer ordering takeout, then just call the building's concierge. You do cook, don't you?" she asked without taking a breath. "I'm only asking because most young women nowadays are so busy with their careers that cooking isn't as much a priority as it was years ago."

A hint of a smile played at the corners of Ciara's mouth. "My mother is a registered dietitian at a nursing facility and my roommate is a chef. Thankfully I've learned to prepare more than a few dishes."

Leona dropped several teabags into a teapot and added boiling water. "Good for you. I have some scones that go very well with tea. Perhaps you would like some?"

"No, thank you."

She wanted to tell Leona Wainwright that she was on duty and sharing afternoon tea with her patient's mother was not a part of her job description. However she had to go along with it. Private nurses were well paid—and in Brandt Wainwright's case, extremely well paid. Ciara estimated her stint with Brandt would probably last two months, give or take a week. Once the casts were removed and he could bear his own weight, then her assignment would be over. After that, her plans included taking two weeks off to visit with her mother in upstate New York before returning to Manhattan for her next case.

Leona poured the tea into fragile, hand-painted china cups, adding a teaspoon of sugar to hers, while Ciara opted for honey. The two women sat sipping tea in comfortable silence until Leona said, "I hope you don't get the wrong impression of my son. I've never known him to be so rude—"

"There's no need to apologize, Mrs. Wainwright," Ciara interrupted. "I'm more than familiar with—"

"Please call me Leona. I always think of my mother-in-law as Mrs. Wainwright."

Ciara smiled over the rim of her cup. "Okay. As I was saying, there's no need to apologize. Brandt's anger and frustration aren't unique to his type of injury. I've had patients who've gotten depressed and refused to eat, talk or even try to do their rehab."

Leona leaned closer, her brow knitting in concern. "What did you do?"

"I recommended a psychiatric evaluation. Some are prescribed antidepressants, but it was usually enough to get them to open up about their feelings of helplessness or loss of independence."

"Do you think that's what wrong with Brandt?"

"I'm a psychiatric nurse, not a psychiatrist. Your son is a professional athlete, and that means that his body is integral to his self-image. The fact that he can't use his legs would affect him more than someone who sits behind a desk for seven or eight hours a day. I don't think Brandt is as depressed as he is frustrated that he needs help with his most basic needs."

"I pray you're right, Ciara. Seeing Brandt in physical and emotional pain is more than I can bear right now." Leona's eyes filled with tears.

Ciara's hands tightened around her cup to prevent her from reaching out to comfort Brandt's mother. She wanted to remind her that her son had survived a horrific accident that could've ended his life. And the fact that he did survive meant he would recover. Whether he'd ever be able play football again was another matter.

"Brandt's going to be all right, Leona. It's just that he's going through a rough time now. Give him another few weeks."

"I'm trying to be patient, but every time he lashes out I don't recognize him. Of all of my four children he is the free spirit, the most fun-loving. When he told me he wanted to be a professional football player, it was the darkest day in my life. I had visions of him being carried off the field or spending the rest of his life in a wheelchair paralyzed from some freak accident. Little did I know that he would still end up in a wheelchair." Leona sniffled, then dabbed at her nose with a napkin. "I'm sorry about becoming weepy. I'm usually not so emotional."

Ciara gave Leona a warm smile. "You're entitled, because that's what mothers do when there's something wrong with their children."

Blinking back tears, the older woman managed a weak smile. "Even when that child is thirty-three?"

"Yes. Even if that child is fifty or sixty-three."

Leona stared at the young woman sitting opposite her. "Do you have any children, Ciara?"

She shook her head. "No."

"Would you like to have children one day?"

"Perhaps one day," Ciara confirmed, staring into her cup of tea.

She'd thought about having a child, but only if she met the right man. Unlike some women, she didn't want to be a single mother and raise a child by herself. Her parents had divorced the year she'd celebrated her tenth birthday, and not having her father in her life had had a negative affect on her relationships with men. Sometimes she hadn't chosen wisely, and when she did choose to commit to a long-term relationship it was for the wrong reason. At the time, Ciara had wanted to prove to her mother that not only could she get a man, but she could also keep him.

William Dennison was in and out of her mother's life so often that Ciara thought he'd worked for the CIA and that he'd had to go undercover for long periods of time. What she didn't learn until she was in her early teens was that her father was living a double life. Although married to Phyllis, he'd also married another woman. His job as regional manager for a major beverage company kept him on the road, so he was able to divide his time between two households with relative ease. Although a bigamist, William never fathered a child with his second wife.

"You're young, so you have time before you have to decide whether you want to have children."

Leona's soft voice broke into her musings. Thirty-three wasn't that young, Ciara thought.

After wiping the corners of her mouth with a napkin, Leona placed it on the countertop. "I think it's time I show you where everything is."

They walked out of the kitchen, passed a laundry room and entered an area off the pantry. The elevator, large enough to accommodate four, was next to a wine cellar filled with bottles of wine too numerous to count. Ciara smothered a gasp when the elevator door opened to a wall of glass, running the length of the hallway and spanning the width of the penthouse.

Leona turned to her left. "This floor is still under construction. Brandt's private quarters have been completed, but the opposite wing is an open space. He said once he's married with children he'll have a contractor build several bedrooms and a nursery."

Ciara was too enthralled by the sight of a rooftop solarium to respond. Palm trees and exotic flowers made the space seem like an oasis in the middle of Manhattan. She stared at the exotic orchids spilling out of baskets, a riot of color in hues ranging from the deepest purple to pure white.

"Who takes care of the plants?"

"Brandt," Leona replied smiling.

"It appears he has quite the green thumb."

Leona laughed. "He installed a programmable irrigation system similar to the ones in supermarket produce sections where a spray of water keeps everything hydrated. The exception is the cacti."

Ciara smiled. Brandt's mother had unknowingly given her something she would use to motivate her patient. If Brandt liked working with his plants, then it was something he could do while still using his wheelchair.

The atrium took up half the rooftop. The other half was open to the elements. Tables, chairs and love seats with weatherproof cushions were set up for dining and entertaining outdoors.

She didn't know what to expect when she walked into Brandt's private suite, but it wasn't a loft-like space with brick walls, aged plank floors, massive beams crisscrossing the ceiling, support columns and crystal chandeliers. A pair of French doors opened out onto the roof, which was filled with large potted palms and exotic plants. The style was bohemian yet elegant and masculine.

Ciara's shoes made soft swishing sounds on the polished wood floor as she walked beyond an area where a chessboard sat on a leather ottoman between straight-back upholstered chairs. She stood under the arched entryway, staring at a collection of swords mounted on a wall. Her eyes were drawn to one that looked very much like a samurai sword. Moving closer, she admired the intricate carving on the handle and scabbard.

"His bedroom is to your left," Leona said behind her.

It was apparent that Brandt Wainwright was more complicated than Ciara thought. His apartment was a retreat high above the noisy city streets.

"Where did he get the columns and architectural cornices?" Ciara asked.

"My daughter works at a gallery dealing in architectural elements from old buildings. Some of the columns come from Hollywood movie sets; the wooden arch support is from a cathedral in Montreal and the lion heads are from an old library."

She and Leona retraced their steps, taking the wrought-iron spiral staircase instead of the elevator to the first floor.

A fully functional gym, home theater with a large, wall-mounted screen and an expansive living room made up the next floor. The library furnishings were unexpected for a professional athlete. There were no trophies or photos, framed newspaper articles or magazine covers. It appeared lived-in, a place were one came to read and relax. Espresso-colored leather chairs and a love seat, a massive antique mahogany desk and dark built-in bookcases completed the room.

Ciara stood at the window, staring down at the bumper-to-bumper traffic inching its way along FDR Drive. They looked like miniature cars from more than thirty stories above the street. "I'd better check on Brandt," she said when Leona joined her at the window. "I have your numbers, so if there's any change in his condition I'll let you know."

Leona smiled. "I know I'm leaving him in good hands." She let out a soft sigh. "Now that you know where everything is, it's time I go home and make certain my household is still intact. I just want to remind you that the cleaning service is scheduled to come tomorrow, and the physical therapist will call to let you know when he's coming. However you plan to deal with Brandt…" Her words trailed off when Ciara gave her a look that spoke volumes. "I'm sorry. I shouldn't tell you how to do your job."

"It's okay. I've had to deal with much more difficult patients than your son."

Brandt Wainwright would probably yell, but Ciara doubted that she would have as hard a time handling him as some of her other patients.

She waited for Leona to leave and then went to see if Brandt was still asleep. Walking into his bedroom, she saw him lying on his back, arms above his head. At first she thought he was asleep, but as Ciara moved closer to the bed she realized he was staring up at the ceiling.

"How are you feeling?"

Brandt turned his head slowly. He'd tried to remember the timbre of Ciara Dennison's voice, but couldn't because of the drug that managed to not only dull the pain racking his body but also his brain. He didn't like taking it because it tended to impair his speech and ability to think. His eyelids fluttered as he fought against the dulling effects of the painkiller.

"Better." He pointed at the armchair near the bed. "Please sit down and talk to me."

Ciara complied, staring at the powerfully built, bearded man with the piercing blue eyes framed by long, dark lashes. "What do you want to talk about?"

A hint of a smile tilted the corners of Brandt's strong mouth. "Anything, as long as it keeps me awake."

"Have you ever thought that perhaps you need to sleep?"

Brandt closed his eyes. "I slept enough when they doped me up in Asheville."

"The term is sedated, not doped," Ciara countered.

Here I Am

"You call it whatever you want, but it's still doping to me."

Sitting up straight, she met his angry glare. "There's no need to get testy, Brandt."

"And you don't have to be so prissy."

Ciara could give as well as she could get but decided to swallow her response, realizing that going head-to-head with Brandt would end in a stalemate. "I'm willing to sit and talk. What I'm not going to put up with is you cursing at me. Save that language for the locker room."

Brandt's eyes narrowed. "Don't tell me you're that prim and proper." As soon as the words were off his tongue he realized he may have misread Ciara Dennison.

"What I am is none of your concern. What you should concern yourself with is taking a shower and washing your hair. After that I'll bring you something to eat."

Brandt ran his fingers through his mussed hair. "I took a shower this morning, but I didn't get around to washing my hair, because there wasn't any shampoo in the bathroom. As for food, I don't want that stuff my mother left in the freezer."

"What's wrong with it?"

"What's right with it?" Brandt asked. "It tastes like hospital food."

Ciara looked away so he couldn't see her smiling. "Are you hungry?"

"Yes. I feel like I haven't eaten in days."

"What do you want? Steak and potatoes?"

Brandt grinned at Ciara, revealing a set of beautiful

straight white teeth. "Steak and potatoes, Philly cheese-steak or sausage and peppers."

"What are you, on some kind of bodybuilding diet?"

"Hell, yeah," he drawled.

"I'm going to set up a swear jar, and every time you curse you'll have to put a dollar in it."

Brandt crossed his arms over his chest. "And what do you intend to do with the contents?"

"Donate it to charity."

"If that's the case, then I'll put a couple of thousand in it beforehand and cuss away."

Ciara rolled her eyes at him. She'd dated a man who after one drink couldn't complete a sentence without using four-letter words. The alcohol lowered his inhibitions and loosened his tongue. After their second date she told him it wasn't going to work out between them.

"Just try and watch your language." A long silence followed as they engaged in what had become a stare-down, neither willing to concede.

"I'll watch what I say if…"

"If what?" Ciara asked when he didn't finish his statement. She then realized he'd closed his eyes. "Brandt?"

"I'm not sleeping."

"What are you doing?"

Brandt smiled. "I'm resting my eyelids."

Ciara rose from the chair. "You rest your eyelids while I go and get some shampoo." Maintaining his personal hygiene was essential to his emotional well-being. She didn't want to give herself kudos, but she was making progress with her patient; she'd gotten Brandt to take his pain medication and he'd agreed to wash his hair. He'd also admitted to being hungry, and that meant he didn't intend to starve himself to death.

"You should find shampoo on a shelf in the pantry, and there're steaks in the freezer." He opened his eyes. "You do know how to broil a steak?"

She'd just discovered who Brandt Wainwright was. He was a big dog with a big bark but with little or no bite. "I've broiled a few. How do you like yours cooked?"

"Medium-well."

"Your mother gave me a tour of your place and I think it would be nice if you eat upstairs. It would do you good to get some fresh air."

Propping himself up on one elbow, Brandt gave his nurse a long, penetrating stare. "Are you going to eat with me?"

"What?"

"'What?'" he mimicked. "I asked if you were going to eat with me, Ciara Dennison, or is that not allowed in your book—sharing meals with your patients?"

"I don't have any hard-and-fast rules, just what is and isn't appropriate between a nurse and a patient. We're not in a hospital setting, so there's nothing wrong with me sharing a meal with my patient."

Lying back down onto the mound of pillows cradling his shoulders, Brandt closed his eyes again. "Thank you."

The seconds ticked as Ciara stared at the bearded man whose very size was intimidating enough without him raising his voice. If he'd thought he'd frighten her into leaving then he didn't know how stubborn she could be. Push and she would push back—harder. Yell and she would yell even louder. Her only focus was making certain her patient received the best possible care.

"You're welcome." The two words were barely off her tongue when soft snoring filled the room. He'd fallen asleep again. Ciara was glad. It would give her time to prepare dinner.

Chapter 5

Ciara positioned the retractable nozzle so Brandt could reach it when sitting on the shower chair. She'd placed a towel around his waist before removing his underwear to provide him with a modicum of privacy. It didn't matter to her whether he was nude or fully clothed. She'd lost count of the number of naked bodies she'd seen in more than a decade of nursing. Some male patients were uncomfortable with female nurses. But even with more men going into the field, there were still too few nurses. She rechecked the Velcro fastenings on the plastic sheath covering his feet and casts, then handed Brandt a plastic squeeze bottle filled with shampoo.

She rested a hand on his shoulder. "I'll be in the bedroom. Call me when you're finished."

Brandt covered her hand with his, increasing the pressure on her fingers when she tried pulling away.

"Aren't you going to help me wash my back?" There was a glint of amusement in his eyes.

Ciara wrinkled her nose. "No. That's why I gave you a back brush."

"Ah, come on."

She couldn't help but smile. "You must really be feeling better."

Attractive lines fanned out around Brandt's eyes when he returned her smile. "You think?"

"I think. Please let go of my hand. I have work to do."

For reasons he could not fathom, Brandt didn't want to let her go. There was something about Ciara that intrigued him. Why, he pondered, did she wear clothes that definitely didn't flatter her figure? And what was up with the bun? The glasses were all right—at least they were stylish. But the rest of her was dowdy. It was as if his nurse had gone out of her way to make herself look frumpy.

He'd seen her smile a few times and the gesture made her look like an entirely different person. It softened her sensually curved, full lips and scrunched up her very cute little nose. Even without makeup her skin was flawless, giving the appearance of whipped chocolate cream. Brandt released her hand and shook his head. What difference did it make to him that his nurse looked as if she were auditioning for a role on *Little House on the Prairie?*

"I'll call you when I'm finished." Ciara had asked him whether he was feeling better. His head was better, but physically he wasn't. Every time he'd tried moving his legs he was reminded of his limited mobility. And he'd decided after dispatching two nurses that he was going to try and cooperate with the third. He wanted to feel better, regain full use of his legs, and he wanted to play football again. Playing football was not only what he did, it had become his obsession.

Ciara changed the linen on Brandt's bed and adjusted the temperature level on the thermostat while she waited for him to finish in the bathroom. The temperature in the bedroom was sixty-two degrees. She'd positioned the ultra-thin, flat-screen television resting on a stand in the sitting area so that Brandt would be able to view it from the bed. Underwear, a pair of shorts and a T-shirt lay across the foot of the bed.

"Come out, come out, wherever you are!" Brandt shouted from the bathroom.

She smiled. Under the mass of muscle was a grown-up boy whose only objective in life was to play ball. "Ready or not, here I come!"

Ciara entered the bathroom, reaching for two towels from the stack she'd left on the bench next to the bathtub. He sat on the shower chair; droplets of water had beaded up on his naked body. Water had turned his palomino-gold hair to a burnished shade.

Brandt tunneled his fingers through his hair, pushing it off his forehead. He went completely still when Ciara came up behind him and towel-dried his hair. The warmth from her body, the subtle fragrance of her perfume swept over him like a cool breeze. But instead of cooling him it generated a swath of heat that settled between his thighs, stirring his flaccid sex like a roused cat.

"Give me a towel!" The demand had come out harsher than he'd intended.

"Whatever happened to please," she hissed in his ear. Ciara nearly slapped Brandt with the towel as she shoved it at him. Taking the other towel slung over her shoulder, she blotted the moisture from his neck and back.

He gritted his teeth as he covered his thighs in an attempt to conceal his growing erection. It hadn't been that long since he'd slept with a woman, so what was it about this woman that had him aroused?

"Please and thank you very much," he drawled sarcastically.

"That's better."

Brandt hoisted himself from the shower chair to the wheelchair after Ciara removed the plastic covering the casts. He suffered her light touch as she drew a damp cloth over and through his toes, dried them and followed with a light dusting of talc.

He met her eyes behind the lenses of her glasses, his gaze lingering on her delicate features. Her face was doll-like: round, wide-eyed, with delicate features. Brandt had overheard men talk about being attracted to the schoolteacher type. Even with her glasses and hair pulled back, Ciara didn't quite fit the category. Twenty-four hours ago he hadn't known Ciara Dennison existed. But he didn't have to have to be a rocket scientist to know that her dowdy style was a feeble attempt to minimize her femininity.

He smiled. "Thank you. I can take it from here."

Ciara gave him a skeptical look. "Are you certain you don't need help getting dressed?"

Brandt nodded. "I'm certain."

She plucked the wet towels off the floor, hanging them up to dry and prayed that Brandt hadn't noticed that her hands were shaking. What she had noticed was his erection, wondering whether it was spontaneous or if she had in some way aroused him.

When she'd worked at the hospital her colleagues would tease her relentlessly about wearing too-large tops. An incident with a male patient early in her nursing career had traumatized her to the point where she refused to wear anything that would reveal the outline of her upper body.

"I'm going to the kitchen to start dinner." She'd marinated the steaks, prepared a salad. All that remained was microwaving the potatoes.

"Are we eating on the rooftop terrace?"

"Yes," she confirmed. "Or would you prefer eating in the kitchen or dining room?"

"No. The rooftop will be nice."

Brandt stared at Ciara's retreating figure. When it came to the opposite sex his radar never failed him. If he met a woman for the first time he was able to conclude after the first five minutes whether he'd wanted to see her again. If not, he knew right away. Ciara was in the former category rather than the latter. But his mother had hired her as his private nurse. She looked nothing like the women he usually dated, yet there was something about her that tugged at him. He wondered if she hadn't been his nurse if he would want to date her.

Releasing the brakes on the chair, he rolled it out of the bathroom and into the bedroom.

Brandt sat across the table from Ciara in an area of the terrace where lengthening shadows offset the lingering heat of the summer sun. She'd prepared skirt steaks, baked potatoes and a summer salad of melon and feta with balsamic vinaigrette. Freshly squeezed lemonade made with sparkling lemon-lime-infused water was a refreshing alternative to water.

He pointed to the salad. "I can't believe you found all of this in the refrigerator."

Ciara set down her goblet of lemonade. "I had to pick through the mixed baby greens to select the ones that were still fresh. You hadn't cut the melon, so it was still ripe." She'd crumbled some feta cheese and added thinly sliced scallions.

"You're an incredible cook," Brandt said, raising his goblet.

She raised her goblet in acknowledgment. "Thank you."

Brandt speared another forkful of salad, savoring the differing flavors and textures on his tongue. "I'd ordered groceries before driving down south, because I knew I wouldn't have time once mini-camp and preseason began."

"Do you usually cook for yourself?"

Brandt nodded. "Not enough, even though I enjoy cooking." He put up a hand. "Before you ask, I'll admit to watching cooking channels. I've learned to make Paula Deen's Southern fried chicken and Aaron McCargo Jr.'s stuffed pork chops."

Leaning back in her chair, Ciara saw excitement light

up Brandt's eyes. It was apparent football, plants and samurai swords weren't Brandt's only interests. "What's your best dish?"

"Shrimp and grits. I'm still trying to perfect an authentic New Orleans po' boy."

"Hey-y-y," she crooned. "So you like Southern cuisine."

"I love it. That's why I bought a place in North Carolina."

Resting her arms on the table, Ciara leaned closer. "Why North Carolina?"

Brandt speared a slice of steak and popped it into his mouth, moaning under his breath. "Delicious. Why North Carolina?" he repeated. "I had a teammate who'd gotten into real estate with his brother-in-law. They gave me a prospectus of new homes and lodges going up around Lake Lure. It only took one visit to convince me to buy."

"Where is Lake Lure?"

"It's near Chimney Rock, around twenty-five miles southeast of Asheville. The long-time locals told me the exterior shots in *Dirty Dancing* were filmed in Lake Lure."

"I thought it was filmed in the Catskills," Ciara admitted.

"I'd thought so, too. It's the same with *Last of the Mohicans*—it was also filmed in North Carolina."

The topic segued from food to movies and music, Brandt confessing he had a fondness for movie soundtracks. Ciara felt as if she'd escaped to another universe devoid of city noise and traffic. If it hadn't been for the sound of passing air traffic overhead she would've forgotten she was sitting on a rooftop terrace in the middle of Manhattan.

The conversation came to an abrupt halt when Ciara's cell phone rang. Reaching into the pocket of her tunic, she stared at the display. It was Leona Wainwright. Excusing herself, she stood up and walked a short distance away so Brandt couldn't overhear her.

"Hello, Leona."

"How is everything?"

Her gaze lingered on the choppy waters of the East River before shifting to the roofs of buildings with water towers and central and cooling units. "It's going well. We're eating dinner on the terrace."

"He's eating?"

Ciara noted the surprise in Leona's voice. "I'm going to be honest with you. He doesn't like the frozen dinners you brought over."

"Did you order in?"

"No. I cooked dinner."

"I hadn't planned on you preparing meals for Brandt. Don't worry. I'll pay you separately for cooking for my son."

"You don't have to, Leona."

"Yes, I do. If I didn't pay you I'd have to pay someone else. And I don't want to get into another argument with Brandt. What matters is that he's eating. The next step is to convince him to start accepting visitors. The entire family traveled to North Carolina to see him, but he was so heavily sedated that he probably doesn't remember who was there. I don't expect you to become a miracle worker, Ciara. But please try and get him to change his mind."

"I'll see what I can do," she said, not willing to promise anything.

She wanted to tell Leona that she had to take it one day at a time. Tonight was the first time in weeks Brandt had gotten out of bed to eat, and she didn't want to force him into doing something he didn't want to do.

"Do you want to call me tomorrow, or should I call you, Ciara?"

"Let's make it every other day—unless something comes up. If Brandt is willing to accept visitors, then I'll call you. Right now I would recommend immediate family members and only one or two at a time. I don't want to be rude, but I'd like to get back to make certain Brandt finishes his dinner."

"I'm sorry, darling. I didn't know I'd interrupted you," Leona apologized. "I'll wait for your call."

Ciara ended the call, slipping the tiny phone into the pocket of her smock. "Sorry about the interruption," she said to Brandt as she sat back down.

Folding his arms over his chest, Brandt angled his head. "I'd like you to answer two questions for me."

"Only two?" Ciara teased, smiling.

Brandt's impassive expression did not change. "For now."

"What are they?"

"Why do you wear your clothes so baggy?"

Her eyebrows lifted slightly. "And what is the other question?"

"How do you maintain a normal love life when you sign up for an extended nursing assignment?"

"The second question is a lot easier to answer than the first. Right now I'm not seeing anyone."

"But you do date?"

"Yes, I date, Brandt. Why are you asking?"

He lifted a shoulder. "Maybe one of these days when I'm not in this chair I'd like to take you out for dinner to say thanks."

"You want to date your nurse?"

"By that time you won't be my nurse. And it really won't be a date."

Ciara stared at him in surprise, recalling his former hostility. "It wasn't that long ago that you ordered me out of your home and now you're talking about taking me out."

"That's before I got to know you."

"Know me or came to the realization that I'm not going anywhere?"

"Both."

"I'm sorry, but I can't go out with you."

"Can't or won't?"

"Okay, won't. I've made it a practice not to date celebrities."

"Have you ever dated one?"

She wanted to tell Brandt to let it go, that he shouldn't take her response as a rejection. "Yes."

"Who is he?"

"I can't tell you." Ciara was more than surprised that he'd asked her something so personal. She was certain if she'd answered his question Brandt would recognize the name.

A slight frown creased Brandt's forehead. His curiosity about Ciara had just escalated. "Are you running away from him?"

"No. Why would you say that?"

"I…I don't know. Forgive me for being intrusive?"

Ciara flashed a sexy moue. "I'll think about it."

"Don't think too long, Nurse Dennison."

"I thought it was going to be Ciara and Brandt."

"Oops. My bad."

She shook her head in amazement. "I'll accept the 'my bad,' but you are much too big for anything resembling 'oops' to come out of your mouth."

Throwing back his head, Brandt laughed. The sound came from deep within his chest and bubbled up like rolling thunder. A moment later her laughter joined his, both laughing until tears rolled down their cheeks. Without warning, he sobered, staring at her.

Ciara stopped laughing, and as their eyes met she felt a shiver run through her when Brandt rolled the chair close to where she felt the warmth of his breath on her face. "What are you doing?" The query was a breathless whisper.

Resting an arm over the back of her chair, Brandt pressed a kiss to her cheek. "Thank you."

"For what?"

"For making me laugh."

Ciara felt his nearness stirring and disturbing. Brandt Wainwright was too large, too masculine and much too attractive a man to ignore completely. "I'm glad I can make you laugh."

Brandt came closer without moving. "And I'm glad you're here."

"Does this mean you're going to do whatever I tell you to do?"

He smiled. "It all depends."

"It depends on what?" she asked.

"It depends on how I feel when I wake up. If I'm going to be in a bad mood, then I doubt I'll be that cooperative. But if I wake up in a good mood then you can have your way with me."

"The only one who will have their way with you will be your physical therapist," Ciara countered.

"Damn, you really know how to kill the mood."

"The mood?" she responded.

"I'd like to think it is. It's been a long time since I've shared the rooftop with a woman—a woman who's hiding behind a baggy top and an old-lady hairdo."

"You forgot the glasses."

Brandt ran a forefinger over her cheekbone. "No, I didn't. The glasses are all right. Even no makeup is cool but the rest…."

Ciara stared, momentarily shocked by his bluntness. "No, you didn't…."

"Yes, I did, Ciara Dennison. There's no doubt you're an incredible nurse but—"

"But what?" she retorted, angrily.

Running a large hand over his face, Brandt tried to gather his thoughts. He had put his foot in his mouth and he had to find a way to extricate it without embarrassing himself or insulting Ciara any more than he had.

"I'm sorry. Forget it."

Her eyes narrowed. "I'll accept your apology, but there's no way in hell I'm going to forget what you've just said."

He held out his hand. "Pay up."

"What are you talking about?"

"You cussed. You owe the jar a dollar."

"The jar is for you, not me."

"Wrong. If I have to make a concerted effort not to cuss, then the same goes for you." He angled his head. "Now pay up, or the deal is off and I will really let loose."

Ciara didn't give Brandt a chance to react when she pressed her lips to his, caressing his strong mouth. The kiss ended as quickly as it'd begun. "I think that's worth more than a dollar."

Brandt was too stunned to reply or react. He sat motionless, watching as Ciara picked up her plate. "Don't start something you can't finish," he warned softly, recovering his voice.

"And what exactly are you going to do sitting in that chair?" she challenged.

There was enough sassiness in her voice to pique his competitiveness. After all, he was a pro ballplayer, always ready and willing to take on any challenger.

"Come over here and I'll show you what I can do."

Ciara blew him a kiss, crooning, "Some other time, cowboy. I don't want you to do anything that would compromise your recovery." She began stacking plates, glassware and serving bowls on the serving cart.

"What I propose will not in way compromise my recovery."

"Slow it down, Superman. There will be plenty of time for that once the casts are off and you regain full use of your legs."

A smile spread over Brandt's face as he watched the confident fluidity in Ciara's movements. Everything about her radiated self-assuredness, as if she was certain of her rightful place in the world. "Will you indulge once I regain full use of my legs?"

Ciara hands did not falter when she placed glassware on the second shelf of the cart. Brandt was asking whether she would permit him to make love to her. There was no way she was going to date another celebrity after what she'd gone through with Victor.

"No."

"No?" Brandt repeated.

Her hands stilled, she glaring at him. "What part of no don't you understand? No, Brandt Wainwright."

"Is it because I am Brandt Wainwright?"

"No. It's because you're a celebrity athlete, and you can't go anywhere without cameras following you. Every aspect of what you say and do is for public consumption."

"And if I weren't what you call a celebrity athlete?"

Ciara wanted to tell Brandt that she'd never dated blonds and in particular blond jocks with inflated egos but decided not to go there. "I'd have to think about it."

While Ciara was thinking about it, Brandt decided to do something about it. He wouldn't put undue pressure on her because that wasn't his style when it came to women. He'd discovered his nurse was someone who intrigued him. Her appearance belied her lively personality. He hadn't expected her to kiss him. He'd enjoyed the kiss, as brief as it was, and wanted to experience it again.

"I'll accept that." *For now,* he added silently.

Brandt maneuvered his chair behind Ciara as she

pushed the serving cart down the hallway to the elevator and kitchen. Sitting in the wheelchair, he stacked dishes, glasses, utensils and serving pieces in the dishwasher after she'd rinsed them in the sink. Working together, they made quick work of cleaning up the kitchen.

She pushed him out of the kitchen and back to the bedroom. "After I take your blood pressure, temperature and check your heart and lungs, I'm going to give you your medication."

Opening his mouth to protest, Brandt closed it quickly. He knew he had to cooperate with his nurse if he wanted to win her over. "I'd rather not take the pain pill until later."

"Okay."

Ciara stared at the thick, pale strands covering Brandt's head as he pushed himself off the chair and onto the bed. He didn't protest when she assisted him out of his shorts, leaving a pair of briefs and a T-shirt. She adjusted the foot of the bed until his legs were slightly elevated, and then the pillows cradling his back and head.

"Can you please give me the remote? The Mets are playing the Rockies in Colorado."

Although she wasn't into sports, Ciara knew baseball games ran an average of two and a half to three hours. That meant the game wouldn't probably end until after midnight. She handed him the remote. "Do you think you're going to get enough sleep, because I'm going to get you up at six in the morning."

"I'll be all right," Brandt said, hoping to reassure his nurse that he was consciously ready to begin what he knew would become a difficult regimen of physical therapy.

"I'll bring you your pain pill at eleven."

"Eleven-thirty."

"Eleven, Brandt," she said in a no-nonsense tone. "The time is non-negotiable."

He gave her a snappy salute as she turned and walked out of the bedroom. "Aye, aye, ma'am."

Ciara had insisted on eleven because she needed to get at least six hours of sleep to be alert. Anything less would put her and her patient at risk of her making a mistake that could prove costly.

She returned with a small case containing a digital thermometer, electronic sphygmomanometer and stethoscope. In addition to his pain medication, Brandt's doctor had also prescribed a multivitamin, an iron supplement and a blood thinner to reduce the possibility of blood clots brought on by his immobility. Any abnormalities were to be reported immediately

Her patient appeared oblivious to what she was doing because his attention was focused on the television screen. He seemed enraptured by the pre-game commentary as she handed him a glass of water from the carafe on the bedside table and then a pill until he'd taken all of them.

"Can you please adjust the air conditioning?" Brandt asked without pulling his gaze from the screen. "It's too hot in here."

Ciara did his bidding, left the bedroom and walked in the adjoining one. She half closed the connecting door. For the next hour or two she would shower, read, give

Brandt his pain medication, then settle down to sleep for the night.

She wanted to forget that she'd kissed Brandt. What she couldn't forget was how pleasurable it had felt. He'd kissed her cheek and she'd kissed his mouth. She and Brandt hadn't known each other twenty-four hours, yet they'd crossed the line between nurse and patient.

Chapter 6

Brandt woke, unaware of time, day or place. The tightly woven shades covering the windows were raised and sunlight had inched its way over the parquet floor. It had been the first restful night's sleep since he'd come home from the hospital. What he had recognized immediately was the fragrance wafting in his nostrils.

"What's the score?"

Ciara lowered the rails to the bed. "I don't know." Brandt had fallen asleep with the television on and when she'd come into the bedroom the image of an infomercial spokesperson had been flickering across the screen.

Pushing himself into sitting position, he stared at Ciara. There was something about her that was different this morning. A knowing smile tilted the corners of his mouth. It was her hair. A ponytail had replaced the unattractive bun.

"I like what you've done with your—" His compliment

was preempted when she placed the thermometer under his tongue.

Ciara stared at Brandt watching her like a predator contemplating his next meal. "I got a text on my cell that the therapist will be here at nine. That means you'll have to shower and eat before he arrives." He nodded as she took his blood pressure, checked his vitals, writing down the results that she would later transfer to her laptop and subsequently forward to Brandt's doctor's office for an update.

He'd noticed something else about Ciara this morning. She was all business. "Everything okay?" he asked when she put her medical equipment away in the canvas bag.

"Your lungs are clear and all of your vitals are within the normal range. I'll wait until after you've eaten to give you your vitamins and blood thinner. I won't give you anything for pain until after your therapy session."

"I'm going to try and do without it today."

Ciara met his steady gaze. "You don't have to be a martyr, Brandt."

He scratched the growth on his chin. "I don't want to become dependent on them."

"I'll make certain you won't become dependent."

Brandt continued to scratch his bearded face. "I think it's time I shave this stuff off my face. It's itching like hell." Ciara's eyebrows shot up. "I know. I'll pay up later."

"I have everything set up for you in the bathroom except your shaving stuff."

Brandt threw back the sheets and, using the strength in his upper body, managed to swing his legs over the side of the bed, wincing from the effort. "There's a razor and shaving cream in a drawer under the vanity. Please bring the chair closer."

It was as if whatever had passed between them the day before hadn't happened at all. He was the patient and Ciara Dennison was the nurse Leona Wainwright had hired for his long recuperation.

Maybe, Brandt mused, he'd come on too strong when he'd pressed Ciara about going out with him. Was he beginning to believe his own hype because he was a Super Bowl MVP? Was it because he'd had the highest quarterback rating for two consecutive seasons? Or was it because women threw themselves at him that he'd believed any woman should be grateful he'd shown them some attention?

It was apparent Ciara was different—in appearance and in temperament—from the other women he'd gone out with. That was something he would make certain to remember in the coming weeks and months.

The women from the cleaning service arrived minutes after the therapist, who wheeled Brandt into his home gym for his first session. Ciara retreated to the solarium to wait. She'd stripped the beds and stored the linens in hampers in the laundry room.

She made a mental note not to have the therapist and cleaning service come in on the same day. There was just too much activity. The sound of vacuuming and people going in and coming out of rooms had upset the calm Brandt needed for his rehabilitation.

Reaching for her cell, she dialed her roommate's

number. "Did I wake you?" she said when hearing her greeting.

"No. I just came in from jogging."

"Since when did you start jogging?" Ciara asked Sofia Martinez.

"Since Bobby invited me to go with him on his morning run."

"You're dating your boss?"

"He's not really my boss, *chica*. His father is my boss. Bobby and I are coworkers."

"Sure. And I plan to join the circus next week," she teased.

"Enough about me, *chica*. You left me a text saying you didn't know when you'd be home. What's up?"

Although she and Sofia were roommates, they rarely saw each other. Whenever Ciara had a private nursing assignment, she usually left a text on Sofia's cell telling her she would be away for several days, or even a week or two. Sofia, who owned the two-bedroom co-op, worked as a chef in a popular Washington Heights restaurant and worked different shifts. There were times when she went in early for the breakfast and lunch crowd, and other times when she worked late for dinner and private parties.

"I have an assignment that will last about six to eight weeks."

"I hope you're going to find someone to fill in for you for my brother's surprise birthday party."

Ciara nodded even though Sofia couldn't see her. She'd committed to helping Sofia coordinate Esteban's fortieth birthday celebration scheduled for the Labor Day weekend. "I'll make certain someone will cover for me." If she couldn't get another nurse, then she would ask Leona to spend the night with Brandt.

"How is your patient?"

"That's why I called you." She told her friend about her initial meeting and confrontation with Brandt, that she'd acted inappropriately when she kissed him and his wanting to date her even though he'd said she looked dowdy.

There was only the sound of soft breathing coming through the earpiece. "I suppose he was referring to your maternity top and bun."

Ciara rolled her eyes. "You don't have to agree with him."

"I'm not calling you dowdy, but you need to start wearing uniforms that fit your body. Whether you realize it or not, you've allowed one ugly incident to determine how you dress. Aren't you the one who's always preaching about not letting anyone control your life? Isn't that why you stopped seeing Victor Seabrook?"

"You're right, Sofia."

"If I'm right, then do something about it. Now, back to your patient. Do you like him?"

"This is not about liking or not liking him, Sofia. I haven't known Brandt Wainwright twenty-four hours and—"

"And what, Ciara? You don't have to know someone twenty-four hours to know there's *fuego* between you. I'm online and I just Googled Brandt Wainwright, and judging from the pictures of him and other women, none of them are featuring maternity tops and buns. Wait a minute. There's a close-up of him and I must say *el hombre es muy guapo.* What do you have to lose by going out with him? Maybe after one date you'll realize you don't want to see him anymore. And poof! It's over."

She smiled. Sofia often used Spanglish when she was excited. The chef was right about Brandt being gorgeous. She'd found herself staring at him like a starstruck teen after he'd shaved. He had a strong, masculine jawline and the slight cleft in his chin was incredibly sexy.

"Maybe I'm just overreacting."

"You're probably overreacting because you've been in a sexual drought."

"It's not about sex!"

"*¡Párelo!* Stop it," Sofia translated in the same breath. "It's always about sex, Ciara. If it wasn't, then the human race as we know it would cease to exist. Remember, his mother hired you, so that makes a big difference if you're going to start with 'I can't get involved with my patient because it wouldn't be ethical.' You may be his nurse, but you're also his companion. Flirt and tease him a little bit. I'm certain that will pull him out of his doldrums. And it's not as if he can chase you around the bedroom in a wheelchair."

Ciara knew she was good for Brandt. She'd made him laugh, eat and take his medication. What she had to figure out was whether he was good for her. Could she afford a dalliance with the superstar athlete behind closed doors? And once he was able to walk, could she walk away emotionally unscathed?

"I'm going to play it by ear," she told Sofia.

"That's my girl. Always leave your options open. Be sure to text me with updates."

"Okay. Thanks for lending an ear."

"*Siempre. Recuerde,* we're *chicas.*"

Ciara smiled. "How can I forget?"

"Because I won't let you. I have to get into the shower. I'm working the lunch shift today. Later."

She ended the call, feeling less anxious than she had before talking to Sofia. Invariably Ciara could count on her friend to give her another perspective on any situation and vice versa. She'd been there for Sofia when she'd ended her short-lived marriage after she'd discovered her husband was sleeping with another woman, and Sofia had been there for her when she ended her relationship with Victor Seabrook. They didn't need to see a therapist to work through their problems. They had each other.

Checking her watch, Ciara estimated Brandt's therapy session would end in another ten minutes. She left the solarium and took the staircase to the first floor. The sound of the intercom chimed throughout the penthouse. Pressing a button on the panel in the living room, she answered the call.

"This is the lobby. Mr. Jordan Wainwright is on his way up."

Ciara hesitated. "Please send him up."

She wasn't about to get embroiled in a family feud, so if Brandt didn't want to see his relative, then let him tell him to his face. She waited in the entryway when the doors to the elevator opened and Jordan Wainwright exited. Living in Harlem, she'd read about the attorney who'd become something of a champion for the poor. But seeing him up close was breathtaking. She stared at the tall, slender man with patrician features, brilliant hazel eyes and a sun-browned face. Everything about him reeked of elegance and sophistication, from his short-cropped black hair to his tailored suit and Italian shoes. It was obvious he was spoken for when she spied the wedding band on his left hand.

Smiling, Ciara extended her hand. "I'm Ciara Dennison, Brandt's nurse."

Jordan returned her smile, attractive lines fanning out around his eyes, and took her hand. "My pleasure. I'm Jordan. Brandt's cousin. Is he around?"

"He's with the physical therapist right now. Please come in and sit down."

Jordan followed Ciara into the living room, waiting until she sat before easing down on a matching chair. "I've been out of the country on my honeymoon, so I was unaware that Brandt had been in an accident until a couple of days ago. My aunt mentioned that Brandt has refused to see anyone, so I decided to come over and check in on him."

"It's difficult for Brandt to accept that he won't be able to stand on his own without crutches or a cane for at least six to eight weeks."

Nodding, Jordan crossed his legs. "My cousin has had bumps and bruises, but he's never experienced any serious injuries. He's also extremely competitive. Not once did he ever let me win, whether it was baseball, basketball or football. I've beaten him in tennis only because I'm faster on the court than he is. But he does have an awesome serve."

"Even with two broken legs, he's still in quite good physical shape," Ciara concurred.

Jordan wanted to ask the nurse if she was speaking of Brandt as his nurse or a woman admiring his body.

"Brandt works out a minimum of two to three hours a day, even during off-season."

Ciara stood up when she heard Brandt's voice raised in anger. Moving quickly, she met the therapist as he followed Brandt who was maneuvering his chair as if he were in a race. She stood in front of him, stopping his progress. "What's going on?"

A redness flooded the therapist's neck spreading to his thinning hairline. "I may have pushed him too hard for his first session."

"May have!" she shouted. "Either you did or you didn't. If you'd read his medical history then you would've been known that my patient has titanium rods and nails in his tibia. Five screws were used to secure it in place, and that the fibula in his left leg was left unaffixed, but will align and heal itself in due time. The key phrase, Mr. Lambert, is in due time!"

"I'm…I'm sorry, Miss Dennison," the flustered man sputtered. "I'd thought with Mr. Wainwright's conditioning he would do well with a more aggressive treatment plan."

Ciara narrowed her eyes at him. "Maybe in two or three weeks." She waved her hand.

"I need to take his vitals."

"I'll take them," she responded.

"But…but I need them for my report," the therapist stuttered.

"I have your number. I'll call you, or leave a message on your voice mail." She turned to Jordan. "Can you please escort Mr. Lambert to the elevator?"

Jordan motioned with his head. "I think it best you leave now."

Ciara grasped the handles to the wheelchair and pushed Brandt out of the living room and down the hallway to his bedroom. One glance at his face told her all she needed to know. He was in pain—intense pain. He'd clamped his teeth tightly together and his face was covered in perspiration.

She was struggling to get him into bed when Jordan walked in. "He usually gets into and out of bed by himself."

Slipping out of his suit jacket, Jordan tossed it on a nearby chair. Anchoring his arms under Brandt's shoulders, he lifted him from the chair and onto the bed. "Come on, cuz. Help me out here." Brandt's two hundred and fifty-plus pounds had become dead weight.

Bracing a hand on the mattress, Brandt shifted until he found a comfortable position. The F-bomb slipped past his lips when stabbing pain shot through his left leg. His eyes met Ciara's. "Sorry."

She smiled. "I'll give you that one." Reaching for the pitcher of water on the bedside table, Ciara filled a plastic cup from a supply wrapped in cellophane. "I'll be right back." Brandt had mentioned a fear of dependence on his pain medication, so she'd stored them where he wasn't able to get to them.

Minutes later she returned with the pill in a tiny paper cup, dropped it in his outstretched hand and watched as he popped it into his mouth and washed it down with the water. She took his vitals, winking at him. "I'll leave you to visit with your cousin."

Brandt smiled for the first time that morning. "Thanks." He waited until Ciara left the room, then turned and looked at his cousin. "Marriage looks good on you."

"Three weeks in paradise with the love of my life says it all."

"So Fiji was nice?"

Pulling a chair closer to the bed, Jordan sat. "Fiji is incredible. I never thought I'd survive without a cell phone or the internet, but after the second day I was so laid-back I'd forgotten my name and the date."

"How's Aziza?"

"Beautiful, sexy and hopefully pregnant."

Exhaling an audible sigh, Brandt closed his eyes. The effects of the pill had kicked in and Brandt felt himself floating outside of himself. "You guys were really serious when you talked about not waiting to start a family."

"We would like to have at least two children two years apart before Zee turns thirty-six."

He smiled. "I'm going to enjoy being Uncle Brandt."

"Any children we have will be your cousins."

Brandt opened his eyes, frowning. "I'll still be Uncle Brandt."

Jordan held up his hands. "It's okay. There's no need to get hostile. Your nurse is rather feisty, isn't she?" he asked deftly changing the topic.

"Feisty isn't the half. There are times when she's downright scary."

"Your mother said you ran the first two nurses off. That's not like you, cuz."

Closing his eyes, Brandt took a deep breath, held it in before letting it out slowly. "I couldn't stand their bowing and scraping."

"I take it Ciara doesn't bow and scrape."

"She's like a Marine drill sergeant. At any time I expect her to order me to drop and give her fifty push-ups."

"I felt sorry for your therapist."

"He's lucky she got in his face, because I was a minute from knocking him on his ass."

"Careful, cuz. You know I don't like taking on criminal cases. Especially those dealing with aggravated assault."

"That's why I rolled out of there while I was still in my right mind." He opened his eyes. "Are you staying in the city or Bronxville?" Aziza owned a charming house in Westchester County and Jordan a maisonette on Fifth Avenue.

"We've decided to live in the house."

"You're commuting?"

Jordan nodded. "I take the Metro North to One-Two-Five, then walk a couple of blocks to the office."

"That's—that's convenient," Brandt said, slurring.

"It is," Jordan agreed. "But I don't know how long I'm going to hang on to the apartment."

"You're selling it?"

"I'm thinking about it. Zee and I can stay with my folks whenever we come into the city."

"You guys can hang out here—that is, if you want more privacy."

"Thanks. When I told Kyle that I was contemplating putting the maisonette on the market, he said the same thing." His law partner owned a townhouse along Striver's Row in the St. Nicholas Historic District.

Jordan noticed his cousin hadn't opened his eyes for several minutes. "It's time I get back to the office. I've got cases piled up on my desk."

Brandt tried opening his eyes, but the effort proved too much. "When are you coming back?"

"Probably one day next week. I'll bring Zee with me."

"Good. I'm not up for having a lot of people over, because I don't want them to see me in a wheelchair."

"Remember, it's only temporary," Jordan reminded him. He stood and reached for his jacket, slipping his arms into the sleeves. He patted his cousin's muscular shoulder before walking out of the bedroom.

Ciara sat on the bench in the hallway, her arms folded under her breasts. She'd called the therapist, leaving the data he needed on his cell's voice mail. "Is he asleep?" she asked, coming to her feet.

Jordan nodded. "He's falling asleep. How is he doing?"

"Pretty well, considering he has two broken legs. He has an appointment to see his orthopedist next week. The plaster casts will be removed, his legs x-rayed, and he'll get ski boot-style lighter casts. He probably won't be able to bear any weight for another month. That's when he can begin more aggressive rehab to reverse muscle atrophy."

"Has he talked about missing the upcoming football season?"

"No. But he did watch a baseball game last night."

When he'd heard that Brandt had been injured in an auto accident, was refusing to see anyone other than his mother and had dismissed two nurses, Jordan had prepared himself for the worst. He knew Brandt would recover physically, but he had his doubts whether he would be able to deal with the possibility that his football career was over.

He knew that after more than ten years in the game his cousin's body couldn't withstand too many more injuries. Perhaps the accident would give Brandt the time he needed to decide whether he should retire.

Smiling, he extended his hand. "Again, it's a pleasure to meet you. Brandt is very fortunate to have you as his nurse."

Ciara shook Jordan's hand. "Thank you."

"I told him I plan to come back this weekend. Will that pose a problem?"

"I don't believe so. Just give me a call before you come. I don't want him to go from having one or two visitors to so many that he'll become overwhelmed."

"That's not a problem. I'll call before I come," Jordan promised.

She waited for Jordan to enter the elevator, the doors closing behind him before she made her way to the bedroom to check on her patient. Ciara knew she had to consciously think of Brandt Wainwright as her patient or she would find herself emotionally too involved.

She'd become a private nurse six months after she'd left the hospital, and most of her patients over the past year and a half had been elderly women, many of whom had opted to live at home rather than in a hospital.

Brandt was asleep, his chest rising and falling in a slow, even rhythm. Her gaze moved slowly over his clean-shaven face, admiring the classically handsome features—the generous mouth, cleft chin and aquiline nose. Sofia was right. Brandt Wainwright was *muy guapo*.

Chapter 7

One step forward, two steps backward. That was how it'd felt to Ciara over the past three days. She sat in the sitting area in Brandt's bedroom, flipping through a magazine. For the past hour there had only been the sound of pages turning to compete with the rain tapping against the windows. When she'd asked him if he'd wanted lunch, and his response was to close his eyes and feign sleep, Ciara waited to see how long it would take before he would finally answer her question.

Brandt's mood had shifted again. He was back to the sullen, surly, disgruntled patient she'd encountered earlier in the week. He barked at her, refused to leave the bed to have his meals, rejected his pain medication and stopped shaving. Whenever Leona called, he'd refused to speak to her, and then issued an order that he didn't want to talk to or see anyone. Ciara had defused the situation by removing the telephone from the bedroom.

Although he'd tried to conceal it, she knew he was experiencing more pain than he had before physical therapy. She'd positioned the railings on the bed to facilitate his getting in and out of it without her assistance whenever he needed to go to the bathroom.

Her cell phone rang and she picked it up before the second ring. "Ciara Dennison."

"Ms. Dennison, this is Amanda at Dr. Behrens's office, returning your call. We have a four o'clock cancellation. We'll send a medical van to pick you and Mr. Wainwright up at three-thirty."

"Thank you, Amanda. We'll see you at four."

Ciara hadn't wanted to deceive Brandt, but she was at her wits' end as to how to deal with his unresponsiveness. Instinct told her that he'd injured or reinjured his legs during therapy. Whether it was machismo or a martyr complex, he suffered in silence rather than ask for something to ease his pain.

Brandt opened his eyes and stared up at the ceiling. "Where are we going?"

"Oh, he speaks," she drawled facetiously.

"Very funny, Ciara."

"Isn't it, Brandt? A thirtysomething grown man pouting like a spoiled child is hilarious."

Brandt glared at Ciara. Why couldn't she understand that he wanted to be left alone? As long as she sat quietly, reading or doing crossword puzzles, he didn't have a problem with her hanging out in his room. It was when she wanted to talk that it bothered him. It was as if she just had to make conversation to prove that he didn't need a shrink.

"I don't feel like talking to my mother, because she

asks me the same questions. 'How are you feeling, darling? Are you better today than yesterday?' My answer is always the same. It's always yes."

Ciara sat up straight, her eyes boring into a pair in shimmering blue. "If it's yes, then why are you eating in bed? Why are you risking getting blood clots by not moving around?"

"I'm not going to get blood clots," Brandt argued, "because I'm taking a blood thinner. Do you mind answering my question?"

"What's that?"

"Where are we going?"

"We're going to your orthopedist. His office called to tell me that Dr. Behrens has to rearrange his schedule for the next week and he would like to see you today." What she hadn't told Brandt was that she'd called the office and asked the doctor to see him.

She swung her legs over the chaise. "I'm going to change, and when I come back I'll help you get dressed."

Brandt sat up, staring at the woman who'd begun hovering around him as if he were preemie. Everything had begun to bother him: his mother's questions and his nurse.

He just wanted to be left alone.

"Do I have time to eat lunch?"

The seconds ticked as they stared at each other. "Yes. Are you going to get out of bed?"

He narrowed his eyes at Ciara. "Do I have a choice?"

Resting her hands at her waist, Ciara gave him a look parents usually reserved for recalcitrant children. "No."

Swallowing an expletive, Brandt reached for the wheelchair and smoothly transferred from the bed to the chair, muscles in his biceps flexing with the motion. "Damn, babe. Why do you have to be so tough?"

Ciara rolled her eyes. "It's my responsibility to get you better so you'll have full use of your legs. Lying in bed is counterproductive to that. And don't call me babe."

"Some of my women like it when I call them babe."

"I'm not one of your women, Brandt Wainwright. Please try and keep that in mind." She didn't understand Brandt. He'd gone from being practically monosyllabic to talking about some of his women, and if she had to choose which she preferred it would be the former.

Brandt turned the chair toward the bathroom. "I'll be there as soon as I wash my hands." Old habits were hard to break. His former headmaster would examine the front and back of each student's hands before they were permitted to enter the school's cafeteria.

He knew he'd given Ciara a hard time only because the pain in his legs had become excruciating—nearly intolerable. He'd decided to forgo the pain medication in the hope that it would ease. Unfortunately, it hadn't.

The medical transport van maneuvered along the curb in front of the building where Ciara and Brandt waited under the canopy for their arrival. The attendant positioned the wheelchair on a hydraulic lift, securing it in the rear of the vehicle. The attendant helped Ciara into the van, where she sat on a seat next to Brandt. Being cloistered in the penthouse for four days had spoiled her—the sound of traffic was deafening, quickly reminding her of the incessant noise of the city.

Brandt, wearing walking shorts, a faded sweatshirt and a baseball cap pulled low over his forehead, sat with arms folded over his chest. He thought he'd conjured Ciara up when she had come into his bedroom to help him put on the shorts. She'd traded her uniform for a pair of jeans, a cotton pullover and running shoes. Without the smock she appeared taller, slimmer. The denim hugging her hips was a testament that she was unabashedly feminine and sexy. Seeing Ciara like this wasn't going to help him suppress fantasies about her wearing next to nothing.

His thoughts were interrupted when the van stopped in front of a townhouse that housed several doctors' offices. Five minutes later Brandt was wheeled into a room on the second floor and placed on an examining table.

Ciara sat on a stool in a corner of the room, staring at Brandt as he clenched and unclenched his right hand. "How bad is it?" Her voice was barely a whisper.

Brandt knew what Ciara was asking, and knew it was useless to lie. "It's very bad." She popped up like a jack-in-the box and walked to the door, his eyes following her. "Where are you going?"

Ciara stepped out into the hallway, motioning to a passing nurse. "Please inform Dr. Behrens before he removes Mr. Wainwright's casts he should be given something for the pain."

The woman with flyaway salt-and-pepper curls nodded. "I'll tell Gene. He's the physician assistant," she said when Ciara gave her a perplexed look.

Ciara waited in the hallway until Dr. Behrens and his assistant entered the examining room. Wallace Behrens, not yet forty, was a highly regarded orthopedic surgeon because of his preference for noninvasive surgical procedures with patients under fifty.

The doctor, redheaded, his brown eyes sparkling like new pennies in a face covered with freckles, shook her hand. "Ms. Dennison. It's a pleasure to meet you. It's always a joy to read your case notes, because not only are they detailed, but also very accurate."

"Thank you, Dr. Behrens." She also shook the assistant's hand, and returned to sit on the stool.

Gene swabbed Brandt's hip with alcohol before using a hypodermic needle to give him a shot of painkiller. Brandt's chest rose and fell in a slow, even rhythm by the time the whirr of the drill cutting through the plaster casts echoed throughout the room.

Without the casts, she was able to see the source of Brandt's chronic pain. The wound above his left ankle was red and frightfully swollen. Dr. Behrens removed the staples, cleaned the area and covered it with sterile bandages.

The surgeon glanced up, meeting Ciara's eyes. "You brought him in just in time to avoid a serious infection."

She said a silent prayer that she hadn't ignored her gut feeling that something wasn't right, that Brandt should not have been in that much pain three weeks post-surgery.

Four hours later, Brandt was back in his bed and able to see his injured legs for the first time in weeks, the scars and fading bruises substantiating the seriousness of his injury.

He gave Ciara a lopsided smile when she pulled up the railings to help make it easier for him to get out of bed. "I...I think we should... We have to celebrate," he said, slurring and stuttering.

She wrinkled her nose. "I don't think so, sport. Remember, you're still under the influence."

"What about tomorrow?"

Leaning over the bed, Ciara stared at the dreamy expression on Brandt's face. She knew he was fighting against the lingering effects of the sedative that had dulled the pain when the casts and staples were removed.

"We'll see how you feel after therapy."

Brandt pressed his forefinger to his mouth. "I need a little kiss."

"Nurses aren't permitted to kiss their patients."

"Come on, Ciara. Loosen up. Do you always have to be so anal?"

Ciara felt as if Brandt had eavesdropped on her conversations with Victor. He'd accused her of being too reserved. Whenever they'd attended social gatherings together, he'd whisper in her ear to "loosen up." What Victor had failed to realize was she was his date, and when they were approached by other people, it wasn't Ciara Dennison they'd wanted to talk to—it was him. The brilliant doctor was much sought after by women looking for advice on cosmetic surgery. After a stint as a plastic surgery expert on a reality show, Victor had become famous. When he wasn't performing life-altering surgeries to improve his patients' quality of life, he was in great demand by those who were willing to pay millions to achieve perfection.

"I'm not anal, Brandt. I just play by the rules. I'm certain you're more than familiar with those rules."

Ciara recalled her conversation with Sofia. What she hadn't admitted to her roommate was her attraction to Brandt. It went beyond patient-nurse. It'd become male-female. Sofia was right. She hadn't slept with a man in more than two years. And whenever her body betrayed her, it was a blatant reminder that she was a woman capable of strong passion.

"But you already broke the rules when you kissed me on the terrace," Brandt reminded her.

Lowering the rail on his right, she leaned closer. The warmth and natural scent from Brandt's body swept over Ciara. She wanted to tell him that she wasn't as unaffected as she appeared. Each time she viewed his nude body she had to call on all of her professionalism to avoid trailing her fingertips over his body like a sculptor.

She'd told herself that she wasn't into sports, and therefore wasn't attracted to athletes whose egos out-weighed their talent but not their paychecks. But Ciara realized that even if Brandt Wainwright had not become a football player, it still would not have diminished his appeal.

He'd been born into money—a lot of money—the penthouse and its furnishings were a testament to that. Sofia had mentioned she'd searched out Brandt Wainwright on the internet, and later that evening Ciara had also looked him up online. There were more than thirteen pages about him, with statistics from his college and pro careers, awards and accolades, photos of his Super Bowl victory and parades. Another site showed photographs of him with women—a lot of beautiful women from all over the world. It was apparent the camera loved him and Brandt loved being photographed. He was smiling in every shot but one. He was gorgeous with his long blond hair.

What do I have to lose? she thought to herself. She doubted whether Brandt was one to kiss and tell, because there had been little or no gossip about him and other women. "You're right," Ciara whispered close to his mouth. "I did break the first rule."

Brandt stared at the lushly curved lips inches from his own. "What's the second rule?"

"Sleeping with a patient. But that's not going to happen."

His eyebrows lifted a fraction. "How can you be so certain?"

"Just am," she drawled.

"Because you're my nurse?"

Ciara nodded.

"What if you weren't my nurse?"

"We'll just have to see, won't we?"

Brandt smiled. Ciara had answered his question with a question. She hadn't said yes, and she hadn't said no either. It wasn't so much the idea of making love to her that had piqued his curiosity—she also had a certain enigmatic quality about her.

"Yes, we will just have to wait and see."

Lifting his head off the pillow and cradling her face at the same time, Brandt slanted his mouth over Ciara's. Her lips parted, as he swallowed her moist breath and deepened the kiss. He felt her stiffen then relax, her mouth becoming pliant against his. As much as he didn't want to, he ended the kiss.

"Thank you very much."

Heat suffused Ciara's face, quickly wending its way down to settle between her thighs. She knew she had to get away from Brandt before she crawled into the bed with him. Securing the rail, she smiled. "You're welcome."

"Do you like Thai food?" Brandt asked.

Ciara smiled, nodding. "I love it. Why?"

"I have a friend who owns a Thai restaurant. If we're going to celebrate tomorrow, then we're going to need food. I owe my mother an apology, so I'm going to ask her and my dad to join us."

"I'm certain she would like that."

"Please bring me the phone so I can call him."

Ciara walked over to the sitting area, picked up the cordless receiver and cradle and plugged it into an outlet beside the hospital bed. Brandt's willingness to be with others was part of the healing process. It wasn't about physical healing; it was about emotional healing. And she'd tired of lying to Leona whenever she called, making excuses why Brandt wouldn't take her calls. Most times she told the woman that her son was sleeping, anything except the truth—that he didn't want to speak to her.

She placed the receiver on the bed where he could reach it. "I'm going to ask the agency to send another nurse in two weeks. I'd agreed to host a birthday party for a friend before being assigned to your case."

"I don't want another nurse."

"You can't be left alone," Ciara argued softly.

"I'll get someone to hang out here until you get back."

Not wanting to argue with Brandt, she adjusted the setting on the thermostat, dimmed the floor lamp in the sitting area and walked out of the bedroom and into her own. Ciara slept with the connecting door open, since there was no other way to know if her patient needed assistance. She'd come to enjoy sleeping in the large mahogany canopy bed.

Before going to sleep, she usually spent time in the kitchen, planning the next day's menu, followed by a leisurely soak in the tub, listening to classic love songs. She reluctantly climbed out of the tub, went through her nightly ritual of moisturizing her face and body, pulled a nightgown over her head and slipped into bed. She woke without an alarm clock, alert and ready.

Chapter 8

Half an hour into Brandt's session with the therapist, Ciara left them alone. Mindful of the previous encounter, Thomas Lambert took a more conservative approach, putting Brandt through a series of exercises focusing on muscle strengthening using weighted pulleys to keep his upper body toned. She'd found herself mesmerized as she watched his pectorals, triceps and biceps flex as he did the exercises. There was still a fading bruise on his upper left chest where the seat belt had dug in. The bruises on his face from the air bag had faded completely.

He used a chair to exercise, lifting his lower legs parallel to the floor. The therapist started out with five reps and indicated it would eventually increase to twenty-five or more. A printout with illustrations of home exercises was affixed to a corkboard on the wall next to a schedule of NFL and AFL games for the upcoming season.

Dr. Behrens had given Brandt a recovery timeline: six weeks to walk with crutches, eight weeks before he would be able to walk with canes. After ten weeks he predicted he should no longer use a cane and then it would be another five months before he would be able to walk without evidence of limping. He had cautioned Brandt against playing any contact sport until a year after the accident. Only then he would be medically cleared and nearly one hundred percent recovered and discomfort-free. Whether Brandt would ever suit up and play football again was something that would be determined by the NFL.

Walking into the dining room, she removed an armchair at one end of the table to accommodate Brandt's wheelchair. The table was set for six. Not only had Leona and her husband accepted the invitation to come for dinner, but Brandt's brothers and sister had also asked to attend.

Picking up a water goblet, she checked it for water spots. She'd returned it to its proper place when Brandt rolled in. "How was it?"

"A lot better than the last time." He maneuvered closer to the table. "You're missing a place setting."

Ciara's brow furrowed. "I don't think so. There's one for you, your sister, brothers and parents. That's six."

"Where's yours, Ciara?"

She gave Brandt a long, penetrating stare. "I'm not eating with you and your family."

"And why not?"

"Because I've made other plans," she volunteered.

She'd searched online for restaurants and cafés on Second or Third Avenue that had caught her interest.

The first thing that sprang into Brandt's mind was that Ciara was going out with a man, and he didn't want to think of her smiling, touching and/or kissing another man. She was his…his nurse, and she was there to… His thoughts trailed off when he realized he had no basis for being jealous of Ciara and another man. He would expect her to seek out male companionship.

"Are you going out with someone?"

Ciara stared at Brandt, baffled. Why would he assume because she'd opted not to eat with his family that she would have a dinner date? "No."

"Then that does it. You will eat here."

"No, Brandt. I don't want to intrude."

"You're not intruding. You've eaten with me every day since you've been here, so why should tonight be any different?" Brandt held up his hand when Ciara opened her mouth to come back at him. "Enough. Please put out another place setting. And I'd really appreciate it if you would stand in as my hostess tonight."

"I'm surprised you ask, because I look dowdy." Her query was dripping with sarcasm.

"That's not even close to being funny, Ciara. You wouldn't be a mess if you didn't wear those smocks."

Ciara glanced down at her light blue top with bright red and yellow butterflies. "I think it's rather cute."

"It's cute if you were a kindergarten teacher. If you need something to wear, then I'll give you my credit card and you can go shopping."

"You want me to go shopping for an outfit and leave you home alone?"

"I'll be all right for a few hours. I'll stay in the sitting area either reading or watching TV."

Ciara looked at Brandt as if he'd suddenly lost his mind. She didn't want to think of going into a boutique to shop, then attempting to pay with Brandt Wainwright's credit card. In no time she would find herself arrested, read her rights, cuffed and entered into the criminal justice system for credit card theft.

"That's okay. I'll use my own card."

Brandt shook his head. "No, you won't. You'll take my card. If there's a problem, then have the store clerk call me."

Ciara worried her lip. "You must not like me very much."

His eyebrows lifted. "Why would you say that?"

"Even if the clerk does call you, I'll still have to go through the humiliation of people believing I'd stolen your card."

The seconds ticked as Brandt stared at the woman who continued to confound him. Most women would've jumped at the chance to go shopping for clothes and not have to pay for them. "Do you have a favorite store?"

She angled her head. "I have a few."

"Name one."

"Barneys."

"Where is it, Ciara?"

"Sixtieth and Madison."

"What if I call the manager of Barneys and let him know you're coming in with my credit card. I'll give him all of my personal information, so that will eliminate a subsequent phone call."

Ciara didn't want to believe her life had become a

rerun. Victor paid for the clothes he'd wanted her to wear whenever they appeared together in public. Initially she'd been flattered when he'd accompanied her on her shopping outings. Then, after a while she'd found it annoying. However, whenever she protested, telling him she didn't need him trailing behind her, it'd sparked a volatile confrontation. It always ended with Victor overruling her.

The only difference this time was she wouldn't have an escort. She could select the store and what she wanted to wear. She'd told Brandt Barneys because she'd never gone there with Victor. "Okay," she agreed.

"I'll call a car to pick you up and bring you back."

She shook her head. "That won't be necessary. I'll have the doorman call a taxi for me."

"Doormen are notoriously nosy and I try to keep them out of my business. Do I need to say more, Ms. Dennison?"

"Say no more, Mr. Wainwright."

His eyes narrowing, he studied the missing chair at the head at the end of the table. "I hope that's not where I'm going to sit."

Resting her hands at her waist, Ciara gave him an incredulous look. "Of course it's where you're going to sit. Why?"

"There's no wineglass."

She approached him. "That's because you can't have wine. Remember, you're taking medication."

"Not today."

"Yes today, Brandt." She usually gave him his medication following the midday meal.

In a move too quick for the eye to follow, Brandt

pulled Ciara down to his lap, tightening his hold around her waist when she tried to free herself. "I told you that I intend to celebrate. And that means having a glass of wine."

Ciara felt his hot breath on the nape of her neck and the muscled thighs under her hips. "Please let me go, Brandt."

He pressed his mouth to the side of her neck. "I will if you let me have a glass of wine."

She giggled like a little girl. "Stop, Brandt."

"'Stop, Brandt,'" he mimicked her voice.

In her attempt to free herself, Ciara's buttocks came into direct contract with his groin. Within seconds, as if he'd been shocked by a jolt of electricity, he'd achieved an immediate erection. Brandt swallowed a groan. The sensation racing through his groin was akin to intense pain—the most intense, pleasurable pain.

Ciara gasped and then exhaled a lingering sigh when she felt a gush of moisture bathe the sensitive folds of her vagina. Feelings she'd forgotten came to life as she surrendered to the strength of the man holding her to his heart. She pressed her hips downward as Brandt pushed upward, rocking back and forth over the swollen length of flesh. She felt the quickened beating of his heart against her back, the rapid breathing in her ear and the sharp nip of his teeth on the sensitive skin of her neck.

She'd challenged Brandt, asking what could he do sitting in a wheelchair. He'd shown her exactly what he could do in a chair, and without penetrating her. He was making love to her, and she was close to climaxing.

"Oh s…" Brandt swallowed the expletive when he felt

the familiar tightening in his scrotum. He was going to ejaculate, but he wanted to be inside the woman gyrating on his lap.

He'd tried holding back but couldn't when his heart felt as if it was going to explode. Then he did something he hadn't done since adolescence. He released himself while fully clothed.

Ciara felt Brandt's large body shudder at the same time the groan, beginning deep in his chest, exploded like the roar of a big cat. The sound was so primal she surrendered to the primordial forces taking her beyond herself. The first orgasm held her captive then it was followed by another and then another. She collapsed, her throat dry, her heart pounding a runaway rhythm and the pulsing reminded her of what she'd missed since walking away from her ex-lover.

"Br-andt…" His name came out in two syllables. "What have we done?"

Trailing kisses along the column of her scented neck, Brandt closed his eyes while enjoying the aftermath of making love with Ciara. "We've done nothing wrong, baby."

"But—"

"No buts, no regrets." He kissed her ear. "Okay?"

A beat passed. "Okay," she whispered.

Brandt hadn't wanted her to feel guilty, because he didn't. He hadn't known her long. But that didn't matter. She was his nurse and he was her patient. That, too, had not mattered.

What mattered was how she made him feel whenever they shared the same space. He'd found himself at odds with Ciara Dennison because of their role reversal. He'd been raised to take care of and protect women, but now it was Ciara who cared for and protected him. She'd gone after the therapist with the ferocity of a mother lion protecting her cub.

Was he upset because of the role reversal?

Yes.

Had he felt vulnerable when he hadn't been able to hide his pain from her?

Yes.

Had he taunted and bullied her? Had he mentioned her frumpy-looking uniform because he hadn't wanted to find himself attracted to her? Had he asked her to kiss him because he'd wanted to taste her sexy mouth again, and not just out of gratitude? The answers were yes, yes and yes.

The first night they'd shared the rooftop dinner he'd realized then Ciara Dennison was hiding her femininity. She'd permitted him glimpses of her natural beauty, however, when she'd exchanged the bun for a ponytail. After she'd exchanged her work clothes for a sweater and skinny jeans, Brandt hadn't wanted to believe she had attempted to hide her long legs and curvy hips under yards of unflattering fabric.

Her sitting on his lap, his arms holding her protectively, felt so right. It was as if she belonged there with him.

Resting the back of her head on Brandt's shoulder, Ciara wanted not to have any regrets, but guilt and shame lingered around the fringes of her mind. If she'd attempted to do what she'd done with Brandt in a hospital setting, not only would she have jeopardized her position, but also her license to practice nursing in the state of New York.

"You're bad for me, Brandt Wainwright."

He laughed. "I'm bad? You're the one who humped me."

"I wouldn't have humped you if you hadn't pulled me down to your lap."

"Don't try and wiggle out of it, babe. You were definitely the humper."

Ciara snorted audibly. "That's because the humpee had a hard-on."

"It couldn't be helped. You know you're kinda sexy."

She glared at Brandt over her shoulder. "I thought I was dowdy?"

"That was before I saw you without the bun and the smock. I couldn't tell whether you were pregnant or you painted in your spare time."

"Neither. Now, please let me get up so I can shower and change my clothes."

Using one hand and keeping his free arm wrapped around Ciara's waist, Brandt deftly maneuvered the wheelchair out of the dining room and down the hallway leading to the bedrooms.

"We can shower together. I'll wash your back and you wash mine."

Ciara grasped the arms of the wheelchair. "We are not going to shower together. And if you don't slow down you won't be the only one with broken bones."

"I'm expert with this baby," Brandt drawled. "Do you want to see me do a wheelie?"

"You try it and you'll find yourself looking for another nurse," she warned.

Brandt slowed the chair, stopping outside the door to her bedroom. There was something in Ciara's voice that communicated she would follow through with her threat. He didn't want to lose her now that he was beginning to peel off the layers to uncover the real Ciara Dennison. He lowered his arm. "I believe this is your stop."

Ciara practically jumped off Brandt's lap and raced into her bedroom, closing the door behind her. In a moment of madness she'd weakened and had found herself bumping and grinding with a man unable to walk on his own.

She made her way to the bathroom, stood in front the mirror, took off her glasses and stared at her reflection. The enormity of what had passed between her and Brandt Wainwright pressed down on her like a lead blanket.

Be careful, Ciara, warned the voice in her head. She hadn't known what to expect with Victor until she was in too deep. But it would be different with Brandt, only because she was willing to become physically and not emotionally involved with him.

Ciara smiled at the driver when he opened the rear door to the Lincoln Town Car, extended his hand and assisted her from the vehicle. "Thank you."

Brandt had made two telephone calls: to the store manager at Barneys and the other to a car service to reserve a car and driver for her. She hadn't been able to count on both hands and feet the number of times she'd stood on a corner—in the rain or snow—waiting to flag down a passing taxi to either take her to work or back home. However, a single phone call placed by Brandt Wainwright, lasting less than a minute, had granted her door-to-door service. She entered the store, exchanging a smile with a well-dressed clerk with expertly coiffed streaked hair. It was impossible for Ciara to pinpoint her age; it was obvious the attractive woman had been nipped and tucked to perfection.

"Good afternoon. I'm Rebekah, and is there anything I can assist you with, Miss…?"

"Dennison," Ciara said. "I need the de rigueur little black dress."

Rebekah's eyebrows lifted a fraction. When the store manager told her Brandt Wainwright's girlfriend was coming into the store, she hadn't expected the tall, slender, bespectacled woman wearing jeans, a white tee and black leather mules. Her thick, dark hair was pulled back in a ponytail.

"Day or evening?" the saleswoman asked.

"It's evening. But it's going to be casual."

"Please come with me, Miss Dennison. I believe I have something that will meet with your approval."

Ciara nodded when she saw the black cotton asymmetric dress with a draped shoulder. It was not only simple, but elegant. It was perfect. Rebekah also had a good eye, because when she slipped the dress over Ciara's body it was as if it had been made for her, skimming her curves and ending at the knee.

Staring at her reflection in the mirror, she studied the back of the dress. "I'll take it."

Rebekah pressed her palms together. There was

nothing better than a quick and easy sale. She pointed to Ciara's bare feet. "Do you need shoes?"

Ciara wiggled her toes, thankful there were no chips in the raspberry polish. "Yes."

"How about peep-toe?" Rebekah asked, staring down at her groomed feet. "Your dress is simplistic chic, so your footwear can be just a little bit sexy."

"How sexy are you talking about?"

"An almost five-inch stiletto sexy," the saleswoman crooned.

Five-inch heels would put her at the six-foot mark. Whenever she'd gone out with Victor, she had been careful not to wear shoes in which she would tower above him. She hadn't been able to understand why, for all his brilliance, he'd had insecurities too numerous to count.

But it would be different with Brandt. He was six-five and she five-seven, and although they wouldn't be seen together publicly, just knowing he was taller was a comfort. "Please let me see what you're talking about."

Minutes later Rebekah returned, dangling a black satin platform slingback with an origami bow at the peep-toe. Ciara recognized the shoe's designer because of the distinctive signature red leather sole.

"What do you think?"

Ciara's smile was dazzling. "Do you have them in five and a half?"

"I'm certain I do."

The heels complemented the dress, while flattering her legs and feet. "I'll take the dress *and* the shoes."

Rebekah's smile matched her client's. "I'll pack up everything for you."

Less than forty minutes after walking through the doors of the Madison Avenue shop, Ciara walked out. The driver placed her purchases in the trunk after opening the rear door for his passenger.

Slumping against the leather seat, she closed her eyes. The style of Christian Louboutin stiletto she'd chosen was called Miss ChaCha. She wasn't going out dancing, but standing in as hostess to Brandt Wainwright when he entertained his family.

She knew her role and responsibilities were becoming more complex—unorthodox, yet it'd had a profound effect on her patient. Brandt was no longer the sullen, grumpy man who'd fired nurses, refused to eat or cooperate with his medication regimen. Getting him mentally ready in his recovery was as important as his walking again.

The driver maneuvered along the curb in front of the high-rise and the doorman came over to open the door. He took the garment and shopping bag from the driver, carrying them into the building for Ciara. He gave them to her before activating the elevator that would take her directly to the penthouse.

The doors opened and she came face-to-face with Brandt. She hadn't left until after he'd showered, changed his clothes and eaten lunch. "Hey, you," she said, smiling.

Brandt returned her smile. "Hey. How was shopping?"

"Splendid." Reaching into the back pocket of her jeans, she handed him the credit card. "Thanks."

"Did you get everything you wanted?"

"Not everything."

"What didn't you get?" Brandt asked.

"There was a diamond necklace in the window at Tiffany's that would've been the perfect accessory," Ciara said, deadpan.

"Do you want me to call Tiffany's and have it delivered?"

Leaning over, Ciara kissed Brandt's clean-shaven cheek. "I'm joking."

His eyes met hers, darkening with an emotion that frightened him in its intensity. Brandt wanted his nurse in the most intimate way possible, and he'd spent the time waiting for her to return, cursing the turn of events that wouldn't permit him to move about without the aid of the wheelchair.

He'd made love to women, yet none had turned him on as Ciara Dennison had done with her impromptu lap dance. And he was certain she was as shocked by the act as he'd been. Not only had it been spontaneous, but the result had been explosive. He'd relived everything that had occurred when sitting on the chair in the shower, and his body had betrayed him for the second time that day.

Fortunately for him, Ciara hadn't been there to hear the curses when he struggled not to take care of his own sexual needs. Once he'd adjusted the water temperature to ice-cold and finished his rant, he was back in control.

"I wasn't joking. I don't remember giving you a spending limit, so you could've bought whatever you wanted."

Ciara felt a shiver race up her back when she met Brandt's penetrating stare. She didn't know what had possessed her to tease him, but apparently it had backfired, because he was serious about her buying anything she wanted. She knew women who would've taken him up on his offer, all the while scheming to take as much from him as they could get. However, she wasn't one of those women. In the past she'd become another wealthy man's darling and she had no intention of it happening again. Even if Brandt Wainwright hadn't become a celebrity athlete he still would be a wealthy man.

She pulled back. "I bought what I needed."

"Are you going to show me what you bought?"

"No."

"No?"

Ciara almost laughed at the shocked expression on his handsome face. "You'll see it later." Stepping out of his reach, she walked through the entryway and great room to the hallway that led to her bedroom. "See you later, baby," she called over her shoulder.

Chapter 9

A chef, sous chef and waiter arrived at the penthouse a half hour before the Wainwrights were scheduled to arrive. When Brandt had informed Ciara that his friend owned a restaurant, she'd believed he would order takeout, not have everything prepared on site.

She'd assisted Brandt in getting into a pair of Dockers men's shorts and into the removable casts before retreating to her bedroom to dress. He'd remained upbeat, his attitude a lot more positive once the removable ski-boot casts had replaced the heavier plaster ones. He was now able to shower without plastic sheaths, but she still had to dry his legs and feet and help him into his underwear and shorts. It would be another three weeks before he would be permitted to use a pair of crutches.

Ciara glanced at her watch, grimacing. She had less than fifteen minutes to dress, make up her face and style her hair before the Wainwrights arrived. Removing her glasses, she deftly inserted a pair of contact lenses. She didn't know why she didn't wear the lenses every day, because they improved her vision appreciably.

She slipped into the dress, pulled up the side zipper, then sat down at the vanity in the bathroom to apply a smoky shadow to her lids and a lighter shade under her brow and a coat of mascara to her lashes, followed by a light dusting of powder bronzer to her face; a plum-tinted lip gloss added color to her mouth. Freeing her hair from the confines of the elastic band, Ciara brushed it until it was smooth, then deftly fashioned it into a loose chignon at the nape of her neck. It wasn't the bun Brandt had complained about, but an elegant variation on the staid style.

Leaving the en suite bath, she walked into the bed-room at the same time there came a light tapping on the door connecting the bedrooms. "Yes, Brandt," she called out, sitting on a chair and slipping her bare feet into the slingback stilettos.

"May I come in?"

She stood up. "Yes."

The door opened and Brandt rolled the chair into the room. Ciara was hard-pressed not to laugh when she saw his expression. He was so still he could've been carved from stone. The only thing that moved were his eyes as they went from her head and slowly downward to her legs and feet. The very air in the room seemed charged with electricity as their gazes met and fused.

She felt the familiar sensation that had precipitated her giving Brandt the lap dance. Closing her eyes, she counted slowly to ten while breathing through parted lips. She had to think of anything but what she wanted to experience again with the man sitting in the wheelchair. Ciara was at odds with herself, because whenever she helped Brandt with his grooming, her touch was impersonal. Nude, he was her patient. Clothed, she wanted to make love to him.

Brandt felt a lump rising in his throat, not permitting him to swallow or speak. He'd tried imagining and fantasizing what his nurse would look like under her unflattering outfits, and he hadn't come remotely close. Seeing her without the glasses made him aware of the exotic shape of her soft brown eyes. His gaze lingered on her mouth—a sweet, sexy mouth he wanted to taste over and over until gorged.

His gaze moved down to the black dress that fit her slender, curvy body as if it had been tailored expressly for her. It was when he stared at her long, shapely legs and slender feet in the black stilettos that he was glad to be sitting, because he doubted whether his knees would've held him upright. Not only was Ciara hot. She was downright sexy!

"What I wouldn't give to be able to stand and walk right now." His desire for her had slipped out unbidden.

Ciara came closer, smiling. "Don't rush it, sport. You'll be walking before you know it."

The lump in his throat fell to his stomach like a stone. She didn't know how much he wanted to be able to get out of his wheelchair, wanted to pick her up and carry her to his bed, wanted to be inside her and make love to her until he passed out from ecstasy or exhaustion— whichever came first.

"You look so beautiful."

Ciara felt a rush of heat in her face from the compliment. "Thank you."

Brandt winked at her. "There's no need to thank me for something I have nothing to do with. I just got a call from the lobby. My parents and sister are on their way up."

She gestured to the door. "Let's not keep them waiting."

Opening the door, Brandt permitted Ciara to precede him, then followed. There was something to be said for *ladies* first, because it gave him the opportunity to stare at her long legs in the sexy heels. She slowed her pace, falling back to walk alongside of him in the wide hallway.

"Are you all right?"

He gave her sideling glance. "Yes. Why?"

"You're breathing heavier."

Brandt stopped. "You can hear my breathing?"

Ciara patted his shoulder. His light blue cotton golf shirt was an exact match for his luminous eyes. "It's my eyes that are less than perfect, not my hearing. My mother used to tease me, saying I must be part bat because of my acute hearing. Now what's up with the increase in respiration?"

"Maybe I'm looking forward to hanging out with my family." Ciara gave him a look that said she didn't believe him. He'd told only half the truth. He was looking forward to seeing his siblings again—his sister in particular. The real reason for the increase in his heart rate was he'd found his body unwilling to follow the dictates of his brain when it came to his sexy nurse.

It had become his custom since he was drafted into the NFL not to become too involved with women from early August until January. Those five months were what he called his dating merry-go-round—he would see a woman, and take her to dinner or a social event, but would not necessarily sleep with her. His focus was staying in top condition and being mentally prepared for every game. It was now mid-August, and although he wasn't physically playing the game, his head was stuck in the off-season.

A soft chime indicated the elevator had arrived. Brandt maneuvered through the living and great rooms to see Fraser, Leona and Clarissa exiting the car. A flash of humor crossed his face. His sister looked as if she'd gained a few pounds, but it was still not enough for her not to appear emaciated.

He extended his arms. "Welcome to my humble abode."

Clarissa Wainwright leaned over and pressed a kiss to her brother's cheek. "Your girlfriend is beautiful," she whispered in his ear.

Brandt smothered a laugh. Clarissa was under the assumption that Ciara was his girlfriend. Nothing was further from the truth even though a part of him had wanted it to be true. "I'd like to introduce my nurse and hostess for this evening." Reaching for Ciara's hand, he cradled it in his larger one. "This is my dad, Fraser Wainwright, and my sister, Clarissa. Dad, Rissa, this is Ciara Dennison. Of course you know my mother."

Leona exhaled an audible gasp when she stared at the woman standing behind her son's wheelchair.

"Good gracious! I didn't recognize you," she gushed, blushing.

Ciara smiled at the tall man with cropped silver hair and soulful blue eyes, knowing what Brandt would look like in another twenty-five years. Father and son had the same lean face and cleft chin. Although the older Wainwright didn't have the muscled bulk of his son, she assumed he either worked out regularly or was very fortunate to have avoided the middle-age paunch. Leona was exquisite in a raw silk lime-green pantsuit and Gucci pumps, while her daughter's all-black attire made her appear pale and very, very thin. Wavy, pale hair fell around her narrow face.

"It's nice meeting you, Mr. Wainwright, Clarissa."

Fraser Wainwright nodded. "The pleasure is mine, Miss Dennison. My wife has been singing your praises, saying you're something of a miracle worker. And I have to agree with her when I see Brandt up and getting around."

Clarissa, resting a hand on Brandt's shoulder, angled her head. "And I'm going to agree with Mother and Dad, because the last time I saw Brandt he was—shall we say—a little messed up."

Ciara gave Brandt's sister a forced smile. She wondered if the Wainwrights were aware of the severity of Brandt's injuries. If it hadn't been for the seat belt and air bag, Brandt would have been more than messed up. He would've died. Bruises, scrapes and broken bones healed, but once an accident report documented time of death, then the family would be faced with the task of making preparations for a funeral.

"Brandt is progressing very well," she said in a quiet

voice. "Give him another few weeks and he will no longer need the wheelchair."

Brandt let go of Ciara's hand. "Dad, please take off your tie and jacket. Tonight we're going to kick back and relax."

Fraser shot his wife an I told you so look. "That sounds good to me."

Leona ignored her husband's glare. "Garth called to say he was picking up Sumner, and they should be here before eight."

Ciara glanced at her watch. They had a forty-five-minute wait before the other family members arrived. "It would be nice to have cocktails in the solarium."

Smiling, Leona pressed her palms together. "What a wonderful idea."

Brandt winked at Ciara. "Please tell the waiter to see me before you go up with the others. Don't worry about me. I'll take the elevator," he teased with a wide grin.

Ciara wanted to tell him that she, too, planned to take the elevator, because she wasn't about to try and navigate the winding staircase in a pair of heels that were just shy of five inches.

"I'm going to hang around down here until Sumner and Garth show up," Clarissa said. "I also want to check out the menu."

Maneuvering the chair in the direction of the living room, Brandt motioned with his head. "Follow me, Rissa." He waited until they were out of earshot of the others, and then slowed the chair. "What's up?" he asked his sister.

"May I help you with something, Mr. Wainwright?" The waiter had appeared as if out of thin air.

Brandt told the man he wanted him to serve cocktails from the built-in bar in the solarium, waiting until he walked away before returning his attention to Clarissa. "Do you want to tell me why you didn't want to join the others?"

"Let's go to your office," Clarissa suggested.

He nodded. "Okay."

"Do you want me to push you?"

"No. Wheelie and I are in perfect synch. Watch this." Brandt executed a one-eighty spin.

Clarissa shook her head, smiling. "Show-off."

"If you've got it, then why not flaunt it?"

Brandt had sobered by the time his sister preceded him into the library. He closed the door. "Now, do you want to tell me what's so secret you don't want the others to hear?"

Sinking down to a leather love seat, Clarissa stared at the toes of her ballet flats. "Harper has been blowing up my cell."

Clasping his hands together, Brandt leaned forward in the chair. "Have you been answering the calls?"

"No. But I want to tell him to stop. I've thought about changing my number, but there are too many people who have it."

"Have you thought about blocking his number?"

"I'd given it a thought."

"What's there not to think about? Block his number, and if he continues to bother you, then call me."

Clarissa's eyelids fluttered as she tried bringing her fragile emotions under control. "I'm telling you because I don't want you to get involved."

"Then why did you tell me? Either I get involved or

you can go to the police and have them charge him with harassment."

"I don't want to embarrass his parents," she argued.

Brandt shook his head in exasperation. He'd never known his sister to be so indecisive. "Either you embarrass him *and* his family, or let him continue to bother you. Make up your mind, Rissa."

Tunneling her fingers through her hair, Clarissa held it off her face. "I'm so confused."

"Why? Are you still in love with him?"

She worried her lip between her teeth. "It's not easy to get over a ten-year relationship like striking a letter on a keyboard. Do I still having feelings for him? Yes. Am I in love with him? I don't think so."

"Why do you think he wants to talk to you?" Brandt asked.

"It's probably to ask me to give him another chance."

He wanted to tell his sister *hell no,* that she shouldn't give Harper Sinclair the time of day, that his need to control her wasn't going to change. He suspected Harper had cheated on Clarissa during the decade-long relationship. But Brandt had managed to remain uninvolved.

"Whatever you decide, the decision has to be yours. I'll stay out of it, Rissa, until—"

Eyes narrowing, Clarissa stared at her brother. She wanted to ask him *until what,* but was afraid to hear the answer, knowing it would result in an injury—to Harper. She'd come to Brandt only because he was the most levelheaded of her three brothers. Despite having a career in one of the most violent sports, Brandt

Wainwright was a teddy bear off the gridiron. Sumner and Garth were different—especially Sumner.

"I'll block his calls."

Brandt patted her arm. "Good girl."

"Enough about me," Clarissa said, her mood brightening. "You look much better than you did when I saw you in the hospital."

"That's because I'm feeling much better."

"She's good for you, isn't she?"

A beat passed as Brandt gave Clarissa a level stare. "Who are you talking about?"

"Your...*nurse*."

"What are you trying to say, Rissa? That she isn't my nurse?"

"There's no need to get defensive, big brother. All I'm saying is that..." Her words trailed off with the distinctive buzz from the intercom. "I'll get that." Rising from the love seat, Clarissa punched the button on the wall panel, activating the speaker feature. "Wainwright residence, this is Clarissa."

"Miss Clarissa. Your brothers are here."

"Please send them up." She returned to Brandt. "We'll talk about your nurse later."

"No, we won't," Brandt countered. "I don't intend to explain Ciara."

He'd never been one to discuss the women with whom he'd been involved with his family—and certainly not with the press. As a professional athlete his life had become an open book, subject to scrutiny and censure, while discretion was something he'd come to covet.

Early in his career Brandt had learned to play the game: show up for photo ops, be seen with the models and actresses and always sign autographs and show up for charitable events. Even when his publicist had suggested he cultivate a bad boy image to sell copy, he'd refused. Occasional profanity was as far as he would go. Behaving badly hadn't been and would never become an option, because he had to think of his reputation once his football career ended.

"You don't have to," Clarissa threw over her shoulder as she turned to walk out of the library. "I'll just ask her what's up between the two of you."

"Let it go and mind your business."

"Uh-oh. Aren't we touchy?"

The doors to the elevator opened and Garth and Sumner Wainwright stepped out into the expansive entryway. There was no mistaking they were related. Both were blond, several inches above the six-foot mark and broad-shouldered. Garth's eyes were a sensual cobalt blue, Sumner's a cool, smoky gray. Both were casually dressed in slacks and shirts, sans ties and wearing lightweight summer jackets.

Garth slapped Brandt's shoulder. "You're looking good, big brother."

Sumner, less effusive, nodded. "You do look great."

Brandt smiled at his brothers. "Great is when I won't need this chair. Thank you, guys, for coming."

"Where are Mom and Dad?" Garth asked.

Clarissa looped her arm through Sumner's. "They're having cocktails in the solarium."

Garth sniffed the air like a large cat. "Something really smells good."

"We're having Thai…" Brandt didn't finish his statement when he realized his brothers were staring at something over his shoulder. He maneuvered the chair to see the object of Sumner and Garth's rapt gazes; he knew what they were experiencing when he found himself ensnared in a similar soporific spell.

It was as if he were seeing Ciara for the first time: he took in the length of her shapely legs, her trim thighs and how the black dress hugged her hips and breasts. Brandt heard his brothers' slow exhalation of breath behind him. It was apparent Ciara had the same effect on his brothers that she had on him.

"Who is she?" Sumner whispered in Clarissa's ear.

"I'll let Brandt tell you," she whispered back.

Brandt, ignoring the whispering going on behind his back, extended his hand to Ciara. "Now that everyone's here, we can go into the dining room."

Garth and Sumner shared a confused look. "Aren't you going to introduce us to the lady?" Garth asked.

"My bad," Brandt drawled, successfully biting back a grin. "Ciara, these are my brothers, Garth and Sumner. Bros, this is Ciara Dennison, my private nurse and our hostess for the evening." The three exchanged smiles and handshakes. "Now that we have the introductions out of the way, I think it's time we eat."

Chapter 10

Ciara, seated on Brandt's right, stared at Sumner Wainwright. His hair was cropped military-style, but it was his cool gray eyes staring back at her that made her feel slightly uncomfortable. She shrugged off the feeling, intent on enjoying the food the chefs had prepared for dinner.

The waiter had filled wineglasses with a pale blush wine and Brandt raised his glass in a toast. "I'd like to toast my family, who had to put up with my bad moods these past few weeks. Thank you for not abandoning me." His gaze shifted to Ciara. "And to Ciara, who stood her ground and wouldn't permit me to wallow in the woe-is-me syndrome. You don't know how much I've come to rely on you."

"Hear, hear," everyone chorused.

Ciara took a sip of the cool wine, her gaze downcast. When she looked up she saw everyone staring at her.

What did they expect her to say? Brandt was her patient, and as his nurse it was her responsibility to take care of him.

The waiter, carrying a tray with a variety of appetizers, shattered the pregnant silence. Placing the tray on a cart, he placed chopsticks at each place setting, and then set out plates of spring rolls, cold noodles with sesame sauce, chicken and beef satay and a variety of steamed chicken and shrimp dumplings along with mixed vegetable dumplings.

"This is the best Thai food I've had since returning from Phuket last year," Fraser said before dipping a piece of spring roll into a plum sauce.

Clarissa stared at her father. "You're not thinking about returning to Thailand, are you?"

Fraser shook his head. "No. Your mother threatened to divorce me if I go back."

Brandt rested his hand on Ciara's knee under the table. "My father represented Wainwright Developers in Thailand when they put up an office building, because he speaks several Asian languages, including Thai, several Vietnamese dialects and fluent Japanese."

"Ciara, have you ever traveled abroad?" Garth asked.

She smiled. "I had the Grand Tour after graduating high school. My mother took me to Europe for the summer."

Phyllis Dennison had promised her daughter if she graduated in the top one percent of her class she would take her to Europe. Ciara studied when she should've been hanging out with her friends, who teased her about becoming a geek. Geek or not, her desire to see another part of the world trumped going to the mall, movies or sleepovers. Boys were interested in her, but she managed to delay dating until college. By that time it was too late to learn the give and take of interpersonal relationships. She'd chosen badly and in the end suffered.

The conversations floating around the table went from foreign travel to movies and finally to the antics of high-profile A-list movie stars as the appetizers were replaced with pad Thai, a spicy crispy-duck salad then entrées of chicken, beef and shrimp with a plethora of sauces that included ginger, basil, green curry, peanut, sweet and sour, and lemongrass. Brandt had requested the chef prepare his father's favorite Thai dish, Bank Kok, crispy fried whitefish with bell peppers and string beans served with the chef's special sauce.

Not only had dinner become a family reunion, but it also served as a peace offering. Conversation was lively, with Brandt smiling and laughing. Even Sumner seemed to shed his dark mood to join the others when Fraser attempted to tell a joke that would've been funny if he hadn't given away the punch line.

"Daddy," Clarissa wailed, "please give it up. You're never going to tell a joke without flubbing it."

Fraser winked at his daughter. "I did it once without flubbing it. Ask your mother."

Leona, resting a hand on her chest, shook her head. "I can't believe you'd ask me to lie for you—especially in front of my children."

"Your children are thirty-three, thirty-two, thirty and twenty-eight respectively," Fraser countered. "So don't talk about them as if they are little kids."

Brandt stared at Fraser. "Dad, why is it when you

and Mom talk about us we're always her children and not yours?"

"Your mother and I agreed that when we had children I would leave the childrearing to her."

"No, we didn't, Fraser Wainwright."

Pushing back his chair, Garth stood up. "I'm sorry to break up this warm, fuzzy gathering, but I have to fly to the West Coast tomorrow morning."

"Who or what is on the West Coast?" Brandt asked.

"An actress, whom I'm not at liberty to name at this time, who wants me to design a small café off Puget Sound for her partner."

Brandt raised his water goblet. "Good for you."

"What would be good is if he'd come to work for Wainwright Developers," Fraser mumbled under his breath.

"Dad, please don't start with Garth," Brandt retorted. "I thought we agreed after I decided to play football that you wouldn't put pressure on *your* children to make them join the family business."

A flush darkened Fraser's face under his summer tan. "Your mother and I did agree."

Brandt closed his eyes for several seconds, reliving the brouhaha that had ensued after he informed his parents that professional football had become his career choice. "If that's true, then, please, let's not talk about it. Not tonight."

He didn't want his father to ruin what had become the best night he'd had since Jordan's wedding. And having Ciara sitting next to him had been an added bonus. She'd surreptitiously communicated to the waiter when to bring each course or refill wine and water glasses, and when she admitted to traveling abroad he wanted to hear all about the places she'd visited.

Garth rounded the table, kissed Leona and patted Fraser's shoulder. "I'll call you and we can get together after I come back."

Fraser smiled. "No problem, son."

"Are you coming, little brother?" Garth asked Sumner.

"I'm an inch taller and at least ten pounds heavier than you. So that makes you the little brother," Sumner teased, rising to his feet.

Leona stood up. "I think it's time we all leave so Brandt can rest." She leaned over and kissed his cheek. "Thank you, darling, for inviting us. And thank you, Ciara, for making the evening even more enjoyable."

Ciara and Brandt waited as the Wainwrights filed into the elevator, the doors closing behind them. They shared a knowing smile. The food had been delicious, the company delightful and the conversation interesting.

She smothered a yawn, chiding herself for drinking two glasses of wine. One was enough to relax her, two usually made her sleepy. "Are you ready to go to bed?" she asked Brandt. It was after ten-thirty.

"Not yet. I'm going to wait until Angaraka finishes up in the kitchen, then I'll go to bed."

"That's not necessary, Brandt," Ciara argued softly. "I'll stay and you go to bed."

"Are you certain?"

"Very certain," she confirmed. "You had physical therapy today, so I don't want you to overdo it."

"I'm not tired."

"And I don't want you to get tired."

Grasping the handles, Ciara pushed the wheelchair into Brandt's bedroom. She removed the casts, helped him undress and lowered the hospital bed to make it easier for him to transfer from the chair to the bed. She dimmed the lamp in the seating area and adjusted the thermostat while waiting for Brandt to emerge from the bathroom.

Brandt maneuvered the chair close to the bed, and with a minimum of effort, pushed off the chair and into the bed. "There's an envelope on the desk in the library. Please give it to Angaraka."

Ciara nodded, adjusting the sheet and lightweight blanket over her patient's legs. She'd reverted to her nurse's persona. "Good night, Brandt. I'll come and check on you later."

"I meant what I said earlier."

"What's that?"

"I've really come to rely on you."

"That's why your mother hired me. To take care of you."

Brandt tried making out Ciara's face in the dimly lit room. Fatigue he hadn't felt before now swept over him, making it difficult to keep his eyes open. "That's not what I'm talking about."

Ciara noticed Brandt was slurring his words, and she attributed it to either fatigue or the glass of wine he'd consumed with dinner. "Go to sleep."

"I like you, Ciara."

"I like you, too, Brandt."

His eyes opened. "You don't understand."

Ciara smiled. "Yes, I do. Go to sleep." She enunciated each word.

Brandt felt the warmth of the body he longed to touch, inhaled the subtle scent of the perfume that was as feminine and sensual as its wearer. It was the first time in a very long time he hadn't wanted to sleep alone, and it wasn't about sex, but companionship. Every night he went to sleep thinking about Ciara, and when he woke it was she he wanted to see.

"Good night."

Ciara heard the soft snoring as she walked into the connecting suite and slipped out of her shoes and into a pair of fluffy slippers. A moan slipped past her lips when she felt the slight ache in her thighs. Miss ChaCha reminded her that wearing stilettos would take some getting used to. She found the envelope on the desk in the library, giving it to Angaraka as he and his staff packed up their equipment.

Twenty minutes after the elevators doors closed behind the caterer, Ciara removed the contacts, cleansed her face of makeup, fashioned her hair into a single braid and slipped into a pair of pajama pants with a matching tank top. She checked on Brandt. He was sleeping soundly.

She went into her bedroom, leaving the connecting door slightly ajar, and got into bed. Interacting with the Wainwrights reminded her that she'd always wanted a brother or a sister. Being an only child had its advantages and disadvantages. She hadn't had to share her toys or clothes and hadn't experienced sibling rivalry; but as an only child she would never become an aunt, couldn't call a brother or sister for emotional support. Maybe if she'd had a brother she wouldn't have had to deal with Victor Seabrook all by herself.

Ciara had thought it admirable that Brandt had stood up for Garth when Fraser hinted at him joining the family's real-estate conglomerate. She was fortunate her mother never tried to dissuade her from becoming a nurse. Phyllis's only comment was that if she wanted a career in medicine, why not become a doctor? Ciara knew she'd had the aptitude and the GPA to get into medical school, but not the patience to commit the time it took to earn a medical degree.

She tended to analyze people when she first met them, but Ciara decided to reserve judgment when it came to Brandt's family. They weren't the Brady Bunch, and yet they weren't as dysfunctional as those featured in TV reality shows.

Unfortunately, the same couldn't be said for her family. Not only had her father cheated on her mother, but he'd also married another woman. Unfortunately for William Dennison, bigamy was illegal in New York. And once his divorce from Phyllis was finalized, he remarried his second wife in what he'd called a renewal of vows when it was actually their first legal union.

Pounding the pillow under her head, Ciara turned over and closed her eyes. She had to stop thinking or she would never fall asleep. Sleep did come and with it an erotic dream of her writhing on a bed with Brandt.

Brandt, pushing into a sitting position, reached across his body and after two attempts picked up the telephone. "Hel…lo," he stammered.

"Brandt! Are you awake?"

He rested his free arm over his forehead. "Of course I'm awake. I'm talking to you, aren't I?"

"Do you know who this is?"

Brandt managed a wry smile. "There's no way I wouldn't recognize your sexy voice."

"I'm going to tell my husband that his cousin is hitting on his wife."

"Jordan would never believe it. It's known that Wainwright men never go after another man's woman. Why the early-morning call, Aziza?"

"I've been calling your cell phone for the past four days. They all went to voice mail. I didn't want to ring your house phone, but I only have a small window in which to respond to a request for you to visit the pediatric wing of a local hospital. When the hospital administration polled the kids as to who they most admire, your name topped the list."

Brandt digested this information. His popularity usually escalated during the preseason, when sportscasters and photographers followed controversial players, interviewed coaches and offered daily reports on those who were still holding out signing contracts in lieu of higher salaries.

"Are they aware that I'm in a wheelchair?"

"You sitting in a wheelchair is temporary, Brandt. Some of these kids will spend the rest of their lives in a chair."

His brow furrowed. "Pile on the guilt, Mrs. Wainwright."

A husky laugh came through the earpiece. "You're the first one to call me Mrs. Wainwright since Jordan and I returned from our honeymoon."

"For better or worse, you are now one of us."

"Jordan reminds me of that every day. Now back to why I called you. Can you make it?"

Brandt closed his eyes. He wanted to decline, but children, whether sick or healthy, were always a priority for him. During his fifth year in the NFL he'd set up a charity focusing on athletic and academic scholarships for high school students from low-income families.

"When and where? Okay," he agreed after Aziza gave him the name of the hospital and the time he was expected to appear. "Will you be there?" he asked.

"I wouldn't miss it. Hang up so I can arrange for a car and driver to pick you up."

"Don't bother. I have my own driver."

"Are you sure?"

"Yes. I'll see you later, Mrs. Wainwright."

"Hang up, Brandt."

"See you later, beautiful."

Brandt had just ended the call when Ciara walked into the bedroom, damp hair falling around her face. He smiled. After the dinner with his family, she'd exchanged her usual baggy outfit for slacks, shorts and blouses. Sandals had replaced her clogs. What she hadn't exchanged were her glasses for the contact lenses.

Ciara returned Brandt's warm smile. "Good morning."

He patted the mattress, and he wasn't disappointed when she climbed into bed next to him. Ciara had stopped putting up the bedrail, permitting him to get in and out of bed unassisted to use the bathroom. This morning he'd washed his face and brushed his teeth, then returned to bed to wait for her. Leaning to his right, he pressed a kiss to her cheek.

"Good morning. We're going out tomorrow afternoon."

Ciara gave Brandt a sidelong glance. Brandt looked good. In fact, he looked better than good. He was delicious. The sun-browned richness of his tanned face gave it a healthy glow. His eyes were bright, shimmering with laugher. She swallowed when she noticed the outline of the bulge under the sheet.

She'd awoken early, lain in bed and called herself every type of fool for even contemplating taking up with Brandt Wainwright. The night before they'd watched a romantic comedy. He'd fallen asleep halfway through the movie and she'd turned off the TV and went to bed.

Sleep had been elusive; she tossed and turned while images of her writhing uncontrollably on Brandt's lap had come back in vivid clarity, followed by more images of an erotic dream wherein she wasn't on his lap, but on her back with him inside her. Never in her thirteen years of practicing nursing had she been so tempted by a man's body as now.

Her relationship with Brandt went against everything she'd professed. Dr. Victor Seabrook was a celebrity, but he paled in comparison to Brandt. However, her ambivalence about her unorthodox relationship with her patient disappeared whenever they shared the same space.

Ciara averted her gaze from his erection, asking, "Where are we going tomorrow afternoon?"

"I've been asked to visit some kids at a hospital."

"Which hospital?" When Brandt told her, Ciara knew she would not have been upright if she'd still been standing. Why, she thought, did it have to be the same hospital where she'd begun her nursing career? The same hospital where she'd met and subsequently dated Victor? The same hospital she'd fled when he'd become more demanding, possessive, when he'd sought to control her life?

Brandt saw Ciara clutch the sheet before her grip eased. "What's the matter?"

She affected a smile that only touched her mouth. "Nothing."

"Please don't lie to me, Ciara. You look as if you've just seen a ghost."

Ciara knew she had to tell Brandt that they were going to a hospital where most of the staff were familiar with her and where she could possibly run into a man who was not what he'd presented—a doctor who was Dr. Jekyll and Mr. Hyde.

"I used to work at that hospital."

"Did you leave on bad terms?"

"No," she answered truthfully. "It was my decision to leave."

"How long did you work there?"

A beat passed. "Ten years."

Brandt studied the face of the woman who unknowingly had changed him and his life. If she hadn't stood her ground he would've chased her out too, leaving him to wallow in a maelstrom of helplessness and self-pity. Ciara was good to and for him, and if there was anything she wanted or needed, he would do whatever was possible to give it to her.

"You're going to have to tell me about it so I'll know how to spin it."

"Are you certain you want to get involved in something that has nothing to do with you?"

Brandt pondered her cryptic query. Ciara's disclosure that she wasn't afraid of anyone or anything had been nothing more than bravado. She *was* frightened. But of whom? "It's too late for that, Ciara. We're already involved, whether you're willing or want to admit it." He didn't have to tell her that nurses didn't kiss their patients or simulate making love with them. Nurses also didn't do double duty as hostesses for their patients. "And if I were able to stand on my own I'd show you just how involved we are."

Ciara found the very thought of making love to Brandt exciting because of her rediscovered sexual awakening. She'd always known of the strong passion within her even if she hadn't recognized her needs. Since breaking up with Victor, she'd realized she had to be alone in order to find out what she really wanted for herself and her future. She knew Brandt Wainwright did not figure anywhere in her future. He wasn't her Mr. Right, but Mr. Right Now.

"I'll tell you later."

Brandt heard the finality in her statement. He didn't want to wait until later to find out what had prompted the woman with whom he'd found himself more involved with each sunrise to leave one of the best hospitals in New York to become a private-duty nurse.

"Talking about it later isn't going to change anything." His voice was soft, coaxing.

Chapter 11

Brandt reached for Ciara's hand, lacing their fingers together and pressing a kiss to her hair. It smelled like fresh coconut. "Talk to me, sweetheart."

Ciara settled against Brandt's chest and closed her eyes. What she was about to tell Brandt she had never disclosed to anyone, and that included her mother. She and her mother had a relationship based on an open dialogue, yet she didn't and couldn't tell Phyllis about her relationship with Dr. Victor Seabrook away from the bright lights and cameras. The closest she'd come to disclosing why she'd walked away from Victor was when she'd confessed to Sofia that he had attempted to control her life.

"What do you want to know?"

"Where did you grow up? Do you have brothers or sisters?"

"I grew up about thirty miles west of Albany. My

parents divorced the year I turned ten, after my mother discovered my father had another wife." Brandt smothered a curse under his breath. Ciara smiled. "My sentiments exactly."

"So," he crooned in her ear, "I don't have to contribute to the cuss jar?"

"Not this time. And to answer your question about siblings, I'm an only child. After high school I enrolled in a downstate college, graduating with a BS in nursing. Less than a year after working at the hospital I was attacked by a male patient...who claimed I'd teased him because I wore my uniforms too tight."

"Did he hurt you, Ciara?"

She shook her head. "If you're asking if he raped me, then the answer is no. If it hadn't been for the other two patients in the room, I can't imagine what would've happened. One rang the nurses' station while the other shouted for help."

"Is that why you wear smock tops?"

"Yes."

Brandt gave her hand a gentle squeeze. "You can't blame yourself for one sick son of a bitch."

Raising her chin, Ciara met Brandt's eyes. They were cold, reminding her of chipped glass. "Tell that to a twenty-year-old."

"How old were you when you graduated college?"

"Nineteen. I graduated from high school at six-teen."

"How old are you now?"

"Thirty-three."

Burying his face in her hair, Brandt pressed a kiss

against her scalp. "And after thirteen years you're still hiding?"

"I only wear the smocks when I have male patients."

"Does it work?" he asked.

"Yes."

"That's where you're wrong, Ciara. It didn't work with me, and do you know why?"

"No. Why?"

"You don't realize how close you came to the truth when you called me Superman. You were deluding yourself when you tried hiding behind those ugly tops because I just happen to have X-ray vision."

Ciara laughed softly and shifted to a more comfortable position. "I'm not that gullible, Brandt."

Brandt kissed her hair again. "Tell me what he did to you. And you know I'm not talking about the patient who attacked you."

She inhaled, held her breath, then let it out in an audible sigh. "I was known at the hospital as the nurse with two looks: working girl and party girl. You're familiar with the working girl and the other night you saw the party girl. It was my party-girl persona that caught the eye of a plastic surgeon—Dr. Victor Seabrook." Ciara paused, waiting for Brandt to acknowledge that he recognized the name.

"Go on," Brandt urged when Ciara fell silent. Although he didn't particularly like watching reality television, he knew the doctor's name.

"The first time Victor asked to take me out I turned him down. I'd gone back to school to get a graduate degree, because I'd wanted to go into psychiatric nursing, so between work and school I had very little time for socializing. A week after I was appointed to a position as a psychiatric nurse he asked me again and I accepted.

"What had begun as casual dinner dates escalated to media gatherings with A-list actors and other celebrities. Victor insisted I have a new outfit for every occasion and he'd accompany me to the various shops and boutiques, personally selecting what he wanted me to wear. I was flattered by the attention, but after a while I felt as if I was being smothered. When I told him how I felt he'd dismiss me with a wave of his hand, saying most women would give anything to have their man pay them that much attention.

"Initially I believed him, because my mother used to complain about marrying a salesman because my father was on the road more than he was at home. I rationalized, telling myself most women would love a man like Victor. He paid my rent, bought the groceries and paid for my clothes. The only thing he wanted was for me to be available for him when he needed sex, or a date.

"I panicked the day he proposed marriage because I had to ask myself if I wanted to spend the rest of my life with a man who controlled every aspect of my life and the answer was no. I told Victor I would have to think about it. That's when he slapped me, saying I was an ungrateful bitch."

Every muscle in Brandt's body tensed. "He hit you?"

Ciara nodded, recalling the incident as if it'd occurred seconds ago. He'd struck her across the face with an open hand. She had been more stunned than hurt, but his intent was more to humiliate than hurt.

"I screamed at him to get out of my apartment, or I would call the police and have him arrested for assault."

"Had he ever hit you before?"

"No. It happened so quickly that it took a minute for me to react. I was so angry I couldn't cry. I applied an ice pack to my jaw, called in sick and twenty-four hours later I'd made a decision that changed my life. I called my supervisor and told her I was sending off a certified letter verifying I was resigning because of burnout. A friend had purchased a two-bedroom co-op in West Harlem, and she was looking for a roommate. I told Sofia I had to get away from my boyfriend, so she sent her police officer brother and some of his friends to pack up my apartment while I moved in with her. I'm certain if I'd told Esteban that Victor had hit me he would've impounded his car, then waited for him to retrieve it and arrested him on some frivolous charge like spitting on the sidewalk."

"You're lucky to have had friends who had your back." Brandt didn't want to think of some man slapping his sister, or any of his female cousins.

"They're the best."

"I take it you haven't run into your ex since you left the hospital."

Ciara exhaled. "I saw him about a month ago at my former supervisor's retirement party. He showed up even though he wasn't invited because he knew I would be there. He said he wanted to apologize, but I wasn't having any of it. I'd asked Esteban to come with me as my date, so when I told him my police officer boyfriend would like nothing better than to arrest him for stalking, he left."

"Is Esteban your boyfriend?" Brandt knew he sounded jealous, but he couldn't help it. He had to know where he stood with Ciara before whatever they had went any further.

"No. Esteban Martinez is a confirmed bachelor. It's his fortieth birthday party that I've agreed to attend. Have you asked your mother to come over and stay with you?"

Brandt shook his head. "No. I'll be all right if I'm home alone for a few hours."

Ciara peered at Brandt's distinctive profile. "I may not get back until late."

"It doesn't matter," he countered. "Now about your ex. Let me handle everything."

"What are you going to do?"

Attractive lines fanned out around his eyes when he smiled. He released her hand. "I'm not going to bitch-slap him, if that's what you're concerned about. I also don't want you to come with me."

"But—"

"No buts, Ciara. I'll tell my agent that I'll need someone to help me from the car to the hospital entrance, and then back again. There are going to be cameras and reporters on hand because it will be a photo op. And I'm certain if reporters start asking questions, then your former coworkers will be more than forthcoming about you and your association with Dr. Seabrook. If he'd showed up to an event where he hadn't been invited just to see you, what's to say he won't seek you out again if he knows you're at the hospital?

"Think about it, darling." The endearment rolled off Brandt's tongue like watered silk. "The man has to have a tremendous ego if he resorted to lashing out physically because you rejected him. After all, he's the high-profile, hotshot doctor who's probably used to women throwing themselves at him. But you'd become the exception and he couldn't deal with it. Guys like Victor Seabrook are dangerous *and* crazy, Ciara, and it would be better if you avoided him."

"What I should've done was have him arrested for hitting me."

"Unless you had proof of physical injury, then it would've come down to a 'he said, she said.' Remember, he's the celebrity and you would've been looked upon as the jealous or spurned girlfriend."

Ciara knew Brandt was right. The reason she hadn't gone to the police to have Victor charged with assault was because she hadn't wanted the publicity. Her position at the hospital would've been in jeopardy and her reputation tainted by the negative publicity. She'd taken the right course of action when she took steps to purge Victor Seabrook from her life.

"Thank you for listening."

"I'm glad you trusted me enough to tell me."

Cradling Ciara's head, Brandt moved his mouth over hers, exploring the soft lips parting under his as he deepened the kiss. The tip of her tongue touched his, pulled back, then emerged again.

His lips left hers to taste her earlobe, her neck, breathing a kiss there before returning to the sexy mouth that had the power to make him say and do things he hadn't thought possible.

Ciara surrendered to the slow, seductive kisses that were as potent as any drug. Shifting, she turned toward Brandt, more than aware of his broken legs. Her hands were busy, tracing the contours of his chest and flat belly. She wanted to reach between his thighs and release his sex to her hungry gaze. Somehow she found the strength to pull away, her breasts rising and falling heavily as she struggled to control her breathing.

She was on fire and she needed him to extinguish it. "Can we, Brandt?"

Eyes wide, Brandt stared at the woman pressed to his side, seeing passion and indecision in her eyes. He knew she wanted him as much as he wanted her. "Yes, we can, darling." His blood-engorged penis was so hard it hurt. "I'll spread my legs and you lie between them."

Ciara shook her head. "No. I'll hurt you."

He gritted his teeth in frustration, not wanting a repeat of what had occurred when she'd gyrated on his lap. "Then sit on me. Please, baby, I want you so much."

Ciara felt hot tears prick the backs of her eyelids. Victor had never wanted her. He'd always needed her. "You're going to have to protect me." Whenever she slept with a man she'd insisted he use protection. She wasn't ready to become a mother, and she was aware of the risks of contracting STDs.

Brandt closed his eyes, praying he wouldn't come before he was able to penetrate Ciara. It wasn't as much about having sex with her as making love to her. "There should be some condoms in the bathroom. They're in the drawer with the shaving supplies."

A sigh of relief slipped past his lips when she left the bed to get the condoms. The tension that had been building between them for days made him feel as if thousands of tiny insects were feasting on his nerve endings. He'd found himself looking for every opportunity to touch Ciara, to kiss her good-night or for the obligatory thank you.

When she'd sat on the bed with him to watch a movie the night before, he knew they'd crossed the threshold where they could sleep together without making love. His disappointment was profound when he woke not to find her beside him. His first reaction was to go to her, but pride had stopped him. What if she didn't want him in her bed? What if she wanted to be the one to make the overture? The questions had assailed him until Brandt realized he wasn't going back to sleep and got out of bed.

Opening the drawer, Ciara found the box of condoms. It hadn't been opened. Taking off her glasses, she left them on the vanity. She closed her eyes, then opened them, staring at the mirror. "What are you doing, Ciara Dennison?" she asked her reflection. "Do you really intend to sleep with a man you've known such a short time? Are you crazy as hell or just plain old horny?"

"Who are you talking to, Ciara?" Brandt called out from the bedroom.

She opened her eyes. "Myself."

"Why are you talking to yourself, babe?"

A wry smile twisted her mouth. "Maybe I'm crazy."

"Do you want to talk about it?"

"I'm already talking about it. I'm talking to myself."

"Either you come here or I'm coming in there to get you."

"Don't move, Brandt. I'm coming." Ciara broke the seal on the box and took out a condom. She walked back into the bedroom, tossing the condom at Brandt, who caught it in midair.

He patted the bed. "Come here, baby. Let's talk about what has you so crazy."

She got into bed, but instead of lying next to Brandt, Ciara sat on folded knees at the foot. "Don't you think it's odd that we're going to make love when a few weeks ago we didn't know each other? Well…maybe you didn't know me."

Crossing his arms over his bare chest, Brandt angled his head. "A week, a month, a year," he drawled. "It's only time."

Sandwiching her hands between her knees, Ciara saw something in Brandt's eyes that made her uncomfortable. It was as if he were looking at her for the first time. "Are you saying time means nothing to you?"

"That's exactly what I'm saying, Miss Ciara Dennison. When it comes to you it doesn't matter whether I've known you one week, one second or one lifetime."

Time no longer mattered to Brandt. Not when he'd lain in a hospital for two weeks, not knowing what city he was in, the day, hour or who'd come to see him. Time had ceased being important because he didn't know how long it would take for him to heal completely. It could take a year—or longer. He went to sleep. He woke up. And in between that time there was Ciara Dennison. She'd become the one by whom he measured his existence.

Ciara was asking questions and he had some of his own. What, he mused, was it about the woman living under his roof, sitting at the foot of his bed that tugged at him in a way no other woman had? He'd never been one to lose his head or heart over a woman, but she was different—she was the total package, something Dr. Victor Seabrook had also recognized. Unfortunately for the doctor with the overblown ego, he'd failed in his attempt to brainwash and control her.

Her indifference to his celebrity-athlete status, or that he was a member of a prestigious New York family, had set Ciara apart from the other women who'd passed in and out of his life. Some he'd dated had beautiful faces with bodies to match, but offered nothing else, because being seen with him was all that mattered. He had tween cousins who had more sophistication than most of them. Yet he'd still played the game—on and off the gridiron—and he'd played it very well.

What he'd found puzzling was that he had resigned himself that his world hadn't stopped because he hadn't joined his teammates for preseason games. He'd turned off his cell phone because he hadn't wanted to talk to any of them, and he hadn't watched a televised game because he did not want to be reminded that instead of tossing a football he was sitting in a wheelchair.

"We're both consenting adults, so I don't understand why you're intellectualizing this, Ciara."

She gave him a long, penetrating look. "I just want to make certain we're both on the same page."

"What do you want?"

Ciara ignored the cold edge in his tone. "When it's over I don't want to have to deal with a lot of drama."

His eyes narrowed. "What are you looking for?"

"Why, sex of course," she said glibly. "Isn't that what men want when they meet a woman?"

Brandt went completely still. He didn't want to believe what he'd just heard. She was treating him as if he were a piece of meat. "You don't want a declaration of love, or expect a happily ever after?"

Ciara wanted to tell Brandt she did, but not with him. She'd dated a man in the spotlight and she didn't want a repeat of what she'd had with Victor. "No. The sex will suffice."

She knew she sounded cold, detached. It had to be that way or no way. Ciara knew she couldn't afford to fall under the sensual spell of the blond giant, who despite his physical limitations was a constant reminder of who she was and what she'd been missing. It'd been more than two years since she'd slept with a man, and the weeks following her separation from Victor had been the most difficult. After a while the urges weren't as strong and then they'd stopped altogether. But now they were back—and stronger than ever. And all because of a man she never would've considered dating if they'd met at a sporting or social event.

Although she'd known Brandt a short time, they had become a couple. They were living together, sharing meals and deliberating what movies to watch. They had even entertained as an unofficial couple. They'd made love without having sexual intercourse, but it was the intercourse both wanted.

Brandt stared at Ciara. She wanted sex while he wanted more than that. Even with two broken legs, he had the option of masturbating to relieve his sexual tension, but he wasn't about to revert to his fourteen-year-old self, for whom it'd become a daily ritual.

He extended his arms. "You've got yourself a deal: no love, drama or happily ever after."

Ciara moved toward him, her hands going to the waistband of his boxers and deftly pulling them off his hips and down his legs. Her hair had fallen around her face, preventing him from seeing her expression when his penis quickly became engorged. Using his teeth, he tore open the condom wrapper and rolled the latex sheath down over his erection.

Brandt stared, hypnotized by the graceful, fluid movements of Ciara unbuttoning her shirt and letting it slide off her shoulders. He swallowed a groan. Swells of brown flesh above the cups of her white lace bra were an erotic turn-on. And not for the first time he cursed the fact that he couldn't move to undress her.

He wanted to reach around her back and unhook her bra to free her breasts. He wanted to take his time removing her shorts and panties, then run his tongue over every inch of her luscious body to discover if it tasted as delicious as she looked. The bra fell away, and he was stunned by the firm roundness of her breasts.

Ciara felt the heat from her soon-to-be lover's electric-blue gaze as she took an inordinate amount of time taking off her clothes. He was fully aroused and the area between her legs was wet and pulsing with a need she'd never experienced before. There was an advantage in remaining celibate, because after being denied something she'd craved for a long time, now the wait would be worth it.

She couldn't control her hands. They were trembling. It took two attempts before she was able to undo the button on her shorts and rid herself of the shorts and bikini panties in one smooth motion. Sleek and lithe as a cat, Ciara slid upward and straddled Brandt. They moaned in unison when flesh met flesh, her breasts flattening against his chest.

Looping his arms around her body, Brandt closed his eyes and let his senses take over. Everything about Ciara seeped into him: the silky softness of her skin, the natural scent of her body. The strong beat of her heart kept tempo with his as she pressed closer. His hands moved lower, cupping her hips and pulling her even closer.

Ciara buried her face against the thick column of Brandt's neck, willing her hips not to move when his hardened flesh pulsed rhythmically against her buttocks. She wanted to enjoy the smell and feel of the man holding her to his heart. She wanted him to infiltrate her senses, erasing the memories of every man she'd known and not just the few she'd slept with. The strength in Brandt's arms was so virile and protective; it had taken her more than half her life to come to the realization that it wasn't love she sought from a man, but his protection.

Brandt eased back, angled his head and brushed his mouth over Ciara's. Deepening the kiss, he took total possession of her mouth, his tongue moving in and out and simulating making love to her. He lifted her effortlessly with one arm, his free hand guiding her down on his erection. There was a slight resistance;

Brandt lifted his hips off the bed as Ciara came down to meet his rigid flesh.

Bracing her feet on the mattress, her knees pressed against her chest, Ciara anchored her arms under Brandt's massive shoulders. She wanted to close her eyes, but couldn't as Brandt's bore into hers. Passion had tightened the skin over his cheekbones, flared his nostrils and quickened his breathing.

The pleasure Brandt found in Ciara's body was so exquisite he feared it would be over much too quickly. She wanted sex—he wanted love. She didn't want drama—and neither did he. She wanted right now—and he wanted now, tomorrow and more tomorrows. His hands circled her narrow waist, fingers tightening on the tender flesh as she moved up and down over his sex like a well-oiled piston.

Heat, chills, waves of ecstasy overlapped and pulled Ciara down into an abyss of passion from which there was no escape. She closed her eyes, gasping when the first ripple of release gripped her.

"Oh, no!" she gasped.

"Let it go, baby." Brandt felt the strong pulsing of her flesh squeezing his penis.

Ciara did let go, orgasms gripping, overlapping and shaking her until she threw back her head and cried an awesome moan of erotic pleasure as Brandt's breath came in long, surrendering gasps.

Resting her cheek against his shoulder, she pressed a kiss to the damp, salty flesh. "Thank you."

Chest heaving, eyes closed, Brandt, smiled. "Thank you!"

They lay together, joined and enjoying the sense of

oneness. Ciara moaned. Her legs were cramping. "I have to get up."

"What's the matter, babe?"

"My calves are cramping."

Brandt released her and she rolled off his body. They lay side by side, holding hands. Ciara's breathing deepened until she slept the sleep of a sated lover. This time there were no erotic images to disturb her peaceful slumber.

Chapter 12

"I'll take it from here," Brandt told the orderly who'd pushed his chair up the ramp to the entrance to the hospital.

Automatic doors opened and the first thing he saw was the oversize poster resting on an easel. It was a photograph of him in uniform, hair falling to his shoulders, his helmet tucked under his left arm and a football under the right. A printed caption with the date, time and location had advertised his appearance. The photo was taken the day after he and his team had won the Super Bowl. Why, he mused, did it seem like a different place and lifetime?

Brandt stared straight ahead, ignoring the whispers and stares of people milling around the hospital entrance. He maneuvered the chair across the expansive lobby to a bank of elevators, where Aziza Fleming-Wainwright waited. A bright smile split his face with her approach.

If marriage agreed with his cousin, it suited Jordan's wife even more. She'd cut her hair into a becoming pixie style. Spending three weeks in French Polynesia had darkened her complexion to a rich mahogany brown. A white-and-black-striped linen coatdress and black patent-leather pumps flattered her tall, slender figure.

"Hey, beautiful," he crooned, taking the hand she extended to him.

Aziza leaned down to kiss her client's cheek, then wiped at the smudge of color with her thumb. "You look fantastic," he continued.

"So do you. Jordan called just before you arrived. He said if you're not doing anything tomorrow, we'll stop by and visit."

Brandt smiled. "I'd love to have you guys over. If the weather holds, we can hang out on the roof."

"Have you spoken to my brother since the accident?"

A beat passed as Brandt and Aziza looked at each other in what had become a stare-down. "No. In fact I haven't spoken to any of the guys on the team."

"I'm not talking about the other guys, Brandt. I'm talking about Alex. You're friends. Pick up the phone and let him know you're okay."

"Okay, I'll call him."

Standing straighter, Aziza glared down at Brandt. He was not just her client—now he was family. When her brother mentioned Brandt Wainwright was looking for a new agent before his old contract expired, she'd met with Brandt over dinner and before the evening ended she'd agreed to represent him. The result was a three-year deal for what she'd thought of as an obscene amount of money for tossing a football, her commission netting her close to seven figures.

"Don't sound so enthusiastic, Brandt Wainwright."

"I said I'll call him, Aziza Wainwright."

Aziza smiled. "Good. Now, let's get you upstairs."

Reaching into her dress pocket, she took out a plastic ID badge marked "Visitor," clipping it to the collar of Brandt's black golf shirt. He looked splendidly fit sitting in the chair. His face was tanned and his cropped hair was growing out. She hoped the children would recognize him without the long hair.

Punching the button for the elevator, Aziza pushed the chair into the car when the doors opened. They were the only passengers in the car that rose quickly and smoothly to the floor housing the pediatric wing.

Brandt felt his heart rate kick into a higher gear when he heard childish voices raised in laughter coming from the end of the hallway. It wouldn't be the first time he'd visit a hospital to entertain young children; it would be the first time he'd come and been able to identify with them.

He maneuvered his chair into an atrium and within seconds the laughter evaporated like a drop of water on a hot griddle. Children lay in beds; others were in wheelchairs with tubes inserted in their noses and hands. Several others sat on love seats, chairs and chaises, staring at him as if he were an extraterrestrial.

The chin of one boy quivered as he choked back tears. "You're not the Viking." His voice was pregnant with disappointment as tears rolled down his face.

Brandt swallowed the lump in his throat. These children were expecting to see a giant of a man with long hair, palming a football with one hand. They wanted to see their hero, but saw someone sitting in a wheelchair they didn't recognize. His head came around, glaring when a photographer snapped several frames in rapid succession.

Aziza sprang into action. She smiled at the stunned faces of the young patients. "When you asked for Brandt Wainwright to come to visit, you thought he would look like the photograph over in the corner."

"Why is he in a wheelchair?" wailed a young girl, also seated in a wheelchair.

Brandt pushed his chair closer to her. "I'm in a chair because I can't walk."

"Why not?" asked a young boy with a tube feeding oxygen into his nose.

"I broke my legs." Gasps followed his statement.

"How?" asked another child.

Brandt told the children and medical staff filling the room about the deer that had appeared in the road in front of his vehicle and how in his attempt to avoid hitting the animal he had crashed his SUV into a tree. Their rapt gazes didn't waver when he told them wearing a seat belt had saved his life, otherwise he would've been ejected from the vehicle.

Videotapes were activated and tape recorders turned on when the children conducted a press conference, asking Brandt questions about how he was rescued, his stay in the hospital, his rehabilitation and whether he missed playing football.

Brandt answered their questions simply, intelligently, and then shocked the children when he asked them if they would sign his casts. Aziza, who'd had a supply of footballs delivered to the hospital, had him personally sign a ball and photographs for each child.

Doctors, nurses and hospital staff floated in and out of the atrium, watching in awe as Brandt Wainwright entertained their young patients, recounting games when he'd had the breath knocked out of him after he was sacked. The children were served cups of ice cream with football-shaped cupcakes before nurses and aides came to escort them back to their rooms, Brandt giving each a high-five or handshake.

He caught a brief glimpse of the man who'd caused Ciara so much emotional pain when he walked into the atrium to talk to a young girl with a dressing over her left ear. When the child turned her head Brandt saw that she was missing her right ear. Dr. Victor Seabrook may have met success as a brilliant plastic surgeon, but he was an abysmal failure when it came to women, Brandt thought.

An approaching reporter shoved a tape recorder under his nose. "When do you think you'll be able to return to playing football?"

Brandt recognized the television sportscaster. "I will answer that question later after my recovery." He motioned for the man to turn off the recorder. "I came here for the kids, not to give you an interview. Now please get out of my face."

Brandt returned to his apartment building emotionally exhausted from his first public appearance since the accident. Not only had he interacted with the children, but had lingered to sign countless autographs for hospital staff. The elevator doors opened and Ciara stood there, hands at her waist, waiting for him. Her smile spoke volumes—she was glad to see him.

"I thought I was going to have to send out a search party," she teased, closing the distance between them and kissing his forehead.

He maneuvered into the entryway. "It lasted longer than I'd expected."

Ciara pointed to his casts. Most of the names were printed. "Who tagged you?"

Resting his hands on the armrests, Brandt leaned over to look at the childish scrawls. "I let the kids sign my casts."

"I'm sorry I had to miss that."

"Don't be sorry," he said cryptically.

"Why?"

"I saw your ex. He'd come to check on a patient."

Slipping her hands into the back pockets of her cropped pants, Ciara pulled the fabric taut over her hips. When Brandt had suggested she not accompany him to the hospital, she'd wanted to tell him that he was no better than Victor, telling her what she should do and where he she could go. But after careful thought, Ciara realized Brandt wanted to protect her from a confrontation with Victor and/or gossip surrounding their former relationship.

"It's good I didn't go with you."

Brandt gave her a tired smile. "Thank you for agreeing with me." He spied the enormous bouquet on the pedestal table between the entryway and great room. "Who sent the flowers?"

"They're from your mother."

"What's the occasion?"

Reaching into the pocket of her cotton blouse, Ciara pulled out a folded check, handing it to Brandt. "Your mother called me to let me know they were coming. She said they're in appreciation for my taking care of you. If you look at the notation on the memo you'll see: cooking duties. She doesn't have to pay me for cooking."

Brandt unfolded the check, his eyebrows lifting a fraction when he saw the amount. "Either she pays you or someone else does it."

"I don't mind cooking, Brandt."

He folded the check, giving it back to her. "Put it in the bank."

"What if I give it back to her?"

"Please don't do that. I'll be the one who will have to deal with my mother when she has a meltdown because she feels you've insulted her."

"You're kidding?"

Brandt rolled his eyes upward. "I wish. Please, babe. Deposit the check and let it be."

"Okay. But tell her I'm not going accept another penny from her." Ciara's per diem salary was much more than she would've earned if her patient hadn't been Brandt Wainwright.

"You tell her yourself. I'm not getting caught up in something that has nothing to do with me. Jordan and his wife are coming over tomorrow night. I'd like you to plan a menu, then we can order from a local restaurant."

"What if we cook rather than order out?" Ciara suggested.

"You'd rather cook?"

"I like cooking, Brandt." Not only did she enjoy

cooking for herself, but she liked knowing exactly what ingredients were going into her body. "I'll take inventory of the pantry and fridge before we come up with a menu. If there's anything we'll need, then it can be ordered and delivered tomorrow."

Brandt noticed Ciara had mentioned "we" several times. "We" meant they had become a couple. "What about an old-fashioned Southern barbecue, complete with ribs, fried chicken, potato salad, coleslaw and baked beans?" she suggested.

Reaching for the handles on the wheelchair, Ciara pushed Brandt into the living room and over to the wall-to-wall, floor-to-ceiling windows. The sun was a large orange ball sinking lower in the sky. She massaged the muscles in his neck. He was tight, tense. Leaning closer, she detected the familiar odor of hand sanitizer.

"I have a recipe for cornmeal-crusted oven-fried chicken that will rival chicken fried in a cast-iron skillet."

"It sounds good."

Ciara stared at the ash-blond strands covering Brandt's head. Shortened, they reminded her of stalks of bleached wheat. She wasn't familiar with the man the media had dubbed The Viking. The man she knew had gone from sullen, obstinate and surly to laughing, teasing and passionate.

"Are you tired?" His head came up, their eyes meeting.

"A little bit."

She turned his chair around. "You're going to take a nap."

"Will you nap with me?" he asked.

She shook her head. "No. I won't be able to sleep later if I go to bed now. Speaking of beds, I think you can now sleep in your own. I'll call the medical equipment company and arrange to have the bed picked up."

"Where are you going to sleep if I move upstairs?" There was only one bedroom on the second floor.

"Where do you want me to sleep?" She'd answered his question with a question.

He studied her face, feature by feature, committing it to memory. And that was all he would have once her assignment ended. Memories of her face and her passion. "I'd like you to move your things into my bedroom."

"Where will I sleep, Brandt?"

A hint of a smile softened his firm mouth. "You will sleep with me, of course."

"Of course? Now that sounds just a little cocky."

"Cocky or confident?"

"Egotistical," Ciara insisted, pushing the chair to the elevator, "smug, brash—"

"Can't you cut me a little slack?" Brandt interrupted.

Ciara maneuvered the chair into the elevator as Brandt punched the button for the second floor. "Why should I? You were nothing short of an ogre when I first arrived."

The doors opened and she pushed the chair out of the elevator and along the hallway leading to his apartment. He peered at her over his shoulder. "Sorry about that."

"Say it like you mean it, Brandt Wainwright."

"I don't know how else to say it. Maybe I can show you."

Leaning down, Ciara pressed a kiss to his ear. "Later," she whispered, nipping his lobe.

While waiting for Brandt to return from his publicity appearance, Ciara had changed the linen on the California king bed in Brandt's bedroom. The transition from sleeping in a hospital bed to a regular bed was certain to improve his mood and speed his recovery.

Brandt stared at the stack of books on the bedside table—he'd planned to read them over the summer and fall. Reading provided him a respite from the frenetic pace of playing football. The season was short when compared to baseball and basketball, but it was much more physical because it was a contact sport. Being and staying in shape was critical, but even the most physically fit player's career could end abruptly with a single tackle.

"I really miss sleeping in my own bed," he said.

Ciara fluffed the pillows. "I can't lower it like the hospital bed, but let's see if you can get in and out of it without too much difficulty."

Brandt pushed the chair next to the bed, then hoisted himself up and onto the mattress with a minimum of effort and movement. "Piece of cake," he whispered.

"Cocky," Ciara countered, reaching over and removing his casts before adjusting the many pillows behind his head and shoulders. "Do you have to use the bathroom before I leave?"

He closed his eyes. "No, I'm good. But I'd appreciate it if you took off my shorts."

"What about your shirt?"

He opened his eyes. "That, too."

Ciara knew it wasn't easy for Brandt to ask her to

dress and undress him. He may have been cocky, but he had more than his share of pride. However, there would come a time when he didn't need her to do anything for him, and that would be when she would walk out of the penthouse and not look back. Clad in a pair of boxer-briefs, Brandt lay on his back while she pulled a sheet up to his chest.

Reaching up, he caught her ponytail, rubbing the blunt-cut ends through his fingers. "What did you do to your hair?"

"I flat-ironed it."

Brandt released her hair. "I like it when you wear it down."

"Maybe another time." Ciara brushed a kiss over his mouth. "I'll be back," she said in her best Arnold Schwarzenegger *Terminator* imitation.

Brandt cupped the back of her head, deepening the kiss. "How did I get so lucky?"

She went still, unable to form a comeback. The seconds ticked as they stared at each other. "I'll come back and check on you after I finish putting dinner together."

"I'd like to eat on the roof."

"I think that can be arranged. Now please let me go so I can start dinner."

He winked at her. "I'll see you later."

"Later, Brandt."

Ciara took a quick inventory of the food on hand to prepare the meal. She added half a dozen ears of corn to her rapidly increasing shopping list, along with white potatoes, carrots and green cabbage. Biting gently on the tip of her thumbnail, Ciara tried remembering what else she wanted to prepare before calling the building's concierge to place her grocery order.

Picking up the house phone, she dialed the extension for the concierge, identifying herself and telling the pleasant-sounding woman what she needed. *That was easy,* she thought, ending the call. Living in the luxury Wainwright high-rise definitely had its advantages. The tenants didn't have to concern themselves with hailing taxis, signing for packages or building security. An added bonus was having the 24/7 concierge to arrange for drop-off and pick-up of dry cleaning and food shopping.

Tonight she'd decided on a one-pot meal: jambalaya. After a few weeks of living with Brandt Wainwright she'd discovered there were very few things he didn't eat. Ciara felt a warm glow through her. Brandt was good for her and she was good for him. If there had a different set of circumstances she would have possibly considered continuing their relationship after his full recovery.

Flickering tea lights and votives, millions of stars dotting the clear nighttime sky and track lighting coming from the solarium provided the illumination for a relaxing evening on the rooftop oasis.

Ciara felt cloistered, wrapped in a cocoon where noise, dirt and grime and the social ills that came with millions of people crowding together in a designated space were only figments of her imagination. She'd heard New Yorkers who hung out on the roofs of their apartment buildings refer to them as tar beaches. Eating dinner on the rooftop terrace, while listening to music coming from speakers in the solarium, she now had her own very private tar beach.

Living with Brandt, albeit temporarily, had spoiled her. All she had to do was pick up a telephone and order most whatever she liked or wanted. Never had the schism between the haves and the have-nots been more apparent to her than now. What puzzled Ciara was despite their wealth, the Wainwrights—at least those she'd met—were ordinary people. They hadn't affected airs of their own self-importance.

She'd worked for families requesting private-duty nurses who, if they hadn't owned the brownstones or townhouses or hadn't leased magnificent rent-controlled apartments, would've been in homeless shelters, scratching out a daily existence. And because they'd wanted to maintain an image that had been so much a part of a long-ago lifestyle they either mortgaged their property or sold family heirlooms to keep up the facade. But even if Brandt hadn't been born into a real-estate dynasty, he still would've been able to maintain his current lifestyle because he was a celebrity athlete.

Sitting up and swinging her legs over the chaise, Ciara came to her feet. "I better get up before I find myself sleeping here all night."

Brandt's rich laughter wafted in the warm night air. "I've done that a few times." He handed plates, silver and serving pieces to Ciara as she began loading the serving cart. She'd concocted the best jambalaya he'd ever eaten. A pitcher of iced tea, brewed with oolong instead of the customary pekoe, and sweetened with honey, was an appropriate beverage complement to the spicy Cajun-inspired dish. "Do you need me to help you?"

Ciara shook her head. "No. All I have to do is rinse the dishes and load the dishwasher. Why don't you look after your plants? I'd noticed some of the leaves were turning brown."

"Are you certain you don't need help?" he asked again.

"I'm good here, Brandt. Go and take care of those pitiful-looking flowers before they die on you."

Brandt knew he'd neglected his plants. Before leaving for North Carolina he'd reprogrammed the watering timetable so a soft mist fell on the plants and flowers like in tropical rainforests. What he could never have imagined was returning to New York sitting in a wheelchair.

Rolling away from the table, Brandt skillfully maneuvered the chair into the solarium. His gaze shifted to a row of clay pots overflowing with rose-pink cyclamen. There were a number of leaves with brown edges. Some men collected cars, stamps, coins, jewelry—a few he knew collected wives. For him it was plants, swords and antique firearms.

The fascination with plants had begun with a fourth-grade science fair. His decision to build a terrarium was the spark that fueled an obsession that had continued into adulthood. He could identify different grasses, mosses, algae, ferns, poisonous and non-poisonous mushrooms, simple leaves and flowers with a cursory glance, and pruning and cultivating new varieties of plants and flowers filled him with a peace that he was unable to put into words.

He had neglected not just his garden, but also his friends. Aziza had berated him for not returning her brother's calls. His cell phone, which had been found in the wreckage of the Escalade, was returned to him along with his credit-card case. Both were in a plastic bag in a drawer in the kitchen. He made a mental note to get the phone and retrieve the messages.

Chapter 13

Ciara, removing husks and silk threads from ears of fresh corn, swayed gently to the music filling the kitchen from the built-in radio. She had gotten up early to marinate meat, boil potatoes and shred cabbage. Brandt had been assigned the task of cutting, dicing and chopping the ingredients that would go into the potato salad, slaw and baked beans. Her head popped up when he returned to the kitchen. He'd made a hasty retreat into the bathroom to splash cold water on his face after dicing onions.

She smiled. "Are you all right, sport?" His eyes were red and slightly puffy.

Brandt sniffled. "I'll survive."

"I wished I'd known you were going to invite another person because I would've ordered more corn."

Brandt approached Ciara, resting his hand at her

waist. "Don't stress yourself, babe. We have more than enough food to feed five people."

"Have you forgotten that two of the five weigh at least two-fifty?" Brandt had invited one of his teammates to join them for dinner.

"I've lost at least fifteen pounds since the accident, so I'm no longer two-fifty."

Ciara moved his hand up to her back after it slipped to her hips. "You can't expect me to cook if you feel me up."

Brandt pressed his face to her side, pulling her down gently to sit on his lap. He tightened his hold on her waist when she attempted to free herself. "Don't move."

She went pliant against his chest. Brandt claimed to have lost weight, but his body was still hard, rock-solid. The upbeat song ended and a soft instrumental piece dating from the seventies filled the kitchen. It was one of her mother's favorites.

Ciara closed her eyes, enjoying their closeness. They'd slept together without touching—Brandt on his back, legs extended, while she'd rolled over on her side in an attempt not to come into contact with his injured legs. She woke before he did, completed her morning ablutions, and when she'd returned to the bedroom, she found Brandt sitting in bed reading.

"Had you always wanted to play football?"

Brandt pressed his mouth to the bandana covering Ciara's hair. She appeared incredibly young with her bare face, tank top and cutoffs. She'd elected not to wear her glasses, and when he looked at her he felt as if he were drowning in pools of liquid chocolate.

"No," he said after a comfortable pause. "It was something I sort of fell into my first year of college."

"Where did you go to college?" she asked, even though she knew the answer.

"Stanford. I was an economics major until I was bitten by the football bug. My roommate was a kid from Georgia and he teased me because I watched baseball. He claimed the only sport worth watching and playing was football. Earl was going to tryouts and convinced me to go along with him."

"What position were you going to play?

Brandt chuckled. "I wasn't going to play any position. I went along with Earl to offer him moral support. The coach saw that I was tall and looked strong, so he had me do twenty-five push-ups and sit-ups, then run the length of the football field twice. I did it without breathing heavily or breaking much of a sweat. What he didn't know was that I'd always been a fitness fanatic, so his little test was like milk and Oreos—sweet!"

Ciara placed her hands over the large ones pressed against her belly. "Show-off."

"You're wrong. I would've been a show-off if I'd given him fifty push-ups and sit-ups, then run the length of the field three or four times. What I lacked in strength I made up with stamina. I got up every morning, rain or shine, to jog three miles."

"Did your roommate make the team?"

"Yes. We were well-known on campus. I played defense my first year, but when our first-string quarterback was injured during practice, and the backup quarterback was on academic probation, the coach asked if I could step in. My first game I threw three touchdowns. And, as they say, the rest is history."

"Are you big for a quarterback?"

Brandt nodded. "I'm heavier than most quarterbacks, but I use it to my advantage. It's a lot harder to sack a six-five, two-hundred-fifty-pound quarterback than one who's six-two and two-twenty. And if I can't get off a pass, then I run with the ball.

"My folks thought playing college football was just a phase until scouts from the NFL starting showing up to watch me. They panicked when I was selected as the Heisman Trophy runner-up and lost it completely when I was drafted in the first round. I witnessed my father losing his temper for the first time. When he threatened to withhold my trust fund until I turned thirty, I called his bluff and signed with the Giants. Meanwhile, my mother took to her bed. How was she going to explain to her fake-ass friends that her son had given up a plum position with his family-run real-estate company to become a common ballplayer?"

"When did you declare a truce?"

"It was just before I was scheduled to play my first pro game. I'd moved into an apartment near Battery Park, and my mother called asking if she and Dad could come to see me. Of course, I said yes. We reached a compromise. They would respect my career choice, and they wouldn't pressure my brothers and sister to join Wainwright Developers. And I promised once I stopped playing ball I would consider joining the company."

Ciara smiled up at Brandt from lowered lids. "That's a nice compromise."

"You win some and you lose some. But for me it's a win-win."

"What happened to your friend Earl?"

"He turned pro, but retired after five seasons because of too many concussions. He married a girl from New England, is the father of twin boys and went into business with his father-in-law. They own and operate a dairy farm in Vermont."

"It looks as if Earl found his happily ever after."

"The last time I spoke to him he said he was happier than a pig in…slop. Gotcha! You thought I was going to say shit, didn't you?"

Ciara held out her hand. "You played yourself, Wainwright. Pay up. You now owe the cuss jar ten dollars."

"How much do you owe?"

"Not ten dollars, that's for sure. You can only run a tab for just so long," Ciara drawled, smiling. "Now it's time to pay the piper."

Brandt's hand moved up and covered her breast. "What if we negotiate an equal trade?"

She frowned. "Don't tell me that a man of your means doesn't have ten dollars on him?"

"Oh, I have a lot more than ten dollars."

"Where is it?"

"Come with me."

Ciara slid off Brandt's lap and walked alongside the chair as he rolled out of the kitchen to the elevator. She followed him off the elevator into his bedroom and to the walk-in closet with racks and shelves filled with suits, jackets, shirts and shoes.

Reaching up, he placed his right hand on a metal plate

with a dimmer switch that changed from red to green. A panel on the far wall slid back to reveal the steel door to a safe. Brandt punched in the code and opened the door. "Plants are my hobby, but I'm also a collector of antique firearms and swords."

Ciara moved closer, peering into the open safe. "Is one of your swords a Katana?"

"Yes. I went to Japan and saw one being made, and I knew I had to have one. I placed an order and it came a year later." Brandt opened a metal box and took out a stack of bills. He counted out five one-hundred-dollar bills. "I think this should cover me for the next month."

Not hesitating, Ciara took the crisp bills. She pushed them into the apron's large patch pocket. "I have to decide whether to donate this to your favorite charity or mine."

"You know about my charity?"

"I may not follow football, but I do know you've set up a foundation for high school kids where every complete pass is worth five hundred dollars and touchdowns are a thousand."

Brandt closed and locked the safe. "I've been accused of being self-serving, but I really don't give a damn. Fans come to the stadium to see the Viking, and whenever I suit up I try and give them their money's worth. I didn't go into football to make money, but to entertain. Sporting events are entertainment, just like the circus. We wear costumes and put on a show for the spectators who come to see us perform."

"Have you always been this cynical about football, or have you changed since the accident?"

Brandt smiled, flashing straight, white teeth. "Aha! Now I get to see the psychiatric nurse in action."

"I'm not trying to psychoanalyze you, Brandt. I merely asked a question."

He sobered when seeing her expression. Ciara wasn't amused. "I play football because I enjoy it. When I stop enjoying it, then I'll know it's time to get out. I'm sitting in this wheelchair not because some three-hundred-pound linebacker landed on my legs, but because a deer picked the wrong time to cross the road. Am I angry with the deer? Hell, no, because I was in his habitat. Am I going to miss not playing this season? Hell, yeah!" He held up his hand. "Don't bother keeping count because I gave you enough money to cover this month and the next one."

"Keep cussin' and it won't last until the end of *this* month." Brandt pantomimed zipping his mouth, and Ciara smiled at his antics. She didn't know why, but she wasn't able to remain angry or annoyed with him for any appreciable length of time. "Let's go, sport. We still have work to do in the kitchen."

"I don't mind helping you, but I'm not going to chop another onion."

"Come on, Brandt. Man up! You claim you watch the cooking channels, and I'm willing to bet you've never heard any of the chefs complaining about chopping onions."

Brandt shook his head. "Why did you have to go and attack my manhood?"

"The word is challenge, darling," she crooned.

"Watch how you use that word," Brandt countered.

"When a woman calls me 'darling' I take it to mean she wants to kick what we have up a notch."

Ciara turned and walked out of the closet. "We can't kick it any higher," she said over her shoulder. "We're living and sleeping together."

Brandt placed his hand on the plate. The green light was replaced with red and the panel slid closed. When Brandt had had the safe installed, the technician had programmed the open-and-close mechanism with fingerprint recognition. It could be reprogrammed with as many as three sets of fingerprints. In the event of an emergency his mother would be able to open the safe.

Brandt wanted to tell Ciara she was wrong. There were other levels to take their relationship.

After all, there was happily ever after.

The elevator doors opened and Brandt smiled as Aziza preceded her husband and brother. Jordan placed a decorative shopping bag on the side table. He knew his cousin would bring his favorite wine.

"Welcome. Forgive me if I don't stand up."

Leaning over, Aziza brushed a light kiss over his cheek. "You're really not a very good comedian."

He winked at her. "I thought I was being funny."

Jordan slapped his cousin on the shoulder. "I don't know who's worse, you or Uncle Fraser."

Brandt squinted at Jordan. "My father isn't that bad."

"Yeah, right," Jordan drawled. "One time he messed up the nursery rhyme about pickled peppers."

Brandt offered his hand to his teammate. "What's up, Al?"

Alex Fleming shook Brandt's hand and gave him a rough man-hug. "That's what I should be asking you. I heard you had a run-in with Bambi and she won."

"Isn't she the showgirl you met in Vegas with the legs that went on forever?" Brandt asked, deadpan.

Alex gave his sister a sidelong glance. "Man, you know what happens in Vegas stays in…" His words trailed off when he saw movement out of the corner of his eye. "Oh, wow…"

Brandt saw the direction of Alex's gaze. Turning slightly in the chair, he saw the object of his teammate's stunned expression. Ciara had changed into a pair of black stretch pants, a matching tank top and black-and-white animal-print mules. She'd worn her hair loose, blunt-cut ends tucked behind her ears. A pair of silver hoops had replaced the tiny gold studs.

Ciara felt the heat from three pairs of eyes. She'd met Jordan Wainwright, so why was he staring at her as if he'd never seen her before? Brandt had mentioned that he was bringing his wife and she assumed that the tall, slender black woman with fashionably cut short hair was his wife. A smile parted Ciara's lips. Harlem's rogue attorney had exquisite taste in women.

Her gaze shifted to the man with cropped black hair standing on Jordan's left. She felt a shiver race along her spine when she noticed his eyes weren't brown or black, but an odd shade of gray that was strangely incongruent in his chocolate-brown face. Talk about eye candy. The man was beyond delicious. He smiled and dimples dotted his lean face like thumbprints in cookies.

She decided to end the impasse. "Hello, Jordan."

With wide eyes, Jordan stared at the woman whose

voice he remembered even if he hadn't been able to recall her face. "Ciara?"

"You know her?" Alex asked.

A hint of a smile tilted the corners of Jordan's mouth. "Yes. We met a couple of days ago."

Brandt extended his hand to Ciara without glancing at her. It was his turn to smile when he felt the light pressure of her palm on his. "Aziza, Alex, this is my nurse, Ciara Dennison." He glanced up at Ciara; she met his eyes. "Ciara, I'd like you to meet my attorney, my agent and my cousin's wife—Aziza Wainwright. The other gentleman is her brother and my teammate, Alexander Fleming."

Ciara angled her head as her gaze shifted from Aziza to her brother. Their parents had passed on the best genes to their very attractive children. A spark of recognition dawned when she realized where she'd seen Alex before. He'd been a contestant on *Dancing with the Stars*.

"It's my pleasure."

Alex took a step, extending his hand to Ciara. "It's definitely *my* pleasure, Ciara."

What the... The expletive reverberated in Brandt's head. He didn't want to believe his best friend was flirting with his woman, girlfriend, lover, nurse. Although he and Alex disagreed occasionally, it was never about a woman.

"I just thought I'd let everyone know," he said as Alex cradled Ciara's hand in his, "Ciara has agreed to be my date tonight."

Jordan stared at his cousin as if he'd taken leave of his senses. "Your nurse is your date?"

Aziza elbowed her husband. "M.Y.O.B.," she hissed between clenched teeth.

"What?"

"She wants you to mind your own business," Alex translated for his brother-in-law.

Ciara decided it was time for her to step into her hostess role. "Brandt and I decided dining on the rooftop terrace under the stars is the perfect way to end the day. Y'all can go on up and we'll be right behind you."

Waiting until their guests made their way to the staircase, she rounded on Brandt. "What were you trying to prove?" she whispered angrily.

Brandt's expression was one of barely contained tolerance as he struggled to control his temper. A foreign and alien emotion held him in a savage grip, refusing to allow him to think with a clear head.

The moment Alex had touched Ciara, Brandt realized he was jealous, and in order to experience jealousy he had to care for her—a caring going beyond their sleeping together. He shook his head. No! There was no way he was falling in love with Ciara. He was probably confusing caring with passion. Yes, that had to be it. He was in love with Ciara's passion.

"Are you deliberately tuning me out, Brandt?"

"No. I'm not tuning you out, Ciara."

"If not, then will you please answer my question?" she countered.

"I didn't want him mauling you!"

Ciara's mouth opened and closed several times. "Mauling? The man just shook my hand."

"The man disrespected me in my own home."

"What!" The single word exploded from her mouth.

"How did he disrespect you? Please tell me," she continued when Brandt's jaw tightened.

"He came on to you not knowing anything about our association."

"You're contradicting yourself, Brandt. Alexander is your friend and teammate. You guys are tight, so if you'd set up a woman for him to meet you would've told him beforehand." She leaned over until their faces were level. "Please tell me what's going on before we go upstairs and we embarrass each other."

Brandt's steady gaze bore into Ciara's. "Would you believe me if I told you I was jealous?"

Her eyebrows shot up. "You, jealous? Of me and Alexander Fleming? I didn't know he existed before he walked in here."

"And I didn't know you existed before you walked in here."

Ciara's heart jolted, her pulse pounded erratically when she pondered what Brandt hadn't said. She felt as if her emotions were on a roller coaster, buffeted from side to side. Brandt was jealous of his friend because he wanted her for himself. What he wanted went beyond their making love with each other.

"You like me, don't you?"

He moved closer without moving. "Of course I like you, Ciara. I've told you that."

She shook her head. "No. I mean you really, really like me."

Brandt picked up a lock of her hair, rubbing it gently between his fingers. "Are you asking if like squared equals love?"

Ciara bit her lip, then nodded. "Something like that."

He pressed his forehead to hers. "I'm not certain whether I love you, because I don't know what it is."

"Maybe you're confusing love with lust?"

"No, babe. I'm more than familiar with lust and what I feel with you right now is not lust. I want you, and I'll probably always want you, but—"

Ciara placed her fingers over Brandt's mouth. "We'll talk about this later. Have you forgotten we have guests waiting for us?"

He caught her wrist, kissing her fingers. "You won't let me forget?"

"Sure," she drawled.

Brandt brushed his mouth over hers. "Love you, babe."

Ciara winked at him. "Love you, too."

Chapter 14

Ciara removed the lids to the chafing dishes. Mouth-watering aromas wafted in the warm summer air. The setting sun lit the rooftop aflame with an orange glow that made light-colored surfaces appear as if they were on fire.

"Do you mind if I pour the wine?" Aziza called out.

"No!" Brandt and Ciara chorused.

Jordan sniffed the air. "I smell baked beans."

Ciara turned and smiled at him. "Give that man a cigar."

"Damn, brother," Alex drawled, "you have a helluva nose."

Brandt beckoned to those sitting at the table. "Grab your plates and come serve yourself."

Ciara hadn't permitted him on the rooftop until after she'd set up the table with a white tablecloth, then added a colorful runner. The far end of the table was covered with flower petals and tea lights. Each place setting held wine and water glasses, cloth napkins and small bowls of water with lemon slices. He'd helped her load the serving cart and set up the chafing dishes on a buffet server.

Ciara didn't treat him like an invalid, and for that he was grateful. He had to be mentally prepared for the time when he was medically cleared to begin walking.

He glanced up to find her leaning over his chair. "Sit down and I'll bring you a plate. Go, Ciara," he whispered in her ear. "You've been on your feet all day cooking, so it's time for you to relax."

"I don't want anyone to think I'm not taking care of my patient."

He took her hand, dropping a kiss on the knuckles. "Remember, I'm your date, not your patient."

Ciara ran the tip of her tongue over her lips, bringing Brandt's gaze to linger there. She knew they were playing a game—one in which both would come up winners. "If I forget, then you'll have to remind me." She walked away with just enough sway in her hips to remind Brandt of what she'd been hiding under her smocks.

Brandt removed the cork from a bottle of merlot, allowing it to breathe before he filled his teammate's glass. He was surprised Alex had requested wine—he usually drank beer. "I do have beer downstairs."

Alex shook his head. "The wine's good. In fact, the food is off the hook. Did you use a different caterer?" Brandt usually hosted a catered New Year's Eve party every other year.

Brandt exchanged a surreptitious look with Ciara. "Tonight's dinner wasn't catered."

Jordan set down his water goblet. "Don't tell me you cooked?" He knew Brandt was an avid fan of cooking shows.

"No. Ciara did."

For the second time that night Ciara found herself in the spotlight, the focus of attention. Cradling the balloon wineglass, she took a deep swallow of the dry red wine. Would it always be that way because of her association with Brandt Wainwright? When she dated Victor he'd always been the center of attention. But it had become the opposite with Brandt.

Aziza touched the napkin to her mouth after she'd swallowed a mouthful of potato salad. "Who taught you to cook like this?"

"My mother."

"Is your mama married?" Alex quipped.

Ciara laughed when she saw the wistful expression on his handsome face. "As a matter of fact, she isn't. But that's not going to help you because my mother's not a cougar. She prefers men in her own age range."

"Do you have a sister?"

"Alexander!" Aziza admonished.

"Aziza!" he mocked. "I'm not looking to get married. All I want is to find a woman who can do more than make reservations. I'm a very simple guy with very simple needs. Tell them, Brandt. Am I complicated?"

All eyes were trained on Brandt. "Do you really want me to lie to these good people?"

The stunned expression on Alex's face was priceless. "I always thought you were my boy and had my back."

"I am your boy, but you're not simple nor is your lifestyle, so don't expect to attract a simple woman."

Alexander turned to his brother-in-law. "Help me out here, Jordan."

"I'd love to, but I'm afraid I wouldn't be impartial. Ciara doesn't know you. Give her your best-case scenario."

The young athlete shook his head. "I'm afraid to ask my sister. She'll be forced to recuse herself because she, too, can't be impartial."

Aziza gave her brother a pointed look. "If I were your attorney I'd suggest you take Jordan's advice and ask Ciara. *Now* I'm going to recuse myself."

The entire table erupted into laughter, Alex joining the others. Pushing away from the table, he stood up. His upper body was silhouetted in the light from the flickering candles and the illumination coming from the atrium. He snapped his napkin with a flourish reminiscent of 18th-century fops. He bowed low to Ciara.

"Milady Ciara. I've come to court to plea my case before thee. Could milady please give me some advice as how to proceed with the young damsels with which I find myself besotted."

Ciara laughed until tears rolled down her face. Alexander Fleming was blessed with enough dramatic flair that he could perform Shakespeare. What she couldn't fathom was how the man with the gorgeous body and face would have a problem attracting women.

Blotting her moist eyes, she waved him over. "Sit down and talk to me."

Still in character, Alex sat down gingerly. His teeth shone whitely against his dark face when he smiled at her. "Thank you, milady."

Placing her elbow on the table, Ciara rested her chin on the heel of her hand. "Do you have a problem attracting women, or holding on to them?" Brandt and Jordan cleared their throats in unison.

Alexander rolled his eyes at them. "I can get the ladies, but something happens after we go out a few times."

"Can you be a little bit more specific?" Ciara asked.

"It's as if they have multiple personalities and I no longer recognize the woman I'd initially asked out."

Brandt shook his head. "I've told Al what the problem is. It's PMS."

Lowering her arm, Ciara glared at him. "Oh, no you didn't go there."

"Did he really say PMS?" Aziza asked.

Brandt held up his hands in a defensive move. "What's wrong with PMS? You ladies do tend to have mood swings during that time of the month."

"Sorry, cuz," Jordan drawled. "I can't agree with you on that because Zee is always the same."

"How's that, cuz?"

Jordan winked at his wife. "Snarky."

Brandt and Alexander pounded the table. "Careful, cousin. 'Snarky' will get you remanded to the sofa for three months."

"I ain't scared," Jordan drawled recklessly.

Aziza placed her hand on Jordan's shoulder. "That's

all right, darling. When I come up pregnant in the three months you're remanded to the sofa, you'll be the one on daytime television. The laugh will be on you when Maury announces, 'You are not the father!'"

This time when everyone laughed, Jordan didn't join in. Resting a hand over his heart, he bowed his head. "Your honor, I'd like to withdraw that last statement."

"What's up with the bad acting?" Brandt asked. "First we have foppish Vicomte de Valmont from *Les Liaisons Dangereuses,* followed by a remorseful Perry Mason. Man up!" he drawled, repeating what Ciara had said earlier.

"Hear, hear!" Aziza and Ciara intoned, raising their glasses.

Ciara was drawn into the warmth and camaraderie of the Flemings and Wainwrights. Although united through blood and marriage, they were friends as well.

When it came to family there was just her and her mother. Phyllis was an only child and she, too, an only child. Her grandparents were gone and Ciara knew of a few distant cousins, but it had been years since they'd gotten together. When she spoke to her mother again she would suggest contacting their Ohio relatives.

Contacting relatives on her father's side of the family was not an option, because the Dennisons had disapproved of William marrying Phyllis. They'd refused to attend the wedding or acknowledge the birth of their granddaughter. The adage "out of sight, out of mind" fit them to the letter. Ciara was certain their disapproval was a factor in William marrying another woman when he hadn't divorced his first wife—it was the second wife the Dennisons approved of and fawned over.

Ciara peered at Alexander Fleming over the rim of her wineglass. She found it hard to believe he was still single. She'd discovered when the conversation segued to a more serious topic that he was twenty-seven, had never married and hadn't fathered any children.

She'd also discovered that Brandt had become Alex's mentor. He'd talked to him about the pitfalls of what he'd referred to as the precarious triangle: alcohol, drugs and groupies—things to be avoided at all costs if he wanted a successful football career.

"I know you're out this season," Alexander stated, "but what about next year, Brandt? Do you plan on coming back?"

Clasping his hands together, Brandt rested them on his head, a habit he'd recently acquired because he found his shoulders and neck stiffening from inactivity. Each time he executed the motion Ciara stared at him. He lowered his hands.

"I do plan on coming back. It's the last year on my contract. Whether I plan to sign another contract is something I have to discuss with my agent." He nodded to Aziza.

Aziza returned Brandt's nod. "And that's something I have to discuss with my client's doctor. If he says he can play, then we'll think about resigning for a year. If not, then Brandt will have to consider his plan B."

Do you have a plan B? Ciara mused. She hoped Brandt Wainwright did, because judging from the X-rays showing the amount of hardware in her patient's legs, she doubted whether he would ever play football again. But that wasn't her call because Brandt was a commodity—a multimillion-dollar commodity.

Aziza moved her chair closer to Ciara's. "You and I have to get together because I want you to teach me how to make your oven-fried chicken, baked beans and what seasonings you use for the dry rub for the ribs. Jordan lived in Massachusetts for seven years and he claims he had baked beans and fried clam bellies at least three to four times a week."

"That's a lot."

"Try telling that to my husband."

Ciara glanced at the magnificent yellow diamond in Aziza's engagement ring. It was as dramatic as the woman who wore it. "We can meet, but it would depend on your schedule."

"I work from home."

"Where do you live?"

"Bronxville. But we also have an apartment in Manhattan. I'm willing to go along with whatever is convenient for you and Brandt."

"He went out yesterday for the first time since his accident and came back a little fatigued."

Aziza nodded. "Interacting with the kids took a lot of his energy. I'd suggested he leave, but he insisted he wanted to stay and sign autographs for the hospital staff. Perhaps he's not aware that he had invasive surgery and it's going to take a while before he'll feel one hundred percent."

"I'll do it, but let me talk to Brandt first."

"No rush. Jordan and I are planning our first dinner party as a married couple in a couple of months, and I plan to cook and cater." Aziza leaned closer, her shoulder touching Ciara's. "I'd like to thank you for helping Brandt out of his funk. His mother told me that he wouldn't talk to or see anyone until you became his nurse. You should have seen the faces of the children when he let them sign his casts. It was like waking up on Christmas morning and finding everything you'd wanted under the tree."

Ciara smiled. "Brandt's got a big bark and no bite."

"He's the best, Ciara. I was reluctant to accept him as a client because I didn't want to have to deal with the overblown ego of a celebrity athlete. After meeting him I realized not only is he an incredible athlete, but he's also an incredible person. If only all of my clients were like Brandt Wainwright."

"How many clients do you have?"

"Five, including Brandt."

"That's not very many," Ciara concluded.

"I know. Jordan and I are planning to start a family, and I didn't want to find myself overwhelmed with running a practice, taking care of my home and a new baby."

"There are two words that should become a part of your vocabulary: *cleaning service.*"

Aziza laughed, satisfaction shimmering in her large eyes. "I like you and your style, Ms. Ciara Dennison."

"Why, thank you so much, Mrs. Wainwright." She'd perfected an authentic Southern drawl. "Do you mind coming with me to bring up coffee and dessert?"

Aziza popped up. "Let's go."

The two women took the elevator to the first-floor kitchen, where Ciara pushed the Brew Cycle button on the coffeemaker, while Aziza set down a platter with cream cheese–topped red velvet cupcakes on a trolley.

Leaning against the countertop, Aziza watched her hostess fill a crystal bowl with sugar and a matching pitcher with cream, moving around the space with the familiarity of someone who'd lived there for more than the few weeks since Brandt had returned to New York from North Carolina.

"You know he likes you."

Ciara froze for a nanosecond, then continued stacking cocktail napkins on a tray with the cream and sugar. "I'm assuming you're talking about Brandt?"

"Who else would I be talking about?"

She gave the attorney a direct stare. "Alex."

Aziza nodded. "You got me there. My brother knew when Brandt called you his date that it was time to dial down the come-on. But you were right the first time. I was talking about Brandt."

"Brandt Wainwright is a very exciting, larger-than-life personality."

"Are you talking about the ballplayer or the man?"

Crossing her arms under her breasts, Ciara leaned a hip against the countertop. "I'm not into sports, therefore I know nothing about Brandt the ballplayer. I was talking about the man."

"I'd like to believe I got the best Wainwright from this generation, but Brandt is more than a worthy runner-up."

"How did you meet Jordan?"

"Brandt introduced us. I needed an attorney to represent me in a sexual harassment suit and Jordan agreed to take the case."

"He won, didn't he?"

Aziza angled her head at the same time she narrowed her eyes. "How did you know?" There were only four people who were aware of the outcome of the suit: Kyle Chatham, Jordan's law partner; her brother; and she and Jordan.

"I would expect no less from Harlem's gangsta lawyer."

Aziza managed to look embarrassed. "Jordan loves it when people call him a gangsta."

"Is he?" Ciara asked, smiling.

"He has a tendency to morph into gangsta mode, but it's his grandfather Wyatt who is a certified gangster," she said. "Jordan's folks usually spend the summer months in Maryland, but you'll get to meet Wyatt when they come back after the Labor Day weekend. My in-laws always have a post-summer soirée at their Fifth Avenue residence, and Christiane invites everyone with a single drop of Wainwright blood, just to tick off Wyatt."

Ciara smiled. "They sound like a lively bunch."

Aziza sucked her teeth. "Don't let the dollar signs fool you. Some of them can get real funky at times. Brandt's brother Sumner is a throwback to Wyatt." The buzzing coming from the coffeemaker signaled the end of the brewing cycle. "To be continued."

"Da-yum," Ciara drawled. "You were just getting to the juicy part."

"The juicy parts are the family secrets that go back several generations. Jordan has hinted there are so many it would take at least a week to disclose all of them. When I ask him what they are, he closes up like a clam.

He's reluctant to tell me because I told him I was going to write a novel based on the Wainwrights. I usually pick up a tidbit here and there whenever there's a family get-together. Invariably someone will have too much to drink and will start spilling the beans."

Unplugging the coffeemaker, Ciara placed it on the trolley. "Would you really write a novel if you gathered enough information?"

Aziza shook her head. "No. I'll leave that task to a direct descendant of Daniel Patrick Wainwright, who came to this country around the turn of the century with twelve dollars and a dream of a better life."

Ciara checked the shelves. "I think we have everything."

The two women retraced their steps when they pushed the trolley into the elevator for the ride to the roof. China cups were filled with steaming gourmet coffee then laced liberally with cream. It was the perfect complement for the moist miniature red velvet cupcakes.

The cupcakes, washed down with several cups of coffee, disappeared quickly. Jordan pulled a sterling cigar case from the pocket of his shirt, offering slender cylinders of tightly rolled tobacco to Brandt and Alexander.

Alexander and Jordan had helped Brandt move to a chaise. They joined him on matching chaise longues, where they lay, staring up at the sky and puffing on cigars.

"I can't believe you don't have any leftovers," Aziza remarked as she filled a large plastic garbage bag.

"I told Brandt that wouldn't be enough food," Ciara said.

"Oh, there was enough. But when you get three guys weighing over two hundred pounds, you don't expect to have leftovers."

"I'll keep that in mind for the next time."

Aziza placed four empty wine bottles in a plastic crate. She hadn't drunk any wine, since she was trying to get pregnant. She would know for certain if she was in another week.

"I'm going to leave these bags for Jordan or Al to take down whenever they decide to get up," she told Ciara.

"When do you think that's going to be?"

Aziza threw up a hand. "It could be in an hour or tomorrow morning. It won't be the first time Brandt has had sleepovers on the roof."

Ciara's jaw dropped. "You're kidding?"

"I wish I was. Too much food and drink provides the perfect excuse for a sleepover. Besides, Jordan weighs too much for me to try and move him."

"Where does your brother live?"

"He has a house in New Jersey. But he'd planned to stay over with us tonight."

Ciara stared at the trio laughing and gesturing in between puffing cigars. She was opposed to smoking, whether it was a pipe, cigar or cigarettes, but Brandt, Alexander and Jordan were adults. They had to be aware of the risks associated with smoking.

"I'm not quite ready to sleep under the stars," she told Aziza. "I can give you a nightgown and grooming supplies in case you have to sleep over."

Aziza checked her watch. It was minutes before eleven. "If Jordan's not ready to leave by midnight, then I'm going to take you up on your offer."

The hospital bed had been removed, freeing up the guest bedroom, and Ciara had moved her things into Brandt's bedroom, freeing up another.

If Alex, Jordan and Aziza decided to stay, there was certainly enough room.

Chapter 15

Sitting on the ledge of the soaking tub, Ciara shook the canister of shaving gel, then squeezed a small amount into her hand. When she rubbed them together the green gel turned into white foam that she then lathered over her legs from knee to ankle. She was fortunate she didn't have to shave her legs that often, but tonight she wanted them silky smooth, because the dress she'd decided to wear to Esteban's birthday displayed more flesh than usual.

She would shower and dress at the penthouse, then do her hair and makeup at the suite in a hotel near LaGuardia Airport. Sofia had decided to have her brother's birthday party at a ballroom in the hotel to accommodate out-of-town guests who were flying in for the occasion. Ciara had called Sofia twice to remind her to bring her dress and shoes before she left home.

"Why don't you let me do that?"

Her hand halted before she could pick up the razor. She hadn't heard Brandt when he'd come into the bathroom, because of the music.

"What are you talking about?"

Brandt maneuvered closer, his hungry eyes lingering over the lithe, naked woman perched on the side of the tub. Her hair was done up in countless rollers that looked like soft rods twisted into open figure-eights.

Four weeks. He couldn't believe it had only been four weeks since Ciara Dennison had become an integral part of his day-to-day life. They went to bed together, woke up together, shared meals and, in spite of his physical limitations, made love. He couldn't, and didn't want to, remember when she hadn't been there. He'd stopped trying to analyze what it was about Ciara that made her so different from the other women he'd known.

"I'll shave your legs."

With wide eyes, Ciara watched him come closer and closer until she felt his warm breath on her bare breast. Even though he'd seen her naked before, she still felt exposed. He'd caught her perched on the side of the bathtub with her legs in such a position that he had a bird's-eye view of her private parts.

"That's okay," she said much too quickly. "I can do it."

"What if you nick yourself? Now how would it look if you went out with those little pieces of tissue stuck to those long, gorgeous legs?"

Ciara picked up the razor, surreptitiously placing her free hand between her thighs. "I'm not going to cut myself."

"Weren't you the one who said you have a problem navigating around one's jugular?"

Their eyes met, her gaze tracing his masculine features and the attractive cleft in his chin. Stubble dotted his lean cheeks. She didn't know whether he'd decided to grow a beard, but he hadn't shaved in three days.

"My legs don't have a jugular, Brandt Wainwright."

The corners of Brandt's mouth twitched as he tried not to laugh. "What do they have, Ciara Dennison?"

"Nerves and bones."

"What types of nerves?"

She gave him an incredulous look. "What is this? An anatomy test?"

Brandt covered her breast with one hand, ignoring her exhalation of breath. The nipple hardened against his palm. "Just answer the question, babe."

Ciara closed her eyes. She couldn't look at Brandt— not when he was feeling her up. "Tibial and sural nerves."

His fingers tightened, thumb sweeping back and forth over the distended nipple. "What are the differences?"

"The tibial is the branch of the…the sciatic nerve extending through the posterior tibial nerve that provides sensations to…to certain muscles of the leg and the sole of the foot."

Brandt pressed his mouth to the side of her neck. "Why were you stuttering?"

"You'd stutter too if I were feeling you up."

"No, I wouldn't." His statement echoed confidence and arrogance.

Ciara opened her eyes, forcibly pushing his hand off her breast. "Let's find out," she said in a challenge.

She didn't give Brandt the opportunity to react when she lowered her legs, turned to face him, unsnapped his cutoffs and, reaching between his thighs, captured his sex and held it firmly in her fist.

He gasped loudly, then groaned as she masturbated him. He hardened quickly. "Recite the Pledge of Allegiance, Brandt."

"I...I...pledge..."

Ciara's hand moved faster, squeezing him, then slowing. She eased her grip. "I can't hear you," she taunted.

Brandt closed his eyes, threw back his head and surrendered to the rush of heat pulling him down into an undertow of the most exquisite ecstasy imaginable. "Yes, yes, yes," he chanted like a litany.

"There's no *yes* in the pledge, darling."

The expression of pure carnal pleasure on her lover's face elicited an intense throbbing between her own thighs. Brandt opened his eyes at the same time as a gasp slipped past her lips, the smoldering flame in his eyes kicking her heart rate into a higher gear.

One moment she was sitting on the edge of the tub and the next she was on Brandt's lap, his hardness inside her. Swept up in a maelstrom of burning desire and out-of-control passion, she rode his erection like someone possessed.

Up and down.

Around and around.

Back and forward.

Brandt's arms circled her body, molding her to his

chest so closely that not even a sliver of light could penetrate. Ciara was so hot, so wet and so good. Each time he penetrated her he nearly lost his breath when her flesh closed around him like a glove a half size too small.

He took her mouth with a savage intensity that matched the sexual mayhem in his groin. His hands moved to her buttocks, his fingers digging into the firm flesh as pleasure, pure and explosive, ripped through his lower body.

Love flowed through Ciara like warm honey. She leaned into Brandt when waves of erotic pleasure scorched her body. Brandt had awakened her dormant sexuality and she couldn't get enough of him. Her tongue dueled with his for dominance, rousing both to peaks of desire that threatened to incinerate them whole. The tremors began, vibrating liquid fire as an orgasm held her captive. She let out a moan, the first of many as the orgasms kept pace.

Brandt's body jerked, jumped and shuddered violently as he released himself inside Ciara, breathing out the last of his passion into her mouth. It wasn't until he felt the secretions leaking from her that he realized the enormity of what had passed between them. He'd made love to Ciara without protection.

Ciara took a deep breath, held it until she felt her lungs burning, then let it out slowly. "Brandt?" The name was a whisper.

"Yes, baby?"

"Are you… Do you have an STD?"

Brandt wanted to laugh, but the situation in which he'd found himself was much too serious. "No." He wanted to tell Ciara that he'd never contracted a sexually transmitted disease, but she hadn't asked. She let out a sigh. "Aren't you concerned about getting pregnant?"

Easing back, Ciara gave him a mysterious smile. "No. We dodged a bullet. I'm expecting my period." If she could count on just one thing, it was her menses coming on time. "What's the matter, darling? Surprised you haven't seen any of my multiple personalities because I'm PMS-ing?"

Brandt rolled his eyes upward. "Are you ever going to let me live that night down?"

He, Jordan and Alexander had fallen asleep on the rooftop, waking up after three in the morning and groggily making their way inside. Jordan found Aziza asleep in one of the guest bedrooms, and Alexander fell facedown and fully dressed across the bed in another room.

It was the morning after their guests had departed that Ciara read him the riot act, calling him sexist for his PMS remark. He'd apologized, exhibiting enough remorse to garner an Oscar, but something in the way Ciara looked at him said she wasn't convinced of his sincerity.

"No."

"That's so wrong."

"What would be wrong is if I found myself pregnant because of bad timing. I'm going on the Pill."

"What would you do if you did get pregnant? Would you keep the baby?"

Ciara struggled with the uncertainty Brandt's question had aroused. The possibility of becoming pregnant when she dated Victor hadn't been an issue, because she'd been fitted with an intrauterine device.

"I don't believe in abortion."

"That's not what I asked you. Would you give my baby up for adoption?"

"It wouldn't be your baby or my baby," she countered angrily, resenting the tone in his voice. "It would be our baby and if we had to make a decision about a child, then we would do it together."

"If you're not pregnant then this conversation is moot. If you are, then let me warn you in advance that I don't intend to get embroiled in a custody battle with you."

"Neither do I," Ciara retorted, "and this conversation is moot." She cradled his face. "I don't want to fight with you, Brandt—"

"There's not going to be a fight," he interrupted.

She closed her eyes for a second. "Please don't interrupt me."

"I'm sorry."

Her fingers dug into his stubble, causing him to wince. "Don't say anything until I'm finished." Ciara couldn't hold back a smile when he nodded his head like a bobblehead doll. "You know I like you—a lot. If I didn't, it wouldn't have mattered how long it'd been since I last had sex. I still wouldn't have slept with you." Easing her grip on his face, Ciara pressed her forehead to his. "You're exciting, easy on the eyes, incredibly sexy and you're nothing like a dumb jock. You're the total package for any woman looking for their happily ever after. But…"

"But what, Ciara?" Brandt asked when she didn't finish her sentence.

She lowered her eyes. "But not for me, Brandt."

Cupping her chin, he stared deeply into the eyes of the woman on his lap. "And why not you? Aren't you entitled to your own happily ever after?"

Ciara affected a wry smile. "Of course I'm entitled."

"Then, what's the problem?"

"There is no problem. You know about Victor." He nodded. "I promised myself I wouldn't make the same mistake twice."

The natural color drained from Brandt's face. His eyes paled, leaving them an eerie pale blue. "You believe that I'm controlling you? Forcing you do things you don't want to do?"

"Don't get it twisted, Brandt. Victor never forced me to do anything I didn't want to do. He wasn't holding a gun to my head or blackmailing me. When I decided I no longer wanted to be his hood ornament, I ended it. What I didn't tell you was that I'd stopped seeing him before he proposed marriage."

"For how long?"

"Three months. I managed to avoid him at the hospital—I had my shift changed and blocked his number on my cell. I lived in a building with a doorman, so he couldn't get in unless he was announced. Victor wasn't able to accept that I no longer wanted to see him after two years of dating him exclusively, so he figured if he proposed marriage I'd take him back."

"Where were you when he hit you?"

"In my apartment."

"I thought you said—"

"I know what I said, Brandt. That he couldn't get

in unless he was announced. I came home one night and he was waiting for me outside the building. He said he wanted to talk, that he, that *we* needed closure. And because I truly wanted it over, I let him into my apartment. He claimed he'd taken up two years of my life without a commitment, so he'd decided it was time to commit. That's when he took out a ring and asked me to marry him. I wanted to ask him if he was for real, but instead said I would think about it."

"The day I went to the hospital I should've asked to see him in private and knocked the hell out of him."

Ciara laughed and shook her head. "Have you forgotten that you're in a wheelchair?"

"Sitting in a wheelchair would not have stopped me from reaching up and grabbing him by the throat for hitting you."

That wasn't an image she had wanted to see: Brandt's large hand and strong fingers tightening around Victor's neck, cutting off oxygen to his lungs. "I don't condone violence, Brandt."

"Neither do I. You don't have to worry too much about me hitting your ex, because I'm bound by my contract's personal-conduct clause—mess up on or off the field and I'm fined, suspended or banned from football. And I'm willing to bet the good doctor would have me arrested for assault. So I can assure you that when I go after him it won't be physical. Now back to us."

Ciara couldn't understand how Brandt could go from talking about Victor in one breath and about their future in the next. Given Brandt's height, weight and strength he probably could break Victor's jaw with one punch.

"Once my assignment ends there can be no us. You're a celebrity, Brandt, and I cannot and will not live my life in the spotlight."

The sweep hand on his watch made a complete revolution before Brandt silently acknowledged Ciara with a nod. She was right. But to Brandt she was so much more: beautiful, intelligent, spirited, charming and the most sensual woman he'd ever known. Ciara had accused him of confusing lust for love. She was wrong. He wasn't in lust with Ciara. He was in love with her.

He successfully hid his disappointment behind a bright smile. "I came in here with the intent of shaving your legs, but somehow I got distracted. Do you still want my help?"

Resting her head on his shoulder, Ciara pressed a kiss below Brandt's ear. "You can shave my legs and share my shower. But you cannot get my hair wet."

"What's going to happen if I do wet it?"

"I will tie you to the bed and give you a Brazilian wax."

Brandt threw back his head and roared with laughter. "Do you know what you are?"

"What am I, sport?"

"You're a very naughty girl with just a hint of mean." It was Ciara's turn to laugh, the low, sensual sound reminding Brandt of a muted horn.

"Do you like naughty?"

"I love naughty."

Ciara scrunched up her nose. "Have you ever been waxed?"

Brandt sobered, remembering when he and Alexander had visited an upscale West Side salon offering services to men and women; the aesthetician convinced his teammate to have his eyebrows waxed. Brandt had recorded the action on his camera phone, complete with audio, as a reminder never to go through the ordeal of having someone slather hot wax on his body and then rip off hair and flesh in an attempt to become metrosexual.

"No."

"Would you consider it?"

"Hell! No!"

"What are you afraid of? You don't want to ruin your macho image?" Ciara teased.

"I'm quite comfortable with my sexuality. It's just that I'm not willing to endure that type of pain because I have a few stray eyebrows."

She gave him a look of incredulity. Brandt had chosen to play a sport where pain was evident with every play. "Don't tell me you'd prefer some three-hundred-pound guy knocking the wind out of you than to go through even two minutes of a little discomfort."

"It's a different type of pain."

"How would you know, Brandt, if you've never been waxed?" He stared at a spot over her shoulder. "How would you know?" she asked again.

"I know because I've seen dudes—big-ass dudes— scream like little girls when getting their eyebrows waxed."

Eyes narrowing, her mouth opening and closing, Ciara glared at Brandt. "Oh, we're back to being sexist? FYI, the male patients I've taken care of moan, groan, scream and complain more about pain than their female counterparts."

"It was just a figure of speech," Brandt said in apology.

"It's a figure of speech that could possibly get you into trouble if a reporter decides to quote you, or someone out to discredit your reputation hears."

He smiled, attractive lines fanning out from his eyes. "Wow. I didn't know you cared."

"I do care, Brandt. I care a lot. Now please let me go so I can take my legs off the arms of this chair. My feet feel like someone is sticking them with straight pins." Sitting on Brandt's lap, her legs dangling over the arms of the wheelchair while they'd made love, had impeded blood flow to her extremities.

Looping his arms under Ciara's shoulders, Brandt lifted her effortlessly, sliding first one leg, then the other off the chair. He couldn't pull his gaze away from her naked body. There wasn't one straight line on her curvy frame. She was all natural: no breast augmentation, lip enhancement or rhinoplasty. Ciara Dennison was natural and real—in-your-face real—without compromising her femininity.

He hadn't planned to make love to her without protection—it had just happened, spontaneously. What Brandt found ironic was that spontaneity wasn't a factor in his personality—at least not consciously or overtly. Even his decision to become a professional athlete had been something he'd thought about for more than a year. When he'd enrolled at Stanford, Brandt's plans had included graduating and joining Wainwright Developers, not playing football.

Ciara mentioned that they'd dodged a bullet, because they'd picked the right time to have unprotected sex. But for him it was the wrong time. If getting her pregnant to hold on to her was the key, then he would become a more-than-willing accomplice and participant. However, trickery wasn't what he wanted to base their relationship on. For him if it wasn't straight up, he wanted no part of it.

There had been women who'd said they were on birth control so he didn't have to use protection, but too many guys he knew had become unwitting fathers that way.

Brandt had always planned to marry and father children, but never had the pull been strong as it was now. And he knew it had something to do with the woman who was his nurse and lover.

"Please give me the towel and razor," he told Ciara when she sat down on the ledge of the tub, "then reapply the shaving cream and put your foot in my lap."

Ciara did as Brandt directed, smiling when he eased the razor over her outstretched leg without cutting her. She'd left Brandt after breakfast to keep an appointment at a salon for her hair, and a mani-pedi. She was supposed to have had her legs waxed, but the waxer had called in sick.

"I reserved a car and driver for you for tonight," said Brandt.

Ciara's head popped up. "I told you I didn't need a car service. The doorman will hail a cab for me when I leave, and I'll have someone bring me back."

Brandt's hand stilled. "Someone, Ciara? You don't even have a name. What if that someone decides to take a detour between here and the airport and something happens? How many women have ended up either missing or dead? Too many," he said, answering his own question. "You will either go with my driver or I'm tagging along—in the chair."

"You're kidding."

"Do I look like I'm kidding?"

She met his resolute stare. "No."

"What's it going to be? Me or the car service?"

A beat passed. "Are you trying to check on my whereabouts?"

The question was out before Ciara could stop it. The first thing that had come to mind was Brandt making certain she wouldn't take a detour, perhaps hang out with another man, before she returned to the penthouse. Clarissa had volunteered to come and spend the night with him, thus alleviating her concern about having to leave the party early.

"Don't ever lump me into the same category as Victor Seabrook." Brandt enunciating each word.

"I didn't say you're anything like Victor," she replied.

"That's not how it sounded to me, Ciara," Brandt countered. "I reserved the car because I want to make certain you'll be protected." What he didn't tell her was the man who would take her to the hotel and back was not only his personal driver, but also a professional bodyguard.

Ciara ran a hand over her forehead. She didn't want to fight with Brandt, not when her body thrummed whenever she recalled his hardness inside her. All of her life she'd craved male protection, first from her father and later from the men she'd dated, but none of them had been forthcoming—until Brandt Wainwright.

"I'm sorry. I misinterpreted your concern. Thank you, Brandt," she whispered.

Raising her foot, Brandt kissed each of her brightly painted toes. "You're welcome."

Chapter 16

The rear door of the Town Car opened and Ciara placed her hand in the outstretched palm of the pale, dark-haired, black-suited man who'd picked her up in front of the high-rise and driven her to the LaGuardia Marriott. She felt the strength in his arm as he helped her out of the car. He took a large, quilted bag from her hand, then led her by her elbow, escorting her to the hotel entrance.

He handed her the bag, reached into the pocket of his jacket and extended a business card. "I'll see you to your room. But I want you to call me when you're ready to leave and we'll meet in the lobby," he said with a distinctive Midwestern accent.

Ciara stared at the card. There was no name, only a number with a familiar area code. She nodded. "Okay." To say her driver was scary was an understatement. He wasn't tall, but what he lacked in height he made up in bulk—he was built like a tank. During the drive from Manhattan to Queens he hadn't removed his sunglasses or his jacket. Only when he reached over to open the door for her did she see the automatic weapon in a holster under his left arm.

They walked through the lobby to the elevators, riding up in silence. Ciara walked the carpeted hallway, her bodyguard following. She stopped at the suite Sofia had reserved for the night, rapping lightly on the floor.

"¿Quién?" asked Sofia from behind the door.

"It's Ciara."

"Coming, *chica!*"

Sofia opened the door dressed in a pair of black bikini panties with a matching demi-bra. Like Ciara, her hair was still in rollers. *"¡Coño!"* she swore in Spanish when she saw the man standing behind her roommate.

Ciara smiled at the driver. "I'll see you later." She walked into the suite, closing the door.

"Who was that?" Sofia asked, slipping into a short silk robe she hadn't bothered to put on when she went to open the door.

"My driver."

Sofia Martinez plopped her petite body down on the sofa separating the living room from the suite's dining area. She hadn't seen her friend and roommate in weeks, but had to admit she looked better than she had in a very long time. Her face wasn't as gaunt as the last time she'd seen her, and even her jeans fit her hips a bit more snugly. When she and Ciara didn't catch up with each other by phone, they usually exchanged emails. Ciara was the ideal roommate. Sofia didn't have to be concerned about Ciara entertaining men, because in the two years they'd lived together she'd never invited one home with her.

"Whoa, *chica. Usted está llevando la gran vida realmente.*"

Ciara understood two words: grand and life. "*Chica.* I'm living *la vida loca.*"

She smiled at the woman who was like a sister to her. The thirty-five-year-old, five-foot-one, hundred-and-ten-pound former dancer was always bubbly and optimistic. She'd given up her dance career after she'd discovered her choreographer husband had been sleeping with a female dancer in their troupe. Sofia moved out of her Tribeca loft, and after her divorce and a sizeable settlement, she bought the two-bedroom co-op in West Harlem.

The two had first met at a dermatologist's office. Sofia had been undergoing a procedure to minimize the appearance of acne caused by her heavy stage makeup. Sofia had shown Ciara an ad for a three-thousand-dollar pair of designer shoes. Ciara had admitted the most she'd paid for a pair of shoes was four hundred dollars, and that had been a bargain, because not only were they last year's model, but the original price was twice that much. Sofia disclosed because she wore a sample size she was able to indulge in her shoe fetish to her heart's content. She'd given Ciara two tickets to her dance troupe's off-Broadway opening. After seeing the performance, Ciara had been awed by the exceptional talent of the woman with the long, black hair, large dark eyes and friendly smile.

Ciara went back to see the performance again, this time with several nurses from the hospital. They were invited backstage to meet the cast and joined several of them for a late dinner at a nearby restaurant. The gathering set the stage for a close friendship between Sofia and Ciara spanning eight years.

The two women had had one argument, when Ciara had offered to pay her share of the maintenance on the spacious co-op. Sofia went into high-drama mode, declaring tearfully that she couldn't take the money because Ciara had let her live with her rent-free during her separation and drawn-out divorce. They finally reached a compromise: Ciara was responsible for paying the cable bill.

Sofia threw up a hand in a dramatic flourish. "My life should be so crazy." She folded her legs under her body. "Now I want to hear all about it."

Ciara, kicking off her sandals, feigned ignorance. "What are you talking about?"

"I want to hear all about you and Brandt Wainwright. I don't need to know the juicy details, because all it's going to do is make me more frustrated."

"Why are you frustrated?"

"*No puedo creerlo.* I can't believe you," Sofia translated without taking a breath. "It's been a long time since I've met a man who makes me want to sleep with him. It's like that with Bobby."

Pulling her feet up under her body, Ciara leaned in closer. "Does he feel the same way?"

Sofia lifted her shoulders. "I don't know. He hasn't sent out any signals that he wants more than friendship."

"Maybe it's because you're coworkers."

Shaking her head, Sofia worried her lip. "I don't think it's that. I believe he thinks I want to get married."

"But you don't want to get married again. Or do you?" Ciara asked when seeing the faraway look in her friend's eyes."

Sofia's eyelids fluttered wildly. "I would *never* marry again, even if I met what I thought was the perfect man, because there's no such animal."

"Not all men are cheaters, Sofia."

"The only thing I'll say is that all men aren't control freaks like that butthead you finally threw out with the garbage."

Ciara recalled her accusing Brandt of monitoring her whereabouts to try to control her. But he hadn't wanted to control her, only to protect her. She knew she wouldn't be sitting in a hotel suite preparing to celebrate a friend's birthday if Brandt were a control freak. After all, she was being paid to care for him 24/7.

"I had to, *chica*. Otherwise I would have ended up as Victor's punching bag."

"Esteban still owes him one for hitting you."

"Well, he would have to stand in line behind Brandt."

Unfolding her legs, Sofia leaned forward. "So you told Brandt about Victor?" Ciara nodded. "Does this mean you and Brandt are beyond the nurse-patient relationship?"

Whispering like a coconspirator, Ciara told Sofia about her reluctance to become involved with her patient because of her ethics, but how after the first time they'd made love she'd felt as if she was finally able to exorcise all the fears she'd had with Victor.

Sofia clapped her hands like a child. "Good for you,

chica. What's going to happen when he stops being your patient?"

Ciara stared at the framed landscape print that was affixed to thousands of hotel room walls. "We go our separate ways to live our separate lives."

"Stop playing, Ciara."

She knew Sofia was serious whenever she called her by her name. "I'm not playing. Brandt Wainwright is a celebrity athlete—"

"Who just happens to like a little chocolate in his milk," Sofia teased, grinning. "The media will have a field day with the two of you, with Brandt as Ken and you as his black Barbie."

Ciara shook her head. "You've got it wrong, Sofia. It's not about what we look like, but who he is."

"He's 'the Viking,' football's golden boy. The gridiron's Brad Pitt."

Running her hands over her face, Ciara wanted to scream at her roommate, but instead counted slowly to ten. "He is a celebrity," she said between clenched teeth, enunciating each word, "and I don't want a repeat of what I had with Victor. The tabloids dubbed him Dr. Eye Candy or Dr. Do Good, and he loved the attention.

"When I asked if he ever tired of the cameras and flashbulbs, he said no. He claimed some people lived all their lives without ever having their fifteen minutes of fame. Victor vowed he would make certain he had his fifteen minutes and then some. That's when I realized he was an egomaniac."

"Maybe it will be different with Brandt."

Ciara heard the wistfulness in Sofia's words, wishing they were true. "I can't afford to take that chance, Sofia.

Maybe if he lived in a small town somewhere in the South or Midwest he would be able to maintain some privacy, but that's not going to happen in New York.

"Don't forget Brandt is a native New Yorker who plays for a New York team and New York is the media capital. In my book that's the trifecta."

Groaning inwardly, Ciara reached up and began removing the rollers from her hair. Instead of wearing her hair swept up, she'd had the stylist set her hair on rods. When removed it would result in a profusion of spiral curls.

Sofia unfolded her lithe body and walked over to the wet bar. "*Hable de hombres suficientemente.* Enough man talk. What would you like to drink?"

"White wine." It was the first thing Ciara could think of.

"Shame on you, *chica,*" Sofia chided. "Wine is when you're sitting down to a nice dinner. Tonight we're going to be anything but nice. There's going to be a live Latin band, *comida deliciosa,* an open bar and so many men to dance with. You have door-to-door car service, so you don't have to worry about driving. Let me fix you something that will make you feel as free-spirited as you're going to look once you slip into your dress and shoes." Ciara had bought a black off-the-shoulder dress that hugged her body like a second skin and a pair of matching peau de soie pumps.

A rush of heat swept up Ciara's neck to her hairline. The dress was an impulse buy. But Ciara wasn't usually impulsive. She attributed it to the fact that she hadn't gone out dancing since attending a wedding a year before. Once she'd gotten to the dance floor, she hadn't sat down. When she got home, she'd collapsed from sheer exhaustion. The night had been memorable because it was the first time she'd attended an event without Victor in years. It had been like being paroled after serving time for a crime she hadn't committed.

"Whatever you concoct, just make certain I'll be able to walk out of this suite without assistance."

Sofia perused the bar, selecting a bottle of gin and some pineapple juice, maraschino liqueur and diced fresh pineapple. "We're both Harlem girls, so I'm going to fix us a Harlem cocktail." She combined all the ingredients with cracked ice in a cocktail shaker, then strained it into old-fashioned glasses, handing one to Ciara. "Here's to a night filled with love and laughter."

Ciara touched her glass to Sofia's, then took a sip. "It's delicious." She took another sip, savoring the differing flavors on her palate. "To love and laughter."

Ciara ate, drank and danced until she was exhausted. Once the band struck the first chord, everyone in the ballroom was up and dancing. Esteban had arrived with friends from his childhood and from the NYPD. Between courses, he went from table to table like a politician—shaking hands and kissing cheeks, thanking everyone for coming to help him celebrate his fortieth birthday.

It was after one o'clock when Ciara wound her way through the crowd to find Sofia. A profusion of curls pinned up at the crown of her head added several inches to her petite stature, while a shimmering navy blue halter dress showed off her dancer's body to its best advantage.

"I'm leaving," she whispered in Sofia's ear.

Sofia frowned. "Some of us are going back to Esteban's house after this ends. Why don't you come with us?"

"I'd love to, but remember I'm working."

"*¡Coño!* I forgot."

She kissed Sofia's cheek. "I'll call you in a couple of days."

"Later, *chica.*"

Ciara left the ballroom and took the elevator to the suite. Opening her evening bag, she took out her cell phone and the driver's card. He answered after the first ring, sounding as alert at one in the morning as he had earlier.

"I'm ready to leave. I'll meet you in the lobby."

She ended the call, tossed her evening bag in the larger quilted bag, zipped it and left the room's card key on the coffee table for Sofia. Making certain she hadn't left anything, Ciara closed the door behind her. When she stepped out of the elevator, she saw her driver looking at her as if she had a third eye in the middle of her forehead. Then she realized why he was staring. She looked vastly different than she had when he'd picked her up. He took her bag, cupped her elbow and led her out into the cool night to the parked Town Car.

Ciara slid into the back seat, sinking into the supple leather seat and closing her eyes. The last thing she remembered before falling asleep was the sound of airplanes overhead.

"Miss Dennison, we're here."

Ciara sat up straight and looked around. She was

in Manhattan in front of Brandt's building. "That was quick."

The driver extended his hand, pulling her gently to her feet. "Traffic was very light tonight. I'll see you upstairs."

She managed a tired smile. "That's all right. I can make it upstairs by myself." Ciara wanted to remind him that the building was monitored around the clock. Everyone coming and going was observed on closed-circuit cameras.

The doorman on duty touched the shiny brim of his cap. "Good evening, Miss Dennison, Mr. Landis."

Ciara acknowledged his greeting with a smile, while her companion stared straight ahead. Brandt had given her an extra card key for the elevator, but she hadn't had to use it, because Mr. Landis reached into his jacket pocket and inserted his into the slot for the penthouse.

The elevator rose swiftly, and the doors opened to a scene that rendered Ciara speechless. A small crowd had gathered in the great room, laughing and talking. A scantily dressed woman, perched on the arm of Brandt's wheelchair, leaned into him, her mouth pressed to his ear. Approaching the revelry, Ciara spied Clarissa sitting on a love seat in the living room, arms crossed under her breasts. A man seemed to be coming on to her, and from her expression she wasn't very receptive.

"Hey, we have a new one!" announced a booming male voice.

Ciara didn't and couldn't react for several seconds after someone had captured her image with a camera phone. She turned back to the driver, who hadn't moved from the elevator. "Mr. Landis, please get them out of here!" Her voice was low, demanding.

The driver and bodyguard nodded. Brandt Wainwright had asked him to protect his nurse, and she had flipped the script, because she now wanted him to protect his employer. Striding forward, he caught the wrist of a woman, forcibly taking the flute of champagne from her hand.

"The party's over and it's time for you to go home, miss."

A stocky man spun around. "Says who?"

"Says me," Ciara announced.

Brandt looked up, his stunned gaze taking in everything as she must be seeing it. "Ciara." Her name came out a whisper.

"I want them out of here, Brandt."

"Go home, Stubbs, and take your friends with you." Brandt's voice seemed to come from a long way off—a voice he almost didn't recognize as his own. His teammate had called, asking if he could stop by. Brandt told him he could, but he hadn't expected Jon Stubbs to bring an entourage and groupies.

"You heard the man," Ciara said loudly when no one moved. "Go home."

Clarissa popped up like a jack-in-the-box. "How many times do you have to be told to get the hell out of here?" Her eyes were shooting daggers at the man who'd tried mauling her. "Mr. Landis, if these people don't leave in two minutes, I want you to call the police and have them arrested for trespassing."

Landis removed his jacket, tossing it on the table between the great room and living room. The butt of the handgun in the shoulder holster looked like a small club against the stark white shirt. "Good night, good people."

As if it had been choreographed, everyone turned and walked to the elevator. The penthouse was as quiet as a tomb when the elevator doors closed.

Brandt broke the silence. "Ibrahim, will you please take my sister home?"

Clarissa rounded on her brother. "I thought I was staying..." Her words trailed off when she was saw Brandt glaring at her. "I'll be right back, Mr. Landis."

Ibrahim Landis slipped into his jacket. "I'll wait outside for you."

Ciara waited for Clarissa to retrieve her overnight bag, then walked her to the elevator, punching the button. "I'm sorry it had to end like this," she apologized in a quiet voice. She and Clarissa had made plans to spend the day together.

"That's okay. I'll probably see you again when my aunt and uncle host their family get-together at the end of the month." She offered a bright smile. "Thank you for taking such good care of my brother. And please don't tell me it's your job, Ciara, because I know it's more than that."

Ciara angled her head. "What is it you know, Clarissa?"

Dark lashes framed a pair of sky-blue eyes that knew too much. "Brandt's in love with you. I'd suspected it when we came for dinner, but when you walked in here tonight dressed like you just stepped off the pages of a fashion magazine, I knew for certain when he looked at you."

"You're imagining things."

"No, I'm not, Ciara. I've seen my brother with more women than I have fingers and toes, and not one of them—"

Ciara held up a hand. "That's enough, Clarissa. I'm tired and I'm certain Brandt's tired, and I need to get him into bed."

Clarissa managed a bright smile. "I'll see you," she said cheerfully, then stepped into the elevator.

Waiting until the doors closed, Ciara slipped off her heels, leaving them under the table in the entryway. Walking on bare feet, she made her way to where Brandt sat waiting for her. She sat opposite him, crossing one leg over the other.

"This may be your home, Brandt Wainwright, but you are still my patient. And you know better than anyone that you can't hang out drinking—"

"I wasn't drinking," Brandt said defensively.

"What's up with the girl on your lap?"

"She wasn't on my lap. She was on the arm of the chair."

"And if I hadn't come in when I did would she have been on your lap?" Ciara asked.

"Why is it you sound like a jealous wife?"

"You wish," she said, glaring. His lids were drooping and the dark circles under his eyes were a testament to his exhaustion. He was entertaining when he should've been in bed.

"Yeah, baby. I wish."

Ciara arose from the chair. "I know it's way past your bedtime, because now you're talking nonsense."

"I say something you don't want to hear and it's nonsense?"

Releasing the brake on his chair, she pushed it out of the living room. "We'll talk about this tomorrow."

"It's already tomorrow."

Ciara tried controlling her temper. "Why are you being so stubborn? Because if you're looking for a fight, then I'm willing to oblige. I come back expecting you to be in bed, not entertaining ladies—and I'm using that term very loosely—"

"They're not my groupies," Brandt said, cutting her off.

"Groupies, whatever. They're all the same, Brandt."

"You forgot ho," he drawled, chuckling under his breath.

"That too. And it's not funny," she chided, pushing him into the elevator off the pantry.

"Did I tell you how sexy you look tonight?"

"Don't try and change the subject, Brandt."

"How many men tried coming on to you tonight?"

"I told you not to change the subject."

"I've got it," Brandt said, taking control of the chair when the elevator reached the second floor.

Ciara was angry with him and he was thoroughly frustrated. His feelings toward her were becoming more confusing with every night she spent under his roof. They shared a bed, but with the dawn of each new day, Ciara was more of a stranger than she had been the night before.

He'd fallen in love with her, but what nagged at him was getting Ciara to change her mind about him. He couldn't help what the media had created—it wasn't as if he could turn the image off and on by flipping a switch. As the Viking he was able to fill stadium seats with rabid fans. But would that success cause him to fail to win the woman he loved?

Brandt entered the bedroom, maneuvering close and transferring from the chair to the bed. He felt Ciara's closeness as she took off the casts and his shorts, his gaze lingering on the spiral curls falling around her face. There was going to come a time when he wouldn't need her help dressing or undressing, and that was when he would have to count down the time when she would walk out of his life, and pride would prevent him from begging her to stay.

There was a lethal calmness in his eyes when he captured her eyes. *Always remember you're a Wainwright. And we Wainwrights don't accept defeat.* His father's mantra came to mind. Ciara may have won a battle when she told him she wouldn't date another celebrity, but she hadn't won the war.

What he had to do was formulate a game plan where he would not only win her love but also her heart.

Chapter 17

Brandt smiled at Ciara. The weather had changed from hot days and warm nights to warm days and cool nights, and so had their relationship. They'd continued to sleep in the same bed, but hadn't made love in more than three weeks. The first week was because Ciara was on her menses and the next two found them in bed together without either making an overture to the other.

Brandt knew it had something to do with Ciara returning home to find the penthouse filled with strangers and her annoyance with his teammate's groupie sitting on his chair. He'd accused her of being jealous, but in truth he was hurt that she hadn't demonstrated a depth of emotion that went beyond their making love to each other. He knew men who had long relationships and never told their women "I love you." He didn't intend to be in that kind of relationship with Ciara.

She'd dated Victor Seabrook for two years, and she

hadn't mentioned loving him. Victor, who'd monopolized two years of her life and had proposed marriage when he'd feared losing her, had gotten an "I have to think about it."

What was there to think about? Brandt mused. He'd dated Courtney Knight for a year before asking her to marry him. Fortunately he'd discovered before they exchanged vows that if she couldn't be a faithful fiancée then she wouldn't be a faithful wife.

Using crutches for the first time, he'd taken half a dozen steps, turned and then retraced his steps. "Congratulations," she crooned.

Brandt winked at his nurse. "I couldn't have done it without you."

Ciara shook her head as she studied the man who'd become more than a patient. "You would have done it without me, Brandt, because you're very competitive and refuse to accept defeat."

He'd ramped up his physical therapy, exercising and pushing himself to extreme limits. If his therapist wanted him to perform twenty-five reps of an exercise three times a day, Brandt would increase it to fifty reps three times a day. He exercised on the days not scheduled for therapy, strengthening his leg muscles while shortening his recovery time.

Switching the crutches to one hand, Brandt used them as support when he sank down next to Ciara on an exercise bench in the home gym. "Let's go out and celebrate."

Ciara was taken aback by his suggestion. "Where?"

"Out to dinner."

Even though Brandt spent time in the solarium or on

the rooftop, she knew he was experiencing cabin fever. Whenever he left the penthouse it was to keep a doctor's appointment. "Okay."

Brandt glanced down at his legs. The casts had concealed the scars. "It's going to feel good to put on a pair of long pants."

"Where are we going?" Ciara asked when she wanted to tell him that she'd enjoyed looking at his legs. They were well-formed and developed. If he hadn't been in tip-top condition, his recovery would've taken longer.

"Someplace local and very casual." He winked at her. "You don't have to change." Jeans hugging her hips and legs, a pastel-pink twinset and her hair pulled into a ponytail made her look like a college coed.

"Do you need help getting dressed?"

"Not this time."

Ciara averted her gaze. "Not this time," she mused. Not this time or the next time. Her patient was rapidly becoming more independent. After the crutches it would a cane or canes, and then he would be able to walk unaided. That's when it would be over for her.

She'd wrestled with her conscience about sleeping with Brandt, then vacillated because the pleasure she derived offset her ambivalence. There were times when she'd called on all of her emotional resilience not to fall in love. It had been easier not to fall in love with Victor once she'd become cognizant of his controlling, possessive traits, but it was different with Brandt. At any time she could call the agency and ask to be reassigned, when it hadn't occurred to her to resign her position at the hospital until the physical altercation with Victor.

Ciara loved nursing, and when she'd joined the

hospital staff her intent had been to begin and end her
career there. The staff had become her extended family
and she still maintained friendships with many in the
nursing department.

"What are you thinking about?"

Brandt's query broke into her musings. "Not much,"
she lied smoothly.

"How much is not much?"

"Nothing worth talking about."

Reaching over, he tugged at her ponytail. "How
would you like a break?"

Ciara stared at Brandt's profile, surprisingly shocked
by his question. "You want another nurse?"

Leaning closer, he pressed a kiss to her hair. "Now
why would I want another nurse when I'm crazy about
the one I have? I was talking about going away for a
week or two."

She wondered if Brandt was thinking about his
aborted vacation. He'd been on his way to North
Carolina when he'd had the accident. "You want to go
to North Carolina?"

"No, babe, I don't want to go to North Carolina. I'd
have a problem getting around on crutches."

Wrapping her arm around Brandt's waist, Ciara
rested her head on his shoulder. Their relationship had
an undercurrent of uneasiness these days. It was as if
they'd reached an impasse: they couldn't go forward and
there was no going back. There was no way they could
undo making love.

"What about your therapy?"

Brandt chuckled. "Do you always have to think like
a nurse?"

It was Ciara's turn to laugh. "Of course. Once a nurse, always a nurse."

"Well, Nurse Dennison, there are some exercises I can do without using a treadmill or bike. Now, where should we go?"

He was offering her a choice—something Victor never had done. It had always been his way or no way. She hadn't thought about or spoken Victor's name since Esteban's birthday celebration, and she knew it was just a matter of time before she would be able to exorcise him completely from her mind.

"We'll discuss it over dinner."

Brandt angled his head and brushed his mouth over her parted lips. "Wherever we decide to go, it will have to be after Sunday. I promised the guys on the team I would come see them play Sunday afternoon."

"What else do you have planned?" she asked, smiling.

"That's it for now. I'm going to have to call my aunt and let her know we'll be away and won't be able to join the others for her fall frolic fête."

Ciara wanted to tell Brandt that reconnecting with his family took precedence over an impromptu vacation, but didn't know his current state of mind. Perhaps getting away was what he needed to prepare himself for the next phase of his life—because there was still the possibility that he wouldn't be able to play ball again. He would always have his family, but even if he'd remained healthy the career of a professional football player was not a long one. He'd chosen a career path measured in mere years and wishes that he would be able to retire physically unscathed.

* * *

Brandt had selected a tiny Italian restaurant two blocks from the apartment building, and what should've taken them five minutes to walk stretched into a laborious fifteen with him stopping to rest every twenty feet. Ciara chided herself for allowing him to perform the task his first day on crutches, but kept silent.

When the waiter recognized Brandt, he showed them to a table that provided a modicum of privacy. Placing a hand over his heart, the man angled his head. "My wife said a special novena for your recovery when we heard about your accident. I will tell her that her prayers were answered."

Brandt smiled. "Let your wife know I really appreciate her prayers."

"I'll give you and your lady time to look at the menu," he said, backing away from the table.

Ciara glanced around the restaurant; like many Manhattan eating establishments, the owner had maximized all available space with the positioning of tables along the brick walls. It was designed to duplicate an underground grotto with a waterfall, gaslight sconces and a cobblestone floor.

"This place is charming," she said, smiling at Brandt across the table. A lighted candle threw long and short shadows over his lean face.

"I like coming here because the service is good, the food is exceptional and I can blend in."

Ciara stared at her dining partner. It was the first time Brandt had alluded to his celebrity status being a hindrance. Even if he hadn't been football's Viking, it would have been difficult for him to blend in, given his appearance.

"Does it bother you when people stop and stare?" she asked.

Brandt lifted a broad shoulder under a cotton sweater. He was dressed entirely in black: sweater, jeans, running shoes and baseball cap. "Not too much. In the beginning I felt uncomfortable because I didn't know how someone would react to me. Were they angry because we hadn't won a game, or were they mad because we had beaten their team? It's impossible to tell what someone is thinking when they come up to me, so I find myself on guard most times."

"When you go out do you usually travel with Mr. Landis?"

A wry smile softened Brandt's mouth. "Ibrahim provides the necessary buffer I need whenever I attend something on the scale of a charity event."

"What about the clubs?"

"I stopped going to clubs a few years back. Alex had just joined the team and we went with several other players to a club in the Meatpacking District. Some dude threw a punch at Alex because he claimed he was flirting with his woman, and all hell broke loose. A running back was jumped by two guys and when it was all over the other guys were unconscious with broken jaws and busted ribs. A bouncer led us out through an emergency exit and by the time the police arrived we were nowhere in sight. That was the last time I went to a club."

Ciara narrowed her eyes. "Please don't tell me you got into the melee."

"Did you actually think I was going to let someone tag one of my teammates without retaliating? There were only two hits: one when I clocked the idiot and the other when he hit the floor. We hauled ass because Alex would've violated his personal conduct clause and could've been banned from the game, while the rest of us would've faced suspension and substantial fines."

"Was Alex flirting?"

"No. It was the woman who'd been coming on to him, but when he told her he wasn't interested, she told her boyfriend he was trying to pick her up. Alex's so-called playboy image is nothing more than media hype. He was seeing a woman for a couple of years, but they broke just before the new year. He claims she was drama personified."

Resting her elbow on the table, Ciara rested her chin on the heel of her hand. "Aren't most relationships filled with drama?"

Brandt stared at the doll-like face of the woman totally unaware of her impact on him and his life. "They don't have to be, Ciara."

Her delicate eyebrows lifted. "Were yours?"

He shook his head. "No."

"What makes you the exception?" she asked.

"It's not about being the exception. It's about recognizing it and taking the necessary steps to avoid it. I don't do well with needy women, or those who crave the spotlight."

"Is it because you're not willing to share the spotlight?"

Brandt recoiled as if he'd been struck across the face. "Is that what you believe, Ciara?"

"It's not what I believe, Brandt. It's what I'm asking."

"The answer is no. It's not easy living in a fishbowl where everything you do or say is scrutinized. It took a while, but I learned to play the game. There are times I smile when I don't feel like smiling, because once you become a so-called celebrity, everybody wants a piece of you. And you can't preen on the red carpet one night then beat up a photographer the next day. You forfeit what you crave most: privacy.

"I could've bought a condo anywhere in the city, but chose the building where I live because it's the most secure Wainwright property in the city. The elevator you take to get to the penthouse only stops at certain floors, because those tenants want to remain anonymous to everyone but the security staff. All of the doormen and security personnel have to go through extensive background checks, and then sign a confidentiality clause not to disclose what goes on in the building. You said you lived in a doorman building, so you know New York doormen are notorious gossips."

"So that little orgy I witnessed was the exception rather than the norm?"

"It wasn't an orgy, Ciara," Brandt spat out angrily. "I thought we'd settled that little misunderstanding. I had no idea Stubbs was bringing his crew with him when he asked to visit."

"Crew? The girls looked more like rump-shaking backup dancers."

"I wouldn't know what they looked like, because I

wasn't interested. And if I had been, what was I going to do sitting in a wheelchair?"

Lowering her arm, Ciara gave him an incredulous look. "I know you didn't ask me that when you know exactly what we did with you sitting in a wheelchair."

Grinning and flashing straight white teeth, Brandt winked at Ciara. "We did some pretty incredible things in that chair. I'll never forget your lap dance as long as I live."

Thankfully she did not have to respond—a waiter set a basket of warm bread and two goblets of water on the table. She picked up the menu and perused the selections, feeling the heat of Brandt's gaze on her.

"Were you jealous?"

She glanced up. "Jealous of whom or what?"

A beat passed. "Were you jealous of the woman sitting on my chair?"

Ciara knew the time had come for her to stop lying to Brandt and to herself. "Yes," she whispered. "I was jealous and angry enough to pull the heifer's bleached blond hair out from her black roots."

If Ciara's admission hadn't been so critical to their relationship, Brandt would've laughed. But he didn't, because he knew that if she was jealous, then her feelings for him went beyond casual sex. Suddenly he was sure of himself and what he had to do to win Ciara over completely.

"You'll never have to worry about me and another woman as long as we are together. Now have you thought of where you'd like to go?" Ciara shook her head. "Would you mind if I make a suggestion?"

"Please."

"Do you get seasick?"

A slight frown line appeared between Ciara's eyes when she pondered his question. She hoped he wasn't thinking of embarking on a cruise. She and her mother had taken a weeklong cruise down to the Caribbean one year and the ship was so large that it took them three days to figure out the shortest route to their cabin.

"No. Why?"

"I'd like to charter a yacht and sail down to the Caribbean. We can use the boat as our hotel when visiting some of the islands."

"It will be just us?"

He smiled. "Yes. Do you want to invite someone else?"

"Oh, no," she said quickly. "I love the idea."

"Good. I'll call and make arrangements tomorrow."

"How long do you anticipate we'll be gone?"

"A week to ten days. Why?"

"I'll have to contact my mother and let her know I'll be out of the country. I also need to stop at my apartment to pick up clothes and my passport."

"Don't worry too much about clothes. We can go shopping when we dock in Miami. I'll have Ibrahim take you home so you can pick up whatever else you'll need before we sail."

Ciara wanted to ask Brandt how many times he'd taken a woman with him yachting to exotic places, but decided what he'd done with other women was none of her business or concern. She would take Sofia's advice and enjoy the ride, then when it was time to get off she would be left with her memories.

"It sounds as if we're going have some fun," she said instead.

"If I can't promise anything else, I can promise you fun."

Chapter 18

Ciara activated the speaker feature on her cell as she folded clothes, storing them neatly in her Pullman. "Yes, Mom, I know what I'm doing. My patient is going on vacation, and I'm accompanying him."

"You know I've never interfered in your business, Cee, but something tells me this man is more than your patient," said Phyllis Dennison.

"And what would the more be, Mom?"

"I can't put my finger on it, but something in your voice is different. You sound happy."

Ciara picked up the top to a hot-pink-and-red-striped bikini, folded it neatly and placed it in the bag. "That's because I am happy. Private-duty nursing is less stressful than working at the hospital, and I get to select my cases."

"Are you dating anyone?"

"No, Mom."

"Why not?"

"Because I don't have the time. What about you? Are you still seeing your history professor?"

Phyllis's distinctive laugh came through the speaker. "Yes. He'd been planning to go to several countries in Africa to do some research for a book he plans to write after he retires at the end of this semester."

"What aren't you telling me, Mother?" Her mother only laughed like that when she was nervous.

"He asked me to go along with him as his wife."

Ciara screamed like an adolescent girl. "What did you say?"

"I told him yes."

Covering her mouth with a trembling hand, Ciara sat down on the chair beside her bed. It had taken twenty-three years, but her mother had found a man who made her happy and secure enough to try marriage again.

"Oh, Mom. I'm so happy for you."

"Thank you, baby."

"When are you getting married?"

"Probably after the new year."

The tears Ciara had tried to keep in check overflowed. "As soon as I'm finished with this assignment I'm coming up to see you."

"James has been talking about driving to New York City to visit some of the museums and libraries, but he has to wait until the end of the year."

"I'll be up to visit you before then. But when you guys come down I'll make certain not to accept another assignment so I can act as your guide."

"I'll let James know."

Ciara talked to her mother for another ten minutes

before ending the call. She couldn't believe it. Her mother was going to marry the widowed history professor who'd waited patiently for Phyllis Dennison to come around and take a second chance on love.

Closing a dresser drawer, Ciara glanced around the bedroom where she hadn't slept in weeks. She'd come to the apartment to pick up her passport and pack a bag with clothes better suited for the tropics. They were scheduled to leave Monday morning at eight from the West Side pier and arrive at the port of Miami Wednesday afternoon.

She zipped the bag, setting it on the floor. Ibrahim was waiting downstairs to drive her downtown, where they would pick up Brandt, then head to New Jersey for the game. Activating the security alarm, she locked the door behind her.

Ibrahim straightened from his leaning position against the bumper of the gleaming black Town Car and met Ciara and took her bag from her loose grip. He seated her before placing her luggage in the trunk. His day had begun early and would end late.

Brandt had called to instruct him to drive Ciara uptown, wait for her, then bring her back and pick him up for the drive to the New Meadowlands Stadium in East Rutherford, New Jersey. He'd been informed that Ciara was his employer's nurse, but instinct indicated she was more—much more to the MVP quarterback. He was paid well for his services and his discretion.

Ciara, awed by the size of the stadium, the thousands filing into the open-air structure and the tangible anticipation of the coin toss and kick-off, was overwhelmed when reporters, photographers and adoring fans surrounded Brandt. She managed to disengage herself from the crowd while he fielded questions, posed for photos and scrawled his name on bare arms, T-shirts and scraps of paper.

She didn't feel sorry for rich people, because all money did was give them a more comfortable lifestyle—it couldn't buy happiness. However, with Brandt there was another factor—fame—and that made his life a bit more complicated. As a public figure he had to put up with being stalked by paparazzi shoving cameras in his face. He had to try to protect his personal space from the crazed or demented person with an ulterior motive.

Ciara attempted to mentally detach herself from her involvement with Brandt, to see him as a superstar athlete and not as her lover. She noticed the way he held his head when listening to someone, the manner in which he'd lean over to talk to a young child, his open smile, the warmth of his laugh and his firm handshake even while supporting himself on the crutches. His hair had grown out enough to touch the top of his ears and neck. A heavy wave flowed across the crown of his head, the flaxen strands shimmering like sunlight on bleached wheat. He was a male trifecta: face, body and brains.

"Viking, do you think you'll be physically ready to play next year?"

Brandt smiled at the reporter shoving a handheld tape recorder inches from his face. "That determination will have to come from the team's physician."

"Is it true that you're not talking to your teammates?"

His smile was still in place, but his eyes weren't smiling. They were cold and piercing. "It depends on which teammate you're referring to." He put up a hand. "Sorry, folks, but I need to get off my feet."

The excitement he'd felt when walking into the stadium was replaced by a panic that made it impossible for him to move his legs. He'd lost Ciara in the crowd. His gaze was wild, frantic when he searched the throng milling around him. Then he saw her. She was standing thirty feet away—and alone.

Their gazes met, his filled with relief. He beckoned to someone from stadium security. "Can you please tell the lady in the red jacket that we're going to our seats?"

The man nodded. "No problem, Mr. Wainwright. I'll escort you there."

It took longer than expected to get to their seats because it was slow going with the crutches, and their progress was impeded when fans ran over to greet or touch him. They were finally seated in a section with league executives and season ticket holders.

It was an overcast day and the air was cooler than Ciara had expected. She'd decided to bring the jacket because she wasn't certain when the game would end. Leaning into Brandt's warmth, she smiled up at him. "You're going to have to explain the game to me."

Brandt lowered his head and kissed the end of her nose. "Didn't you have football at your high school?"

"The year before I went to high school the school board disbanded the team after a boy died after being tackled in practice. At first they thought he'd suffered a concussion, but two days later he lapsed into a coma and was declared brain-dead. His parents signed the order to have him taken off life support and donated most of his organs. That left us with just basketball and baseball."

"There are thirty-two teams, divided into the NFC and AFC, and each conference is divided into zones: east, north, south and west. Each team plays the other three teams in their division twice—once at home and once on the road."

"How long is the season?" Ciara asked.

"Seventeen weeks, sixteen games."

"That's not very long, Brandt."

"Long enough to get your brain scrambled. I usually don't feel the pain when I'm playing, but the next day, depending on where I got hit, it's no joke. That's why I had the contractor include the sauna and steam room at my apartment. There's nothing like moist heat for aches and pain."

Ciara listened intently when Brandt gave the background on the game, but it ended when the teams took the field. She watched the action on giant screens. Her image appeared on the screen with Brandt's and the stadium erupted in ear-shattering cheers. She sat, transfixed, when Brandt's name was announced and he rose, using the crutches for support, and waved to the crowd and the players. Their images lingered when he sat, draped an arm over her shoulders and pulled her close. It was as if the entire world knew she was with Brandt Wainwright.

Brandt kept up a continuous commentary, explaining each play, shouting at the top of his lungs when his team scored the first touchdown, then covering her mouth with his, sucking the air from her lungs and leaving her struggling to breathe.

He loves this game. The four words taunted her. Brandt loved football, and the million-dollar question was, would he ever play again? Her cell phone vibrated at the beginning of halftime. Ciara pulled it out of her jacket pocket, staring at the display. Sofia had sent her a text: saw Viking suck yur face on prime time. U go Chica. She tucked the tiny phone into her pocket. If Sofia had seen her so did millions of others. The image was frozen in time for posterity.

The second half started with Brandt's replacement getting sacked twice and throwing three incomplete passes. The hometown crowd booed and shouted obscenities. Epithets like *bum* and *loser* were chanted until the Giants moved the ball down the field and the placekicker kicked a field goal. The score seesawed back and forth, ending in a tie when the clock ran out.

"Let's leave now while we can," Brandt said in Ciara's ear. "It's going into overtime." Again, the cameras followed them as they left their seats, fans applauding. Smiling, he raised a hand in acknowledgment.

They made it to the parking lot, where Ibrahim waited for them. He took the crutches, storing them in the trunk after Brandt slipped onto the back seat next to Ciara. A loud roar went up in the stadium when the driver took his position behind the wheel. A rare smile parted Ibrahim's lips. "We won."

Brandt sat up in bed, watching Ciara pace the width of the bedroom. She'd opened the casement windows and cool air flowed into the space. "Are you coming to bed, or do you intend wear a hole in the rug?"

She stopped pacing, her hands in tight fists, and glared at him. "I can't believe they put that footage on the late news for the world to see."

"It was just a kiss, Ciara. Why are you acting as if it was something more risqué? Besides, you're hardly recognizable."

"My roommate recognized me, Brandt. She sent me a text saying she saw it."

"That's because she knows I'm your patient."

"Please, Brandt, don't try and minimize it. Nurses don't go to professional football games with their patients then kiss them in front of millions of viewers."

He patted the mattress on his left. "Come here, baby. There's always a solution to every problem." Brandt smiled when she approached the bed and climbed in beside him. He pulled her close until she lay over his chest. "If there's any talk, then we'll just say you're no longer my nurse. I'll call my mother and have her tell the agency she doesn't need your services any longer. Meanwhile she'll pay you directly."

Ciara pondered Brandt's explanation. "Just what would I be to you?"

"You'd be my girlfriend."

"Why does it sound so simple?" she asked.

"That's because it is. Don't move." He reached for the cordless receiver on the bedside table. He dialed his parents' number, apologizing to Leona for waking her, then told his mother what he wanted her to do and why.

"Go to sleep, Brandt. I'll call them right now."

"Thank you, Mom."

"There's no need to thank me. There isn't anything I wouldn't do for Ciara. And I want you to tell her that."

"I will."

"What did she say?" Ciara asked when he placed the receiver on the cradle.

"She said she's going to call them right now. And she told me to tell you that there's nothing she wouldn't do for you."

Ciara smiled. She wanted to tell Brandt that it was nothing Leona wouldn't do for her son. The Wainwrights viewed her as a miracle worker, giving her credit for pulling Brandt out of his funk. It might have taken more time, but he eventually would have tired of wallowing in self-pity. Not only was Brandt a competitor, but he played to win.

"You can tell her thank you for me."

Brandt tunneled his fingers through her hair, massaging her scalp. "Are you ready for tomorrow?"

"I was born ready."

And he was ready to make love to her, but decided to put it off until they were out to sea. He had at least ten days to show Ciara how much he'd come to love her. Not only did he love her, but he was in love with her.

Victor Seabrook lay in bed, watching the late news. He went completely still when video footage of the football game flashed across the wall-mounted flat-screen. Talk about luck! He'd fired a P.I. because the man hadn't been able to come up with anything on Ciara Dennison and there she was, cuddling with Brandt

Wainwright at a football game at the newly built stadium for the world to see.

White-hot rage swept through him, making breathing difficult when he saw the ballplayer kiss Ciara. *"Bitch!"* The word slipped out, filled with venom Victor hadn't known he possessed. When she'd threatened to tell her boyfriend that he was stalking her, Victor never would've thought the man was the Giants' quarterback. That's why she'd turned down his offer of marriage. She was holding out for someone wealthier and with more visibility. Dr. Victor Seabrook was a celebrity doctor, but Brandt Wainwright, born into a real-estate dynasty, was a celebrity athlete and media superstar.

He'd waited two years to pay Ciara back for not appreciating what he'd done for her. He'd made her, provided her with what she needed to step into polite society with a minimum of effort. She'd met people who wouldn't have given her a cursory glance if she hadn't been on the arm of Dr. Victor Peter Seabrook.

Reaching for the cell phone on the bedside table, he punched "Contacts" and scrolled through the directory until he found the name he wanted. He smiled when he heard the husky female voice.

"Hey, you," he said, repeating her unorthodox greeting. "I've got something for you that should sell out your next edition."

"Shall I come over now?"

Victor frowned. "I'm in bed."

"When has that ever stopped us from conducting business, Dr. Seabrook?"

"You're right, Poppy." He didn't want Poppy Rayburn

and she didn't want him. But that didn't mean they didn't need each other. "Come on over."

Tapping a button, he ended the call and swung his legs over the side of the bed, reaching for pajamas. Even though it wouldn't make a difference to Poppy if he did come to the door without clothes, he didn't want her distracted from what he planned to divulge to her.

Chapter 19

Ciara stood at the rail, staring at the choppy waters of the Atlantic as the sleek yacht sliced through the ocean with a minimum of rocking motion. She and Brandt had arrived at the pier at seven and been shown to a stateroom that had every convenience of a hotel. The crew of seven was as inconspicuous as they were efficient.

A steward had unpacked their luggage, putting everything away, and half an hour after sailing the on-board chef served them a buffet breakfast of herbed scrambled eggs, sausage patties, baked country ham, buttermilk biscuits, homemade jams, navel oranges, hot coffee and tea and fresh orange juice with champagne.

Closing her eyes, she wrapped her arms around her body. The autumn sun was hot, but it was the wind that chilled her exposed flesh.

Ciara opened her eyes when she felt another source of heat. Brandt had replaced the crutches with two tripod canes; he admitted the canes helped him with balance and stability. She turned and smiled up at him. She'd gotten so used to seeing him seated that she was overwhelmed by his towering height and the breadth of his shoulders.

"How was your nap?"

Brandt stared at Ciara from under lowered lids. Barefoot and wearing a sweatshirt over a pair of shorts and with her ponytail whipping in the wind, he found her more tantalizing than when she wore the body-hugging dress and stilettos. She looked so incredibly beautiful, delicate and innocent that he found it hard to draw a normal breath.

"It would've been better if I had someone to share it with me."

Looping her arm through his, Ciara went on tiptoe to brush her mouth over his. "Why didn't you ask me?"

"I did, but you told me you wanted to stay on deck and enjoy the ocean."

Ciara pressed closer, her breasts molding to the contours of his hard chest. "Ask me again, Brandt."

Lowering his head, Brandt trailed kisses down the column of her scented neck. "Ciara Dennison, will you come to bed with me?"

Curving her arms under his shoulders, she rested her cheek over his heart while counting the strong, steady beats. "I'd thought you'd never ask."

He let out an audible exhalation. "What I wouldn't give to be able to pick you up and carry you downstairs."

"Patience, sport. That time will come," she whispered.

Ciara lowered her arms, wrapping one around his waist as she led him below deck.

Brandt knew he would eventually regain enough strength in his legs to lift more than his body weight. It was the realization that Ciara might not be around when he reached that milestone that had him anxious and frustrated.

His taking her away was to give her a break from what had become a mundane ritual of checking his vitals, examining his legs, preparing meals, conferring with the physical therapist and accompanying him for his scheduled visits to the doctor's office.

His routine hadn't varied much: he spent time in the solarium reading or pruning his plants, exercising, occasionally viewing movies from his extensive collection and sharing meals on the rooftop with Ciara, weather permitting. It was when they retired to bed that the floodgates opened and they talked—about anything and everything but themselves and what they wanted for their futures.

Brandt was able to keep his balance as he followed Ciara into their stateroom. He could've reserved the Wainwright family yacht the *Mary Catherine* for the trip, but that meant driving down to the shipyard on the Chesapeake. The *Mary Catherine* was smaller, sleeker, but this one was better able to ride out a storm if they were to encounter rough seas—there still were another two months before the official end of hurricane season.

There were three decks of cabins and salons, with the crew occupying the lowest deck. The interior staterooms were luxurious—walnut, teak, a gleaming stainless-steel stair on the main aft deck and ebony-and-cherrywood tables bespoke elegance and grace as seen in the finest homes.

Ciara hung the Do Not Disturb tag on the doorknob, then closed the door and turned the security lock until she heard the soft click.

Brandt sat on the bed, watching her intently as she closed the distance between them. He extended his arms and she walked into his embrace, burying her face in his hair. He felt so good and smelled even better.

"I think I'd better close the curtains or the crew will get an impromptu peep show."

She pulled the heavy fabric over the porthole, shutting out sunlight and endless miles of water. Turning back, Ciara met Brandt's eyes as she pulled the sweatshirt over her head, then the tank top. Her shorts and panties followed, leaving her completely naked for his rapacious gaze.

She felt no fear or shame whenever she took her clothes off for Brandt, because it always felt so natural. Perhaps it was because within hours of meeting Brandt for the first time it had been she who'd gazed on his magnificent nude body. He may have been her patient, but he was also a man—a very attractive man who made her feel things she didn't want to feel. Her fingers were steady as she unbuttoned his shirt, pushing it off his broad shoulders. He pushed her hand away when she attempted to unsnap his khakis.

"I can do it."

Ciara nodded. For weeks she had performed the task of helping him to dress and undress, so it'd become a habit. She knew Brandt didn't like relying on her for what was a basic human function, but he'd endured it until he was able to reestablish a modicum of independence. She got into the bed, lying on her side and watching as he relieved himself of his pants and boxer briefs.

Brandt lay on his back and swung his legs into the bed, smiling when he executed the move without pain. Using the strength in his upper body, he turned on his right side, facing Ciara, and rested a hand over her breast. Her eyes fluttered, then closed.

His eyes ate her up, from the hair spread out on the pillow to the rapidly beating pulse in her throat and heaving breasts. He forced himself not to stare at the area below her waist, because he wanted to visually savor her for as long as he could without penetrating her. Once inside Ciara, Brandt experienced a loss of control and common sense.

Whenever he was buried in her moist heat he found himself swept up in a magical journey where he could see himself growing old with her, surrounded by their children and grandchildren. Even as a child he'd been a realist, never giving in to flights of fancy like some children who'd pretended they were superheroes. The only place where he'd achieved superhero status was on the gridiron. Blessed with quick reflexes, an accurate throwing arm and the uncanny strength to stave off being sacked, he'd become the Viking, a real-life flesh-and-blood superhero to the media and football fans.

He was close enough to Ciara to see the outlines of her contact lenses. "Thank you."

A slight frown appeared between her eyes. "For what, Brandt?"

"For being here with me."

She gave him a mysterious smile. "I should be the one thanking you."

"Why?"

"Because I'm supposed to be working, but you're spoiling me."

"You're not working, Ciara. Remember, my mother terminated your services last night. You're Brandt Wainwright's girlfriend, and as such I'm going to try to do everything I can to spoil the hell out of you."

"You don't have to try," she countered. "You're doing it." She was on a luxury yacht with a crew at her beck and call. She didn't have to cook, do laundry or make her bed. All she had to do was get up, shower, dress and go up on deck to lie in the sun.

"I'm going to ask one thing from you as my girlfriend," Brandt said after a comfortable silence.

Ciara felt her heart kick into a faster rhythm. Now it's time for the other shoe to drop, she thought. "What is it?"

Brandt's hand moved from her breast to her hip. "Why do you make it sound as if I'm asking you to do something you don't want to do?"

"I didn't mean for it to come out like that."

He kissed her forehead. "You are precious to me, baby. What I'm asking is for you to give yourself to me and I'll give you all of myself in return."

Ciara stared at the attractive cleft in his strong chin. "Is that it?"

"If you want me to ask for more, then I can come up with a laundry list, baby," Brandt said, chuckling softly.

"No, Brandt. I don't have a problem with what you're asking for."

He sobered, meeting her eyes. "It's just not your body I want, Ciara." The seconds ticked by as they stared at each other.

"You want me to love you," Ciara said perceptively. To her surprise, Brandt showed no reaction, and she knew that she'd read him correctly.

"Am I asking too much from you?"

She felt a momentary panic before it disappeared like a wisp of smoke. Brandt was asking her to love him when she'd used everything in her emotional arsenal to fight her deepening feelings for her patient. She'd rationalized, telling herself she had no time for love and that when she walked away from Brandt she would take her love for him with her.

"No, darling. You aren't asking for too much."

Brandt's gaze softened, becoming a caress when he stared into her eyes. "I love you, Ciara, and because I do I would never do anything to hurt you."

Ciara placed her fingers over his mouth. "Let's enjoy what we have." Her mouth replaced her fingers when she caressed his mouth, silently communicating her love for the man holding her to his heart.

Reaching down, Brandt placed Ciara's leg over his. He bit down on his lip when his penis hardened quickly. He still couldn't make love to Ciara using positions that would bring them maximum pleasure, but at least now he didn't have to rely on her straddling his lap.

He longed for the day when he could place her on her back and he would start at her neck and taste every inch of her fragrant body until they experienced the full range of lovemaking. Grasping his erection, he guided it between her thighs, closing his eyes and moaning when her moist heat closed around his sex.

Making love facing each other made Ciara feel vulnerable. She wasn't able to hide her reaction to Brandt's lovemaking from him. He hadn't put on a condom because she was now using a contraceptive, and without the barrier of latex the sex was more intense.

Brandt raised her leg, resting it over his waist, while he angled his lower body for deeper penetration. He rotated his hips, pulled back and pushed, each time deeper, harder. If it were possible, he wanted to stay inside her until hunger or forces of nature forced him to pull out. Whenever he made love with Ciara he felt as if he'd come home. She was safe haven, a sanctuary where he found a peace he hadn't known was missing in his life.

"Open your eyes, baby." He smiled at the dreamy expression on her face. "I want you to look at me when I tell you that I love you."

A rush of tears filled Ciara's eyes, spiking her lashes. "I'm listening." The two words were whispered.

Brandt clamped his jaw and went completely still in an effort not to release himself inside her, but not making love to her for weeks had tested his resolve. He went to bed wanting her, woke with an erection and craved her throughout the day. There were days when he deliberately avoided her because he feared forcing her into a situation she hadn't agreed to. He always wanted their coming together to be by mutual consent. She was not his possession, something he could use, put away and use again at his whim.

"Not only do I love you, but I'm also in love with you."

Ciara smiled through the watery tears threatening to overflow. Her chin quivered. "I hate you for making it so easy for me to fall in love with you."

"You love me and you hate me. What's up with the ambivalence?"

"I didn't want to get involved with you."

"But you did," Brandt confirmed.

Ciara closed her eyes for several seconds. "I didn't want to even like you."

"But you do," he countered.

She flashed a sexy moue. "Not only am I involved, but I'm also in love with you, Brandt Wainwright."

He kissed the end of her nose. "How did I get so lucky?" He'd asked her the same question weeks ago.

Ciara moaned when Brandt began moving again, reigniting her passion. Heat and cold clashed, sweeping her up in a maelstrom of desire that made her feel faint. They established a rhythm, choreographing a dance of desire, as shivers of delight eddied up and down her spine.

Brandt's groans overlapped Ciara's, his hips moving faster and faster. Then it happened. The tightening in his scrotum, the burning sensation at the base of his spine, then the rush of semen, leaving him unable to speak or breathe.

Ciara Dennison was the first woman with whom he'd slept without a condom. And she was the only woman with whom he'd made love that he wanted to have his child. He hadn't lied to Ciara. He did love her—more than he could've imagined loving any woman.

* * *

Brandt and Ciara stood at the rail, watching as the shoreline of Charlotte Amalie grew smaller and smaller as the yacht sailed in a northerly direction. They'd spent the day shopping and touring the island by car.

Over the past week their ports of call had been Miami; Key West; San Juan, Puerto Rico; and St. Thomas in the U.S. Virgin Islands. They were going home, with a stop in Miami to refuel before continuing on to New York. The weather had decided to cooperate. It'd rained twice, during the early morning hours, and when they had disembarked it was to days filled with sunshine and tropical trade winds.

Their days began with leisurely lovemaking, shared showers and hearty breakfasts eaten on the top deck. Days at sea were spent sunbathing, watching movies or playing chess. The midday meal was always served buffet-style with fresh salads, tropical fruit, cold fish platters and fruity beverages. Dinners were extravaganzas fit for visiting royalty. Each evening the chef prepared a special dish, cooked on deck with accompanying wines, and served by white-jacketed waiters.

Brandt felt the vibration against his leg. It was the first time someone had called his cell phone in eight days.

Reaching into the pocket of his slacks, he took out the BlackBerry. A frown appeared between his eyes when he saw that Jordan had called him. He retrieved the voice mail message. His cousin had sent him an email he thought would be of interest to him.

Walking over to a deck chair, Brandt sat, placing the canes on deck beside the chair. When he accessed his email account and read the article Jordan had forwarded, Brandt knew if he hadn't been seated he would've lost his balance. Ciara's greatest fear was manifested. Her association with him had become fodder for the tabloids.

"Is something wrong?"

He glanced up as Ciara sank down on the chair next to his. "No." When he punched a button, the article was replaced by the phone's wallpaper. "Why do you ask?"

Ciara stared Brandt through the lenses of her sunglasses. "You had this strange look on your face."

Brandt was faced with the dilemma of showing her the email or waiting until they returned to New York. Within seconds, he decided on the latter. He wouldn't take any action until he spoke directly to Jordan.

"Someone sent me a bunch of chain letter emails," he lied. "I hate those damn things clogging up my inbox."

Ciara rested her hand on Brandt's forearm. His sun-browned skin and ash-blond hair reminded her of a magnificent palomino. Two days. They had forty-eight hours before returning to New York and reality.

Chapter 20

Ciara walked into the kitchen and threw several newspapers and a magazine at Brandt, hitting him in the chest. "You knew about this, didn't you?"

They'd returned to New York at seven in the morning, and twelve hours later during one of the televised entertainment shows, her worst fear had become a reality. The photos of her and Brandt kissing at the New Meadowlands Stadium had opened a Pandora's box, releasing a swarm of lies, rumors and scathing innuendos.

She'd left her cell at the penthouse, and when she'd retrieved her messages there were several from her mother, Sofia and many of the nurses she'd worked with at the hospital. All of the messages carried a similar tone: *We're here for you if you need us.*

Ciara hadn't known what they were talking about. She'd called her mother, but there was no answer at home and the call to her cell went directly to voice mail. It was then that she'd called Sofia, who was forthcoming about what had become the latest celebrity gossip.

An anonymous source had told gossip columnist Poppy Rayburn that Ciara Dennison was a gold digger, trading in men every two years as if they were leased cars. The article went on to say that she'd used celebrity plastic surgeon Dr. Victor Seabrook and when she tired of him she'd moved on to Brandt Wainwright. The article ended with: *Who's her next target?*

Brandt closed his eyes, hoping to shut out the photograph of Ciara clinging to Victor Seabrook's arm that had been taken at a fundraising event to benefit juvenile diabetes, but the image of her beautiful face when she'd smiled at the camera remained.

He opened his eyes. "Yes, I did."

Sitting on a stool at the cooking island, Ciara glared at him. "When did you know?"

Brandt's gaze shifted to the images on the screen of the muted television. "I found out from Jordan. He emailed me when we were on the ship coming back from St. Thomas. I wanted to tell you, but I knew it would upset—"

"Upset me!" she spat out, cutting him off. "I'm livid because you lied to me, Brandt. I asked you if anything was wrong and you told me no. I don't know what kind of women you're used to dealing with, but in case you haven't figured it out I am not a girl. Did you think I was going to have a meltdown? Or did you want me in a good mood so we could continue to—"

"You don't know what the hell you're talking about!"

Ciara went completely still. "I know you'd better not

ever raise your voice to me again." Her threat was low, cutting.

"Or you'll what, Ciara?" Brandt challenged, his temper rising to meet hers. "You'll leave me like you left Victor Seabrook? I don't think so."

Her eyes narrowed like she was a cat ready to pounce. "You don't believe I'd walk out on you?"

"No. Because if you do, then you'd just validate the lies. You know what you are and I know who you are," he continued, his voice softer, more conciliatory. "What you have to do is try and come up with the name of someone who'd want to discredit you."

Covering her face with her hands, Ciara shook her head. "I don't know."

"Think, Ciara. What about a vindictive girlfriend or boyfriend?"

She lowered her hands. "Maybe I'm naive, but I never had a problem with anyone at the hospital. Not with my coworkers or supervisor."

"What about an old boyfriend?"

"I dated one boy when I was in college, but we ended it after a year. He eventually married a girl from our graduating class. I went out with another guy a couple of years before I began seeing Victor. We'd see each other for a couple of months, break up, then we'd reconnect six months later. We both knew it wasn't going anywhere, so we decided not to continue to waste each other's time and ended it."

"I need their names."

Anxiety spurted through Ciara when she thought about Brandt's request. "What are you going to do?"

"Nothing."

"Nothing?" she repeated. "Then why do you need to know who they are?"

"Jordan's coming over to talk to you about this. He'll let you know what he needs to sue Poppy Rayburn and that rag she writes for for slander and defamation of character."

Hot tears pricked the backs of Ciara's eyelids. She was hoping if she kept a low profile the gossip would eventually go away. But it wasn't going to go away. Not when the Wainwrights were talking lawsuit.

She shook her head. "No, Brandt. I don't want my life disrupted with what amounts to silliness and a 'he said, she said.'" Ciara couldn't blame Poppy for writing the article. She blamed herself, because she'd known what to expect when she'd been seen with a man in the public eye.

"It's too late, baby. This is just not about you or me. It's about us."

"Us because you're a Wainwright?" she asked sharply.

"It's about…" The intercom rang and, using only one cane, Brandt limped over to answer it. "Jordan's on his way up."

Sliding off the stool, Ciara walked out of the kitchen and into the living room. She wanted to cry, but couldn't. She wanted to scream, but didn't. It had taken only one public appearance with Brandt to start tongues wagging about her identity, and one kiss to defame her character.

She heard the distinctive chime indicating the elevator had arrived at the penthouse level. She sat straighter when Jordan and Brandt and an older man who bore a striking resemblance to Jordan walked into the living room. Both wore dark blue pinstripe suits, white shirts, dark ties and wingtips. Brandt dropped down beside her, holding her hand, while she studied the other two men.

Waiting until his cousin and great-uncle sat on the love seat, Brandt squeezed Ciara's hand. "Ciara, I'd like you to meet my uncle, Wyatt Wainwright. Wyatt, Ciara Dennison."

Wyatt Wainwright rose, extended his hand and smiled at the young woman who had caused quite a stir because of her association with his nephew. "Miss Dennison."

Ciara smiled at the elegant man with a head of shocking white hair and piercing blue eyes. He and Jordan shared the same lean face, jawline and patrician features. She recalled Aziza mentioning that her husband's grandfather was an old-school gangster.

"It's a pleasure to meet you, Mr. Wainwright."

Wyatt retook his seat, his eyes taking in everything about Ciara Dennison. He had been watching the football game when he saw Brandt kiss the young woman sitting next to him. He'd known the gesture was certain to elicit curiosity as to who she was. What he hadn't known was that she'd been romantically linked to the celebrity plastic surgeon.

Wyatt found the nurse attractive, and there was something behind her eyes he recognized as determination. She was no shrinking violet. "I'm sorry I didn't get to meet you at the family fall get-together, Ciara. If I had, then I doubt whether I'd be here tonight."

"Why are you here, Mr. Wainwright?"

Crossing one leg over the opposite knee, Wyatt stared

at the toe of his polished wingtip. "I wanted to see for myself the woman who is responsible for dragging the Wainwright name into sleazy rags."

"Grandfather!"

"Uncle!"

Brandt and Jordan had spoken in unison, but Wyatt waved at them as if they were annoying insects. "Stay out of this!" He redirected his attention to Ciara. "I also came because I want to hear the truth, Miss Dennison."

Annoyance snaked its way up Ciara's spine. If Wyatt thought he was going to intimidate her, then he was mistaken. Like she'd told Brandt, she didn't scare easily. "How do you know what you read in the paper isn't the truth?"

Black eyebrows lowered over the penetrating blue eyes. "One thing I'm not, Miss Dennison, is a fool. So don't take me for one," he chastised. "Jordan has agreed to represent you when we sue Poppy Rayburn and that rag she calls a paper, but we need to know about your past relationship with Victor Seabrook."

Ciara felt as if she'd been ambushed by the Wainwrights, and she wondered why they were focusing on Victor. Had they uncovered something she didn't know? She exchanged a sidelong glance with Brandt. He squeezed her hand again.

"You have to tell them, babe."

Her voice was low, calm when she told them everything from her initial introduction to Victor, to when she ordered him to leave her apartment and when he showed up uninvited to the retirement party for her former supervisor.

The muscle in Wyatt's jaw twitched. "You didn't have him arrested for assaulting you?"

Ciara shook her head. "I just wanted to be rid of him. But if he'd continued to harass me then I would've had him charged with stalking."

"His blowing up your cell was enough to have him charged with harassment," Jordan said.

Wyatt snorted. "In my day we didn't go to the police, but meted out our own form of street justice. If a man hit a woman, then he found himself with a broken arm. And if he beat her up, then it was both arms and legs.

"That's because you were an OSG," Brandt said under his breath.

Jordan shot his cousin a "no you didn't say that" look before he redirected his attention to Ciara. "Who, other than Dr. Seabrook, would know where he'd purchased your clothes?"

"Other than the salespeople at the boutiques and department stores, I wouldn't know. Victor had his favorites: Bergdorf Goodman, Saks Fifth Avenue and Bloomingdale's. He also shopped at Wolford, Montmarte and a few other shops at Columbus Circle. Anyone could get this information off the internet. There are more than forty pages on Victor if you search for his name."

Jordan reached into the breast pocket of his suit jacket and took out a small leather-bound book. He flipped to a flagged page. "I had someone look up Victor Seabrook, and Montmarte and Wolford weren't mentioned anywhere."

Wyatt slapped his thigh. "I told you the son of a bitch gave Poppy that information. The article was too detailed for hearsay, and that poor excuse for a journalist slanted it to sound as if Seabrook was the wronged party. That he was so in love with Ciara that he proposed marriage, but she'd laughed in his face and then left him to hook a bigger fish. When I first read the article I was under the assumption that a woman had fed Poppy the information, because most men, unless they're clothing designers, could care less about labels or the stores that carry them."

Ciara closed her eyes, not wanting to believe Wyatt. But she knew there was some truth in what he was saying. Not only was Victor controlling, but he was also guarded. He only shopped in certain stores and ate at certain restaurants because then he could control his environment.

When she opened her eyes Ciara saw three pairs of eyes staring at her. "I'm sorry, Jordan, but it sounds too simple."

"So was breaking into the Democratic National Committee's office at the Watergate back in '72," Wyatt drawled. "It's the smart ones who end up outsmarting themselves."

"Whether simple, crude or sophisticated," Jordan said with deceptive calmness, "the person or persons who persuaded Poppy Rayburn to print that article managed to humiliate you and get their fifteen minutes of fame— even if vicariously."

Ciara nodded. Jordan was right. The article had become an exposé of her past relationship with a man who was admired as much for his medical expertise as for his humanitarian work. Dr. Victor Seabrook had become a much-sought-after plastic surgeon and medical expert. Meanwhile, the article had portrayed Ciara as a parasite, a gold digger who'd taken advantage of a man she'd snared in a carefully spun web of deception.

"If someone was out to hurt me, then they've succeeded. Who's going to hire me if they believe I'm going to take advantage of a family member—especially if they're male and wealthy?"

"Don't worry about it, Ciara," Brandt said, joining the discussion.

She rounded on him. "I have to worry about it, Brandt. It's my career that's in jeopardy, and I'm not ready to give it up because some vindictive cretin decides to feed malicious lies to the media. What's next, Brandt? Or is it who's next? Should my next patient be an octogenarian worth billions? This time I'll persuade him to marry me, and then convince him to change his will so I'll stand to inherit everything. Of course there will be the proverbial fight when his family decides to contest the will because their beloved wasn't of sound mind and body when he disinherited them."

Brandt's expression was a mask of stone. He knew Ciara was upset, but he preferred her screaming and throwing things to her cynicism. "We're going to get Poppy to print a retraction."

"How, Brandt? By using your uncle's method of breaking her arm?"

Wyatt chuckled. "That is a thought." He sobered like quicksilver. "This isn't only about you, Ciara. Except for an incident or two, the Wainwrights have managed to remain scandal-free. Brandt is the most recognizable Wainwright, followed by Jordan, but so far the others have kept a low profile. And as the head of the family that's the way I want it.

"You're Brandt's nurse, and it is also obvious you two have something else going on. I don't want to know what it is, but as long as you're involved with my grand-nephew you'll be afforded the same protection as anyone with a drop of Wainwright blood. If you and Brandt decide to separate, then you're on your own."

"My grandfather's right," Jordan confirmed. "As your legal counsel, I'm going to insist you not speak to anyone about this."

"What about my mother?" Ciara asked.

"Have you spoken to her?"

"No. I called her, but she hasn't called me back. When she does, what do you want me to tell her?"

"Tell her you're not going to publicly rebut anything, and if anyone approaches you your reply will be 'no comment.' Let your mother know she's not to talk to anyone about this."

Ciara nodded. "Should I tell her that you plan to sue the paper?"

Jordan shook his head. "No. The fewer who know about the suit the better."

Easing her hand from Brandt's loose grip, Ciara massaged her temples with her fingertips. Tension made her feel as if she had a vise around her head. She'd spent the most incredible ten days of her life with a man she loved, only to return home to accusations that she preyed on wealthy men like a scavenger on carrion.

Brandt rubbed the back of Ciara's neck. "Why don't you go upstairs and lie down? If Jordan needs anything else, he can talk to you tomorrow."

"Okay." She stood up, Jordan and Wyatt rising with her. "Thank you for everything."

Wyatt and Jordan waited until Ciara left the room, then sat down again. A hint of a smile played at the corners of Wyatt's mouth when he met Brandt's angry expression. He was impressed that his favorite nephew had managed to keep his temper in check.

"You've got yourself a live one, boy."

Brandt wanted to laugh, but he didn't feel like laughing given the seriousness of the situation that had prompted his cousin and uncle to come to his home. It wasn't often Wyatt displayed his softer side.

"I like her," Jordan stated without guile.

"I like her spirit," Wyatt said.

"I'd like to buy that rag and then fire Poppy," Brandt mumbled.

Wyatt and Jordan exchanged a smile. "That can be arranged," the older man said.

Brandt leaned forward. "Are you thinking what I'm thinking?"

Jordan crossed his arms over his chest. "In today's economic climate, advertising revenue is down and papers are issuing pink slips left and right, so it has to be just as bad or worse for the tabloids. A journalist isn't legally bound to reveal his or her sources, but I think if we…"

"What are you hatching, Jordan?" Brandt asked when his cousin didn't finish his statement.

"I can't tell. If I do then that would you make you culpable."

"Culpable to what?"

Jordan flashed a sinister smile. "Just say I'm prepared to make the owner of *The Informer* an offer he can't refuse."

"What if he refuses your offer?"

"Then I'll sue the hell out of him, Poppy Rayburn and his rag."

Brandt put up a hand. "Do what you have to do to clear Ciara's name."

Bracing both feet on the floor, Wyatt leaned forward. "How serious are you about this girl, Brandt?"

Brandt decided to be forthcoming. "Very serious."

"Serious enough to marry her?"

Brandt knew going away with Ciara had changed him and her. A few times he'd fantasized they were married and on their honeymoon. Her presence offered him a peace he hadn't thought possible. It'd been six weeks since she'd walked into his life, and in less than six weeks she would walk out.

"Yes. I'm in love with her."

"Have you told her?"

Brandt smiled. "Of course."

"What did she say?"

His smile faded. "Why the cross-examination?" he asked.

A sudden iciness flashed in the older man's eyes. "I need to know when I write a check to clear your girlfriend's name. The price goes up if she's your wife, because then she'll be a Wainwright."

"I don't need your money."

"I know you don't, Brandt. But as head of the family—"

"Your patriarch status is null and void where it concerns Ciara," Brandt countered. "You take care of what belongs to you, and I'll take care of what belongs to me. Jordan, once you find out whatever it is you need to seal your deal, let me know and I'll forward you a bank check. I don't want to appear rude, but I'm going up to check on Ciara."

Jordan stood up. "No problem, cuz. I forgot to tell you that Zee won her sexual harassment case. Rather than go to trial, Kenneth Moore took a plea. His license was revoked, and he won't be able to practice law for the next ten years. He'll also have to give up two and a half million for her pain and suffering. Zee plans to use the money to set up a foundation for sexually abused women."

Brandt smiled for the first time in hours. His brilliant attorney cousin had brought down the sexual predator that had harassed the woman who would become his wife. Now he was counting on Jordan to clear the name of the woman he wanted as his wife.

"The slug got off easy. Uncle Wyatt, how were sexual predators dealt with in your day?"

Seventy-eight-year-old Wyatt Wainwright blushed to the roots of his snow-white hairline. "I never witnessed it, but I did hear of some guy losing his family jewels in a botched circumcision. He almost bled to death, but somebody called the cops who took him to the hospital. Word was he was never the same."

Jordan grimaced. "Damn. I suppose Moore did get off easy." He rested a hand on Wyatt's shoulder. "Let's go, Grandpa. Zee and I are staying in the city this weekend, so that will give us time to talk about how we're going to deal with *The Informer*." He gestured to Brandt. "Don't get up. We'll see ourselves out."

Brandt sat staring at outside long after his uncle and cousin left. The Wainwrights had closed ranks because they sought to protect the family name. He wanted to go to Ciara and reassure her that she had nothing to fear, that he would protect her, but the slanderous article had driven a wedge between them.

He had no doubt Jordan and Wyatt would do what they needed to do to clear the Wainwright name, and Brandt knew what he had to do to secure his future and Ciara's.

Chapter 21

Ciara woke to find the spot next to her empty, but the impression on the pillow indicated Brandt had come to bed. After she'd left Brandt and his uncle and cousin in the living room, she'd talked to her mother, showered, swallowed two aspirin and gotten into bed. Within minutes of her head touching the pillow she had fallen asleep.

Sitting up and swinging her legs over the side of the bed, she stared at her feet. They were as dark as the rest of her body. She'd forgone wearing shoes when on deck. If she'd been more uninhibited, she would've sunbathed without her top, but hadn't wanted to embarrass herself or a member of the ship's crew.

Ciara left the bed, walking on bare feet to the adjoining bath, stopping when she saw Brandt sitting on a stool, shaving. "Good morning."

He smiled at her in the mirror as she walked to an

area of the bathroom where the commode and urinal were concealed behind a half wall of frosted glass. "Good morning."

"You're up early," Ciara called out.

Brandt drew the razor over his jawline. "I have a press conference."

There came the sound of toilet flushing, running water, the whirr of a toothbrush followed by gargling. He'd splashed cold water on his face and patted it dry when Ciara came up behind him.

"A press conference for what?"

He met her eyes in the mirror. "To announce my retirement."

With wide eyes, Ciara stared at Brandt, unable to process what he'd just said. "Why?"

Shifting slightly on the stool, Brandt grasped her wrist, pulling her down to his lap. "Why not?"

"But you love football."

He gave her a tender look his mother had given him whenever he had taken the time to make rather than buy a gift for her. "I love you, too."

Ciara shook her head. "No, Brandt."

"No what? You think I'm doing this for you?"

"Aren't you?"

"No. I'm doing this for us. I expect to recover completely, but I also know that I'll never be able to play football again. One tackle, I go down the wrong way, then I'm messed up again. Maybe the next time I won't be so lucky to get a nurse who'll knock me upside the head when I want to throw in the towel."

Looping her arms around Brandt's neck, Ciara rested

her forehead against his. "You're the worst liar I've ever met, Brandt Wainwright."

He winked at her. "I thought I was pretty good." His expression stilled, grew serious. "Our living together and sharing a vacation was a wake-up call that something was missing in my life."

"A woman."

"No, Ciara. Not any woman. You. I had to lie flat on my back, unable to get out of bed and perform the most basic functions by myself to realize I needed more than the cameras, the adoring fans and the Super Bowl ring. I put you in the line of fire when you went to that game with me. I made you a target even when you'd told me that you didn't want to be in the spotlight. If I'd listened to you, baby, Poppy would've never written that article."

"That's where you're wrong, Brandt. If someone was out to get me, it would've happened sooner or later. I spoke to my mother. She told me 'this too will pass.' I think she was referring to what she'd gone through when she found out my father was a bigamist. She had her pity party, then she got it together because she had to take care of me. I hope your uncle and Jordan don't think I'm ungrateful, but I really appreciate them coming to my defense."

"That's because they think of you as a Wainwright."

"But I'm not a Wainwright, Brandt."

"You would be if you married me."

"Why?"

Grasping her shoulders, Brandt eased her back to

where he could see her face. "You have to ask me why? Isn't loving you enough, or do you want more?"

"Hell, yeah, I want more, Brandt Wainwright. I have your love, but I also want you to promise you'll be a faithful husband, a loving and supportive father and you'll let me do whatever it takes to make you happy."

His smile was dazzling. "Did you just say yes?"

Ciara sucked her teeth. "I can't believe I've fallen in love with a dumb jock."

The last word had just slipped past her lips when she found herself straddling Brandt's lap, his hardness pressing against her mound over her nightgown. Gripping the front, he pulled at the cotton fabric, rending it from neckline to knee.

"No!"

Brandt flashed a feral grin. "Oh, yes." Anchoring his hands under her knees, he pulled her legs up and over his shoulders, her back resting on his thighs, her head dangling over his knees. "Let the games begin," he crooned, cradling her bottom in his large hands.

Ciara cried out, then swallowed a moan when his mouth covered her mound; his tongue moving in and out of her vagina made her feel as if she were having an out-of-body experience. Arms flailing and head thrashing wildly, she forgot to breathe, leaving her lightheaded and close to fainting.

She felt the flutters growing stronger and stronger. Ciara gasped again when Brandt lowered her legs and entered her in one sure, strong thrust. Now they were equals. Anchoring her hands on the sides of the stool, she moved up and down on his erection.

Brandt was transfixed by the firm bouncing breasts

and the expression of pure carnality sweeping over her sensual features, unable to believe she was his—forever. Their lovemaking was different, deeper, more satisfying. She'd become a Wainwright—his Wainwright woman even before they'd exchanged vows.

Her hot flesh squeezed his tightly, eased and then squeezed him again—this time tighter and longer than the previous one. "Oh, baby! Please, please, baby!" he pleaded shamelessly. "Please let it go."

Ciara did let it go, love flowing from her heart and her body. "I love you, I love you," she chanted over and over until it became a litany.

Brandt waited for his heart to resume its normal rhythm, then buried his face between her neck and shoulder. "Game over."

Ciara giggled. "Who won?"

"No one. It's a tie."

Running her fingertips up and down his moist back, Ciara exhaled audibly. "Yes," she whispered after a comfortable silence. "Yes, Brandt, I will marry you."

"When, baby?"

"Next year. After the Super Bowl."

Brandt pressed a kiss under her ear. "Would you be opposed to a destination wedding?"

"I'd love a wedding on the beach with the ocean as the backdrop."

Lines fanned out around his eyes when he smiled. *No tie!* "How many babies do you want?"

Her hands stilled. "Let's start with one, then take it from there."

"I thought you'd want at least two or three, only child."

Ciara laughed softly. "Slow down, sport. There's plenty of space on this floor to put in at least four bedrooms."

"I can live with that."

"Can you live without football, Brandt?"

Her question gave Brandt pause. He didn't want Ciara to think he was giving up the game for her; he was giving it up because it was time for him to walk—if not limp—away. "What I don't want to live without is you. Playing football was a temporary detour in my life's game plan. Fortunately, I have options many other athletes will never have. I can join the real-estate business, or I can go into business for myself."

Ciara realized she didn't know the man she'd promised to marry as well as she should. "Why type of business would you set up for yourself?"

"I don't know. Maybe you can help me make up my mind." Brandt didn't tell her that he'd contemplated buying *The Informer*. He knew nothing about running a newspaper, but he'd always been a quick study.

"I'm certain if we put our heads together we can come up with something viable," Ciara said. She shrugged what was left of the nightgown off her shoulders. "You owe me a nightgown, Brandt Wainwright."

"Sorry about that, babe. I guess I got a little excited."

Ciara's eyebrows lifted. "Only a little?"

"Okay, a lot, only because you're a helluva sexy chick."

"This sexy chick better let you get ready for your press conference. Where is it?"

"Aziza made arrangements for it to be held in one of

the conference rooms at Wainwright Developers. I want you to come with me."

"No, Brandt. You have to do this alone. I'm not going anywhere. I'll be here when you get back."

He ran a finger down the length of her nose. "We're going to get the person who leaked that information to Poppy, and when we do they'll pay."

"It doesn't matter anymore. You know what they say about karma."

"Yes. It's a bitch."

Ciara sobered, wondering if it was Victor who harbored a grudge because she'd rejected him. What, she mused, was her recourse? Would she be able to sue him over disclosing factual information? His defaming her character by calling her a gold digger was another matter. He was a control freak, but he was also a brilliant, selfless surgeon who'd helped countless people reclaim their lives. She had to determine what was more important—her pride or his brilliance.

"If it was Victor, then I don't want you to do anything to him. My marrying you is punishment enough. His knowing I'm going to lie down next to you every night and see your face when I wake every morning is enough. And when I give birth to your babies and not his—that will, as they say in the South, 'take the rag off the bush.'"

Brandt stared at Ciara, his eyes making love to her. "How did I get so lucky?"

Curving her arms under his shoulders, Ciara kissed Brandt's thick neck. "I keep asking myself the same thing, and so far I haven't come up with an answer.

Maybe after we celebrate our golden anniversary we'll come up with an answer."

"Do you think I'll still be able to get it up fifty years from now?" Brandt teased.

"Of course. There is no excuse for erectile dysfunction with the number of pills on the market."

Throwing back his head, he laughed loudly. "I suppose Daddy will still be smoking."

"Daddy will be all right as long as Mama doesn't put out his fire." They laughed, sharing the moment when all was right in their world.

Brandt set Ciara on her feet, then reached for the canes several feet away. "After the press conference, I'm coming back to pick you up and we're going shopping for rings. I'll also make arrangements for your mother to come down and meet the family."

"What if we let our mothers select the locations, and then we just show up?"

Again, it wasn't for the first time that Brandt couldn't believe he'd found someone like Ciara. He loved her. His family liked her. And she'd charmed the pants off Wyatt Wainwright.

Football had been good to and for him, but spending the rest of his life with Ciara was something even more special, and he couldn't wait to make her a Wainwright woman.

* * * * *

Fru·gal·is·ta [froo-*guh*-lee-stuh] *noun*
1. A person who lives within her means and saves money, but still looks good, eats well and lives *fabulously*

THE TRUE STORY OF HOW ONE TENACIOUS YOUNG WOMAN GOT HERSELF OUT OF DEBT WITHOUT GIVING UP HER FABULOUS LIFESTYLE

NATALIE P. MCNEAL

Natalie McNeal opened her credit card statement in January 2008 to find that she was a staggering five figures—nearly $20,000!—in debt. A young, single, professional woman, Natalie loved her lifestyle of regular mani/pedis, daily takeout and nights on the town with the girls, but she knew she had to trim back to make ends meet. The solution came in the form of her *Miami Herald* blog, "The Frugalista Files." Starting in February 2008, Natalie chronicled her journey as she discovered how to maintain her fabulous, single-girl lifestyle while digging herself out of debt and even saving for the future.

THE *Frugalista* FILES

Available wherever books are sold.

HARLEQUIN®

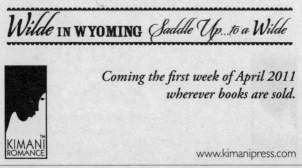

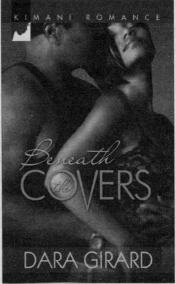

REQUEST YOUR FREE BOOKS!

2 FREE NOVELS
PLUS 2 FREE GIFTS!

KIMANI™
ROMANCE

Love's ultimate destination!